ADVANCE PRAISE FOR *RIGHT ON CUE*

"Falon Ballard is a master of chemistry-filled banter and lovable characters! No one does it like her!"

—Sarah Adams, author of *The Cheat Sheet*

"Falon Ballard is the queen of sharp wit and swoony romances. With delicious, intricately crafted love stories, and dynamic, wonderfully flawed characters, I will devour everything she writes and beg for more." —Mazey Eddings, author of *The Plus One*

"*Right on Cue* is a perfectly crafted rom-com that weaves together a charming cast of characters with witty dialogue, heartfelt moments, and sexual chemistry that leaps off the page. It will leave you with a smile on your face and a full, happy heart. Ballard is *right on track* with this delightfully satisfying read."

—Sophie Sullivan, author of *Ten Rules for Faking It*

"Falon Ballard's writing sucks me in like a best friend sharing a juicy story. Grab your ice cream and wine and get comfy because once you start *Right on Cue*, this adorable, charming, and spicy rom-com will hold you captive until the very last page."

—Meredith Schorr, author of *Someone Just Like You*

"Full of winks to the rom-com genre and packed with steamy tension." —*Library Journal*

PRAISE FOR *JUST MY TYPE*

"[A] charming ode to writers' passion and love."　　—*PopSugar*

"Seth and Lana have instant chemistry on the page, and it's a joy to read their snarky banter that transforms into something more heartfelt. Their longing for each other, and the obstacles in their way, feel realistic. . . . A compulsively readable second-chance romance that's full of pining and laughs."　　—*Kirkus Reviews*

"This entertaining rom-com from Ballard . . . , which refreshingly sees both protagonists undergoing therapy for their respective issues while reassessing their personal and professional goals, is one of healing and emotional growth as much as romance."

　　—*Publishers Weekly*

"A clever, upbeat rom-com that will leave a smile on readers' faces and joy in their hearts . . . A great showcase for Ballard's talents: Her voice is fresh and flirty, her characters well developed, . . . and her pacing brisk and never boring. Romance readers—of all types—will be immensely entertained."　　—*BookPage*

"A unique and humorous tale. Ballard hits all the right notes in a second-chance romance with smart, appealing lead characters."

　　—*Booklist*

"This spicy, tropey read will have most rom-com fans declaring, 'It's just my type of book!'"　　—*Library Journal*

PRAISE FOR *LEASE ON LOVE*

"[A] fun and light read . . . Ballard intersperses the book with text conversations (emojis and all) between Sadie and Jack, as well as her group conversation with her friends, that make readers feel like they're really part of the story. When Sadie and Jack's feelings for one another are finally realized, you can't help but celebrate alongside the characters." —*USA Today*

"Laugh-out-loud banter, smart characters, and heartfelt charm . . . this rom-com has it all!" —*Woman's World*

"[A] cozy romance." —*PopSugar*

"[A] quirky, heartwarming contemporary romance . . . This is a treat." —*Publishers Weekly*

"A fantastic read . . . a sharply funny roommates-to-lovers, opposites-attract rom-com." —*Booklist*

"This charming story of new beginnings and emotional growth has a sassy and likable narrator in Sadie, and the novel keeps a light tone despite touching on difficult subjects like toxic families and grief. . . . Readers who enjoy female entrepreneurs, found family, and gentle romantic leads will enjoy." —*Library Journal*

"The romantic beats and the slow-burning attraction between [Sadie and Jack] are things to savor. . . . Ballard sweetly explores the ways they complement one another and also how they hope to reinvent themselves following catastrophic personal changes."

—*Kirkus Reviews*

"A delight on every level. Ballard delivers a soft, sweet story with enough shadows to make the happily ever after feel that much more earned. . . . A beautiful love story about finding something precious that seems out of reach."

—Denise Williams, author of *Do You Take This Man*

"A hopeful, heartwarming debut. With a relatable disaster of a protagonist and an adorably nerdy hero, this opposites-attract, roommates-to-lovers romance is a true delight."

—Rachel Lynn Solomon, author of *Business or Pleasure* and *The Ex Talk*

"Sadie is a firecracker of a protagonist who's very aware of her flaws, and Jack is her perfect counterpart, embracing all of her rough edges with softness and understanding. *Lease on Love* warmly and wittily underscores that none of us are perfect, but we are all worthy, we are all enough: we all deserve to be loved, not just by others, but by ourselves too."

—Sarah Hogle, author of *You Deserve Each Other*

"A crackling, compulsively readable debut about forging new career and romantic paths, finding strength in found family, and discovering what it truly means to be 'home.'"

—Suzanne Park, author of *So We Meet Again*

Also by Falon Ballard

Just My Type

Lease on Love

RIGHT

ON

A Novel

CUE

FALON BALLARD

G. P. Putnam's Sons
New York

PUTNAM
— EST. 1838 —

G. P. PUTNAM'S SONS
Publishers Since 1838
An imprint of Penguin Random House LLC
penguinrandomhouse.com

Library of Congress Cataloging-in-Publication Data
Names: Ballard, Falon, author.
Title: Right on cue / Falon Ballard.
Description: New York: G. P. Putnam's Sons, 2024.
Identifiers: LCCN 2023044615 (print) | LCCN 2023044616 (ebook) |
ISBN 9780593712900 (trade paperback) |
ISBN 9780593712917 (ebook)
Subjects: LCGFT: Romance fiction. | Novels.
Classification: LCC PS3602.A621125 R54 2024 (print) |
LCC PS3602.A621125 (ebook) | DDC 813/.6—dc23/eng/20231004
LC record available at https://lccn.loc.gov/2023044615
LC ebook record available at https://lccn.loc.gov/2023044616

Printed in the United States of America
1st Printing

Book design by Shannon Nicole Plunkett

This one's for me.

RIGHT
ON
CUE

People's *Exclusive Interview with Screenwriter and Hollywood Darling Emmy Harper*

After a several-years-long hiatus from the rom-com world, perennial favorite and beloved nepo baby Emmy Harper is returning to the writers' room with her latest film, No Reservations. We sit down with Emmy for a no-holds-barred interview where we discuss her return to her screenwriting roots, that surprise Oscar-winning masterpiece from last year, and how she's still working through the grief over losing her father, Hollywood icon Tom Harper. You don't want to miss this exclusive peek into the life of one of today's most treasured stars.

PEOPLE: *Emmy, first let us start by saying we are such huge fans of your work.*

EMMY: *Thank you so much. I'll admit, even after all these years, I never get tired of hearing that!*

PEOPLE: *Let's just dive right in, shall we?*

Emmy laughs nervously, sipping from her (full-fat) latte.

EMMY: *I suppose we shall.*

PEOPLE: No Reservations *is your first romantic comedy since the death of your father four years ago. What was it like returning to the genre that defined your early career?*

EMMY: *It was so many things. Heartbreaking and difficult at times, but also rewarding. It truly felt like coming home. I've always loved making people happy, and happiness is something I haven't had a lot of in recent years, so it was nice to lose myself in this world of love and laughter.*

PEOPLE: *Back when you first started writing screenplays—at the ripe old age of twenty, might I add—many hailed you as the next Nora Ephron. And, of course, your parents, the late Tom Harper and the fabulous Diane Brenner, are both legends in their own rights. Was there a lot of pressure on you to succeed?*

EMMY: *Of course!* [There's another hint of that laughter.] *My parents have always been very supportive and the complete opposite of stage parents—I think it's well known by now that they essentially refused to let me get involved in the business until I was a teenager—but the pressure comes with the family name. I know I've had a huge advantage having them as my connection in the industry, and I never wanted to disappoint anyone.*

PEOPLE: *I think it's safe to say you've never let anyone down! You've written some of the most commercially successful rom-coms of the past decade, but also some more serious fare. Let's talk Midnight Sunset, your now Oscar-winning foray into writing a more sober film. What was that shift like, and what inspired you to go down a darker path?*

Emmy goes quiet for a long moment, thinking about her answer and taking a long breath before she starts speaking, like she needs to steady herself before she can respond.

EMMY: *I guess the easy answer to that is I was in a dark place. Losing my dad so unexpectedly . . . I'm not sure if I'll ever truly be over that, if you can ever truly be over that. There was just no way for me to sit down at my computer and write a happy love story when my world felt so encompassed by grief. My parents have always been the inspiration for my films. They are—or were, I guess—a real-life happily ever after. Seeing what* *happens after the happily ever after ends was a real punch in the gut. Midnight Sunset was the movie I needed to write at the time, and I'm very proud of how it turned out.*

She clears her throat after a long pause.

EMMY: *But I'm thrilled to be returning to rom-coms and making more movie magic of the lighter variety.*

PEOPLE: *With* No Reservations, *you're also taking on a producer role for the first time. How has that been?*

EMMY: *Amazing. I've really loved getting to see the process from beginning to end. And with Liz* [Hudson, Emmy's best friend, former college roommate, and esteemed director] *leading the charge, I know my baby is in good hands.*

PEOPLE: *Word on the street is that Jonathan Brentwood has been cast as the leading man?*

EMMY: *Word on the street is correct. I adore Jonathan, and he is the absolute perfect person for this role. I couldn't imagine anyone else taking it on.*

PEOPLE: *And for the leading lady?*

We catch Emmy grimace, even though she tries to hide it by sipping from her empty cup of coffee.

EMMY: *We'll let you know as soon as we know.*

CHAPTER

ONE

IT BECOMES CLEAR AS SOON AS THE PRETTY BLONDE opens her mouth that she is not the one. The whole room knows it, with everyone shifting subtly in their seats and shooting one another knowing glances. But she keeps going, and so does her scene partner, although Jonathan does glare at me from across the room.

Everyone is glaring at me, actually, if the tiny daggers I feel digging into my back are any indication.

Eventually, the poor, sweet actress finishes her scene and leaves with a wave and a smile. The room lets out a collective breath when the door bangs shut behind her.

"That was the last one for today." My best friend and now producing partner, Liz, pushes back her chair with a loud scrape. She stalks to one corner of the small room, pivots sharply, and then marches to the opposite side.

Everyone waits for her to finish before speaking; that's the kind of power she commands.

She comes to a halt in front of where I'm sitting, at the end of the table of exhausted and frustrated production team members. Her hands grip the edge of the plasticky wood, and she leans toward me with that look in her eye. "Emmy."

"No." The word is an immediate reflex—I know what she wants before she even asks for it.

She brings her eyes level with mine. "I'm a half second away from begging."

"I can't do it."

"She's not the only one about to beg," Kurt, our executive producer, says from his position at the other end of the table. "To be frank, Emmy, we're getting to the point where begging is going to morph into insisting."

I swallow down another automatic no because Kurt sounds more serious than usual. And he's the one who controls the purse strings. "You guys know I can't. I'm not an actress; I'm a screenwriter."

Jonathan Brentwood, our adored leading man and a college friend, joins Liz at the front of the table. "You could have fooled me, Em. When you read with me at my audition, your performance seemed pretty perfect."

"I agree." Kurt rises, and his already imposing presence looms over me even further. "We've been stuck in these auditions for weeks, and we haven't seen anyone nearly as strong as you were. We're scheduled to start filming in two weeks. We don't have time for this anymore."

Liz crosses her arms over her chest, but she doesn't appear to be worried about Kurt's declaration. "What are you saying, Kurt?" If I didn't know better, I'd almost say there was a hint of smug in her question.

"You have twenty-four hours. Find me our Isobel, or I'm pulling the plug." He claps what is probably meant to be a comforting hand on my shoulder. "You know how much I care about you, Emmy. Your dad was like a brother to me, and I've watched you grow up, but I'm not about to put my name and my cash in jeopardy because you're holding on to some baggage from the past." He swings his bag over his shoulder and strides toward the door. "Let me know what you decide."

The rest of the production team, along with Jonathan, scurry out of the room behind Kurt, leaving me alone with the woman who knows me better than almost anyone.

"Pancakes?" Liz asks.

"Pancakes," I agree.

WE ARRIVE AT VILLAGE BAKERY A HALF HOUR LATER, ordering our food before finding seats in the back of the café.

"I can't do it," I say the moment our coffees have been dropped off. I know well enough by now not to deliver bad news to Liz before she has caffeine in her hands. "You know I can't. And you know I won't."

"I understand that you *think* you can't. But I know with one hundred percent certainty that you can. And not only that, but you should." She tousles her white-blond pixie cut, which perfectly frames her pale, heart-shaped face, and turns her piercing blue eyes on me in what I know is a challenge.

I blink first, turning my gaze to the brightly colored chairs, the art on the walls, and the bud vase sitting in the middle of the table. "I'm not an actor, Lizzie, you know this. I haven't been in front of the camera in more than fifteen years. And I prefer it that way."

We accept our food from a server, two stacks of

pancakes as big as my head. Liz doesn't say anything while she butters hers and pours on an avalanche of syrup. The stress must really be getting to her, because Liz is one of the most health-conscious people I know; she only calls for pancakes in the most dire of circumstances. She shovels in a huge bite, chewing slowly before she turns her puppy-dog eyes back on me.

I hold up a hand in front of my face so I don't have to see her. "No. Do not even try that. I am immune to your begging."

"Then why are you hiding?"

I lower my hand, peering out cautiously, only to be hit with those big, baby blue buckets of sadness. "Liz. I can't. You know what happened last time."

She puts down her fork and reaches across the table to take my hand in hers. "Last time you were just a kid, Em. Look at how far you've come, at this amazing career you've had. You won a goddamn Oscar last year, and you're going to let something that happened a million years ago keep you from doing what you love?"

"That's the thing though: I don't love acting. At least not anymore. I'm a writer. And I'm perfectly happy doing what I'm good at and nothing more." I squeeze her hand before pulling mine away, lest the simple touch somehow reveal the fact that I'm lying. Not about being a writer. I do love it, and it does make me happy. Just maybe not totally and completely happy.

"You might not love acting—although the way you jumped at the chance to read for Isobel in Jonathan's audition begs to differ—but you love this character." She shovels another bite into her mouth, but I don't fill the silence while she chews. "I know you do, Em, because I could hear it in your performance. And I know how much this movie means to you."

I purse my lips to hold in my retort. She's not wrong. Isobel, the female main character in *No Reservations*, is one of my favorites I've written. When we found ourselves in need of a reader for auditions for the male lead, I *did* jump at the chance. But it was meant to be a one-time-only, special-occasion, never-happening-again performance. Even if it was the most fun I've had in a really long time.

Unfortunately, I may have filled the role a little too well. Liz has been on me to play the part ever since, especially as we get closer and closer to our scheduled start date and seemingly further and further from finding our Isobel. I never would've pushed for my best friend to direct this project if I'd known how much whining and cajoling would ensue.

I've been stalling, certain that the perfect actress would make her way to auditions. Meanwhile, I've had to tell Liz at least once a day that there is no way in hell she is casting me in my own movie.

Safe to say, things are not going as planned.

And the most annoying part is that I don't want Isobel in the hands of someone unqualified. Someone who doesn't get her, doesn't get my words.

But I don't know if any of that is enough. Yes, I love this movie and this script and this character. But do I love her enough to forget about the past and try it all again?

Liz can tell I'm wavering. I know she can because there's a hint of a smile pulling on her stupidly full lips. "You know you and Jonathan would be awesome together, and he'd be an incredibly supportive costar." I open my mouth to speak, but she holds up her hand. "Don't make any decisions right now. Take some time to think about it. But not too much time." Her hint of a smile fades. "You heard Kurt."

"Do you think he was serious about the twenty-four hours?" The thought of losing our funding on this film is a knife to the heart. It took me a long time to fall back in love with writing about love, and if *No Reservations* doesn't even make it to the screen, I don't know how I'll push through to write another.

"I think Kurt is always serious." She hits me with her most formidable stop-being-an-idiot look, one I've been on the receiving end of frequently during our many years of friendship. "So promise me you will seriously consider doing this. We need you."

"Fine. I'll think about it," I grumble, happy to put a pin in this whole conversation. "But don't get your hopes up. I'm sure the right actress will come along just in the nick of time."

The all-too-knowing smile she gives her pancakes makes me come close to hurling up my own.

AFTER WE LEAVE THE CAFÉ, I SIT IN MY CAR FOR A solid ten minutes, unsure of what to do next. I probably would've sat for longer if some asshole hadn't started honking at me to give up my parking spot. If I'm being honest, I know there's only one person I really need to talk to about my dilemma. And I'm dreading it, not because I don't want to talk to her, but because I'm pretty sure I already know what she's going to say.

Pulling into the driveway of my mom's house in the Hollywood Hills brings on its usual flux of competing emotions. Her house is adorable and perfect for her and the fresh start she desperately needed after my dad passed away four years ago. It's also an overpriced reminder that I'll never step foot in my childhood home again. And although I understand why she needed to leave—not just to escape the memories, but because the house was too much for her to care for on her own—it doesn't take away the sting of losing one of my last tangible connections to my father.

My parents had the kind of relationship you don't often see in movies because it's what happens after the film ends, when the two people so perfectly suited for each other build a real life together. They had a classic showmance, one of the few that lasted well beyond the first movie they ever made as costars, one that landed them on every list of Hollywood's top power couples. It was easy to write epic love stories when I had my very own example to study. It's been a lot harder since my mom lost her partner and best friend.

I would sit in my car for another ten minutes here, too, but I know she's already seen me pull up. If I don't climb out soon, she'll have no problem coming outside to find out why. So I trudge up the steep steps to her front porch and push open the door she's already unlocked for me.

"I'm in the kitchen," she calls, as if I wouldn't have been able to easily locate her in the tiny two hundred square feet that comprise her living room, dining room, and kitchen.

I kick off my shoes and sink onto the couch, swinging my feet up on the ottoman that doubles as a coffee table.

"Coffee?"

"No, I'm good. I just had one with Liz."

She comes in a minute later, two mugs in her hands, passing one off to me before folding herself into the armchair across from me.

"Why do you even ask if you're going to bring me one anyway?"

"I thought writers subsisted solely on coffee." She flashes me a smile while trying to disguise her look—you know the one, the one moms level at you when they're trying to figure out what you're hiding. When I was a teenager, I hid secret crushes and an occasional bottle of alcohol. As an adult, I stick to hiding my emotions. Not that it ever works.

I ignore her alien brain probing and focus on taking a long sip of coffee, which of course is prepared exactly how I like it.

She clears her throat and raises her eyebrows in some kind of mom power move. "So, to what do I owe the pleasure?"

"Can't a daughter just swing by and check on her mother for no specific reason?" I shift my body, angling myself slightly away from her just in case her brain probe is real.

"Yes. But you obviously have a reason." She sets down her coffee on the side table next to her chair and clasps her hands together in her lap. "Why don't we skip the song and dance, and you just tell me what's going on?"

Purely on instinct I open my mouth to argue with her, but then I think better of it.

"Liz wants me to be in the movie."

The lack of surprise on her face makes it clear that Liz has mentioned this to her already, which is honestly rude and should be illegal. My mom and Liz hit it off the moment they met on move-in day back during our freshman year of college and have had their own pseudo mother-daughter relationship ever since. "And?"

"And I don't *want* to be in the movie." I study her face, watching for even the smallest of hidden messages in her reaction, but the woman is a three-time Best Actress Academy Award winner and gives away nothing.

"So tell her no."

"I did. Several times."

"Then what's the problem?"

I glare at her for being purposefully obtuse. Is this what it's like to have a child? Because no thank you. "The problem is she keeps pressuring me."

"If you don't want to do it, then who cares? Liz is your best friend. If you don't want to be in the movie, she'll find someone else to be in the movie." She picks up her mug and watches me carefully over the rim as she sips.

"What if she can't find someone else?"

"You mean to tell me that in the entire city of Los Angeles, the entertainment capital of the world, esteemed director Liz Hudson can't find a single actress to be in her film? Back in my day, girls would've been lining up for the chance to audition."

"It's *our* movie," I grumble. "And there are girls lining up to audition. They're just not exactly what we're looking for. And Kurt threatened to pull funding if we don't make a decision, like, today."

She shrugs. "Then pick whoever's second best."

I grit my teeth and try not to snap the handle off my mug. "I don't want someone who's second best."

"Then I guess that means you'll have to play the part." Her smile is as sweet as my coffee.

"Your mind games don't work on me, Mom. I'm not thirteen anymore."

Her eyes open wide with false innocence. "I don't know what you're talking about, sweetie. I'm just trying to help you figure out your problem."

"You're a menace." I carefully set my coffee cup on the gold tray sitting on the cushioned ottoman.

She leans forward, resting her arms on her knees. Thanks to the small space, it leaves only about two feet between us. "Why are you hesitant about taking this part, Emilia?"

"Ouch, okay, there's no need to full-name me here. I'm not in trouble or anything."

Instead of responding to my deflection, my mom simply holds my gaze.

I sit back in my seat with a sigh. "I'm a writer, not a performer. And you know I hate being on camera." It's even harder to lie to her than it is to Liz.

"Is this about that idiot boy?"

A small smile tugs on my lips. When it comes to holding a grudge, I learned from the very best. We Harper women do it well. "No, this is not about that idiot boy. At least not directly."

She reaches across the short divide between us, taking my hand and gently pulling me forward so my position mirrors hers. "If you really don't want to do this, you know you don't have to, no matter how much Liz is pressuring you. She's a big girl; she'll get over it."

"But?"

"But if you're saying no because you think you can't do it, because you think you might fail, then that's bullshit and you need to get over yourself."

"Wow, Mom, thanks so much for your love and caring support."

She gives my hand a squeeze before returning to her upright position. "You know I'm right."

I remain folded in half, elbows resting on my knees, head hanging down. "There's a part of me that does want to say yes. Mostly because I feel like Dad would agree with you and encourage me to do it. He'd tell me to fuck the haters and not to be afraid to try something different, to go for what I want." A tissue appears in front of me, and I didn't even realize I was crying. I take it and blot at my eyes.

My mom rises from her chair and joins me on the couch, tugging me into her embrace. "I'm pretty sure that's exactly what he would say."

My head falls onto her shoulder.

"But you also can't do this only for him, Emmy. Just like you can't do it for Liz, or even to get back at that idiot boy."

"Is this the part where you tell me I need to do it for myself?"

"Hey, it may sound after-school-special, but it's true."

I let her hold me for longer than I probably should, telling myself she needs to deliver this comfort as much as I need to receive it. It makes me feel better about being over thirty and still needing my mom. Although, in her very own words, fuck the haters; you're never too old to need your mom.

I finally sit up when the crick in my neck starts to hurt. Because yeah, that position definitely isn't as comfortable now as when I was younger.

"So you're going to do it?" She tries to hide the glee in her voice but doesn't do a very good job.

And because I'm still a petulant teenager at heart, I lie. "I'm not sure. I'm going to take the rest of the day to think about it." I stand, taking my mug to the kitchen and rinsing it out before grabbing my keys and crossing the few steps to the front door. "Thanks for listening."

She pulls me into a hug. "Literally my job."

"Do not even think about calling Liz when I leave."

She opens her eyes wide in mock outrage. "I would never."

"Uh-huh."

"You know how much Liz hates talking on the phone. We text."

This time the outrage is mine and hardly mocked at all. My own mother shoves me outside, and I can see her tapping away on her phone before the door even closes behind me.

"Traitor!" I call over my shoulder as I bound down the steps and slide into my Prius.

Well. Fuck.

Screen Scandals

In some delightful casting news today, we are happy to report that everyone's favorite rom-com writer Emmy Harper is going to be stepping in front of the camera in her brand-new love story *No Reservations*—a classic rom-com about a big-city girl who gets stranded at a small-town inn and finds herself falling for the charming owner. Harper has penned some of our favorite romance movies of recent years (not to mention her killer foray into the more dramatic space with her brilliant and Oscar-winning *Midnight Sunset*), but this will be her first time on-screen. Or, I guess we should say, this will be her first time in a *long* time.

That's right! Not only has Harper starred in a movie before, but she had the pleasure and good fortune of starring opposite our ABSolute (emphasis on the abs, always) favorite action hunk, Grayson West! How have you never heard of this cinematic masterpiece before, you might be wondering. Well, the simple answer is it's terrible. No really. Both West and Harper were just starting out in their careers, and their chemistry is all over the place—from jumping off the screen during their one shared kiss to borderline murderous in basically every other scene. It's no wonder it's been all but stripped from our memories.

Lucky for Harper, she'll be starring opposite super-hunk Jonathan Brentwood in her upcoming, hopefully triumphant return to the screen. We can't wait to see some sexy small-town hijinks from these two hotties!

CHAPTER

TWO

MY HAND REACHES OUT TO ADJUST THE VOLUME ON my car stereo, turning down the blare of my "Let's Get Pumped" playlist so I can focus on the directions on my GPS screen. Because loud music makes it harder to navigate and all. Especially because said music needed to be loud enough to drown out the fact I most definitely cannot hit Mariah Carey's high notes. Just a few minutes away from my destination, it's time to focus.

Luckily, the adorable, postcard-perfect inn in Pine Springs, California, where I'll be spending the next six weeks, is right off the main road, blanketed in fluffy white snow, despite it now being early March. Pine Springs is close enough to LA to make for easy travel, but far enough away to have real weather. That seasonal flaw aside, the inn is gorgeous with its robin's-egg-blue facade and bright white trim. It's a fitting centerpiece for *No Reservations*.

Because yes, I succumbed. Somehow, the combined powers of my mother and my best friend, plus the threat of losing all of our funding, were enough to convince me to take on the role of Isobel, despite all my trepidation. It's been just two weeks since I signed on the dotted line, and I've enjoyed every second of the wait until shooting begins, delaying the inevitable for as long as possible. Because despite my excitement about stepping back on-screen (shocker: Liz was right and I have been itching to stretch my acting chops once again), the closer we've gotten to actually starting filming, the more anxious I've become.

And here we are. On set. In the snow. About to try my hand at one of the few things in life I haven't ever managed to do well, with no chance to turn back now.

Shit.

I park my Prius in the small lot off to the side of the inn. Throwing my purse over my shoulder, I collect the trash from my six-hour road trip—two empty coffee cups and one or two or ten empty bags of gas station snacks—and open the door, stepping out into the chilly midafternoon air. And it's legitimately chilly, not just LA chilly. The cold bites through my thin sweater, and I rush to the front steps of the inn as fast as my not-made-for-snow boots will allow.

A gust of warmth greets me the second I push through the bright yellow door, bells tinkling as I nudge it closed behind me. For a second, I pause in the entryway, letting not just the heat but also the atmosphere of the lobby wrap around me like a soft, fluffy blanket. A soft, fluffy blanket that comes with freshly baked cookies and a puppy. That's how perfect it is.

Directly ahead of me is the front desk, crafted from dark wood and strung with a floral garland, even though spring definitely has not sprung just yet. To the right of the check-in desk is a staircase, the railing made from a matching dark wood. A sitting room is visible through a doorway to my left, with a stone fireplace and lots of overstuffed-looking armchairs. The smell of pies baking in the oven permeates the space, giving off serious cottage-core vibes—the kind that are legit and can't be picked up on a trip to Target.

It's absolutely perfect, and just being in the room sends a little bit of a thrill through me. Maybe this won't be so bad. Maybe deciding to jump into this project headfirst isn't the stupidest decision I've made in a really long time.

"You must be Emmy." An older Black woman with graying hair tucked into a smooth bun beams at me from behind the front desk. She's wearing a soft purple sweater and immediately reminds me of every favorite TV sitcom grandma ever.

I beam back, because I can't not, and cross over to her. "That's me." I reach out my hand to shake hers before realizing I'm still carrying an armload of trash. "Oh, sorry. Is there somewhere I could throw this away?"

"Of course." She gestures for me to hand it over.

I fumble a bit, dropping an empty bag of peach rings. By the time I pick it up and hand it over the counter, the rest of the evidence of my terrible road-trip snacking has been disposed of. "Thank you so much. And yes, I'm Emmy Harper." When I stick out my hand this time, grasping for some semblance of professionalism amid the nerves, the woman pushes it away, instead coming around the counter to wrap me in a warm hug.

"Welcome, Emmy. I'm Linda Parkson, and we are so excited to have you here."

"I'm so excited to be here, Ms. Parkson."

"Linda, please, dear." She crosses back around the counter and starts fiddling on her computer. "You are the first one to arrive, and I would say that gets you the best room in the house, but truth be told, I already assigned you the best room in the house."

I lean both elbows on the counter. "Oh, that's so sweet of you, but I certainly don't require any special accommodations." Not that I've ever been one to turn down a free upgrade. It's not often that writers get special treatment, so twist my arm and give me the fancy room.

"Nonsense. You're the reason all of this is happening." She taps for a second on the keyboard before pausing to give me a conspiratorial look. "I managed to charm a copy of that script you wrote out of your location scout, and I think it's absolutely delightful."

Heat rises in my cheeks at her kind words. "Well, thank you. I'm glad you liked it. And I have to say, your inn is exactly what I imagined as I was writing it."

"I can't wait to see you bring it to life." She hands me a key, a real metal one, on an actual keychain. "Your room is upstairs, down the hallway to the right, last door on your left-hand side."

"Thank you so much. I'm just going to grab my bags from my car, and I'll head up and get settled." I tuck the key in the back pocket of my jeans and give Linda a little wave before turning back toward the front door. I don't register the tinkling of the bells until my head connects with a chest. A very hard chest, luckily covered by a very soft sweater. "Oh, shit, I'm so sorry." Taking a step back, I tilt my head up. And up. And up. "Oh. Shit."

Competing emotions roil around in my brain like glitter

in a snow globe that's just been turned upside down and shaken. Violently.

Because attached to the hard chest is a gorgeous face.

A gorgeous, scowling face.

A gorgeous, scowling face that takes me thirty seconds of open-mouthed staring to properly recognize.

"What the fuck are *you* doing here?" I blurt out before I consider who else might be around to overhear me.

That gorgeous, scowling face furrows. "I'm sorry, do I know you?"

My mouth drops open even farther. "Do you *know me*? Is that some kind of joke?"

Perfectly crystal-clear blue eyes squint before looking me over from head to toe. "Nope. Not a joke."

A throat clears over my shoulder, and Linda steps up next to me, placing a soft hand on my forearm, which may or may not be tightened and about ready to punch something. Or someone.

"Grayson West, I'm Linda Parkson. The producer called me earlier about the change, and I have your room all ready for you."

"What change? What producer? *I'm* the producer!" I look back and forth between the two of them. "This inn has been reserved for cast and crew only. You are not allowed to be here." Linda's soft brown eyes are trying to telegraph something to me. Probably something along the lines of *Please don't punch this man in my lobby.*

Grayson's eyes are looking everywhere but at me, roaming around the room, his furrows growing even deeper by the second.

"This was a mistake," he mutters under his breath.

"What was a mistake?" My voice rises in volume and pitch as Linda digs her nails into my arm.

The bells over the door tinkle once again, and our fearless director, the woman who is supposedly my best friend—although what happens in this room in the next five minutes could very well change that fact—strides in, shivering and rubbing her arms for warmth. "Fuck, it's cold here." She pauses for a second, taking in the scene before her.

Grayson, avoiding and furrowing.

Me, rabid and glowering.

Linda, holding me back.

"Fuck me." Liz sighs, running a hand through her hair. "I was hoping to beat you here, Grayson."

"Liz, you have about five seconds to tell me what the hell is going on before I call TMZ and tell them every single thing I know about you. And include college spring break photos." I gently shrug off Linda's grip and take a step closer to Liz, boxing Grayson *fucking* West out of this conversation.

Linda turns to the golden-haired behemoth, gesturing to the front desk. "Let's get you checked in, Mr. West." She tucks her hand into the crook of his arm and leads him away. "I have to say, I'm a big fan."

"Traitor," I grumble at her retreating back.

Liz takes my arm and pulls me into the sitting room, kicking the swinging door closed and pushing me down into one of the armchairs closest to the roaring fire. She remains standing, pacing back and forth in front of the worn stone of the hearth. Her mouth opens and closes about ten times, but nothing comes out.

"Jesus Christ, just say it." I cross my arms over my chest and glare at her.

"Jonathan had to drop out. I only got the call late yesterday. He broke his leg snowboarding and is going to be in a full cast for the next two months." The words pour out of her mouth in one quick jumble. "I pushed for someone else—anyone else—but Emmy, I swear he was the only one who could get here on time and not put us seriously behind schedule. And Kurt made it clear, in no uncertain terms, that we are *not* to delay the schedule." She plops into the chair next to mine. "I'm so sorry. I know you hate him. I get it, I do, but we had no choice."

I purse my lips to keep from screaming. "You know what it took for me to agree to do this, Lizzie."

"I know." The guilt is evident in the puppy-dog eyes she flashes me.

But her guilt doesn't mitigate the dread. "I can't do this with him, Liz. I just can't." Panic starts to rise in my chest as my brain begins to fully compute what is happening. And what this all means. And who this is happening with.

She reaches over and grabs my hand. "You can. I know you can. He's just one dumb actor."

"One dumb actor who ruined my damn career," I bite out. "You know what he said about me. You know how incapable he was of being professional on set." I push out of my chair, taking my own turn pacing. "And do you know what's even worse than what he did when we were teenagers?"

"His horribly inflated ego?"

"No!" I pause in my pacing, my hands on my hips. "I mean, yes. But also no." I pinch the bridge of my nose, attempting to force a calming breath through my lungs. "He doesn't even remember me." I collapse back into the squishy chair. "The man is responsible for the downfall of my career, and he doesn't even remember me." That knowledge might sting even more than the events of our complicated past.

"And now you have to pretend to fall in love with him." Liz sums it all up in one succinct sentence.

I blink away a sheen of tears, low-key mortified I'd even let Grayson fucking West bring on the waterworks. "And now I have to pretend to fall in love with him."

Liz takes in a deep breath, blowing it out loudly and forcefully. "Well, shit."

Linda enters the room from a swinging door in the corner, two wineglasses in her hands. "I don't mean to be presumptuous, but it looked like you might need—"

"Yes," Liz and I say in unison, each gratefully accepting a glass of red wine.

I take down half of mine in one gulp, folding myself into the soft cushions of the chair. Liz's eyes bore into the side of my face, but I ignore them, instead focusing on laying out my options.

Option one: I don't even bother to take my bags out of my car. I drive back to LA and return to a life behind the scenes. It's not a bad life. I have plenty of money, and I like writing, and the hours are nice. And I never have to fake make out with assholes.

Option two: I don't let Grayson West get the best of me this time. Sure, it's been a while since I was in front of the camera. But I'm a professional. I can do this. I'll just close my eyes and pretend he's Chris Hemsworth.

Fuck. Why couldn't we have gotten Chris Hemsworth?

Liz snorts. "He'd be perfect, but you know he'd never do a movie like this."

Guess I said that last part out loud. "Good point. On that note, why the hell is Grayson West doing a movie like this? One that involves feelings and emotions and doesn't have any explosions in it?"

"To be totally honest, I have no idea why he agreed. Rom-coms are definitely not in his wheelhouse, but I got instant confirmation from his manager that he was interested. Even if we could've found someone else, I don't think it would've been wise to turn him down. He's got the kind of name that can bring in a big audience. And that's good for all of us."

I swig the last of my wine as if it can wash away the truth I've known since we first sat down. "There really wasn't anyone else?"

"There really wasn't anyone else." She hands me the rest of her wine like the good best friend she is, swapping her half-full glass for my empty one.

Staring into the depths of the crimson, I swirl the wine around before taking another swallow. "I'm going to need you to have my back."

"Always." She holds out the empty glass, raising it toward me. "I know this process isn't starting out how you wanted it to, but I promise, I'm going to take care of you and we're going to rock the shit out of this."

I clink my glass against hers. "I need to update the rider clause in my contract. I'm going to require a case of wine."

"Done."

"And a lot of chocolate."

"You got it." She sets her glass on the side table between us and gives me a serious look. "You know I will always have your back, Emmy. But I do think we should make some things clear."

"You're the boss here." I set my own now-empty glass on the table, knowing where this is going before she has to say it. "I know we have to have some boundaries."

"Let's maybe try to keep the Grayson-related venting purely professional, shall we? We can't let drama from more than a decade ago dictate life on set, even if he is an asshole." She stands and tugs on my arm. "Let's go get settled in."

I give Liz a resigned nod and let her pull me out of my seat. "I can do this?"

She takes my face between her hands, squishing my cheeks like I'm a chubby baby. "You wrote a beautiful script, Em. And this is the perfect role for you. I know it's taken a long time for you to feel like you could step back in front of the camera, and I promise I'm not going to let you blow it. Especially not because of some dumb man."

I pull her into a quick hug. "Thanks."

After collecting Liz's key from Linda, we brace for the cold and head back out to our cars to grab our bags. Because it's just Linda working at the front desk today, we haul them up the carpeted stairs ourselves, turning right at the landing. I drop off Liz at her room and continue on down the hallway to the last door on the left.

It shouldn't come as a surprise, given the perfection downstairs, but my mouth still drops when I open the door to my room, my new home for the next six weeks. There's a large four-poster bed topped with a yellow quilt and a mountain of throw pillows. The furniture is all antique heavy wood. Heat radiates from the fireplace, with my own squishy, floral-covered armchairs in front of the flames. I cross over to the large picture window, complete with window seat, and take in the view. Nothing but snow and trees as far as the eye can see.

I'm about as far out of my comfort zone as I could possibly be. But Liz is right. I'm not going to let anyone or anything blow this opportunity for me. Not my insecurities or my hang-ups or my past.

Not even Grayson fucking West.

I inhale a long, deep, cleansing breath before cracking my neck back and forth. Like I'm preparing for a fight. Which I very well might be. But better to have one tiny fight now—before filming starts, before the rest of the cast arrives and Grayson and I have to pretend to like each other—than a big blowup that could surely derail the entire production later on.

Checking my appearance in the full-length mirror on the back of the door, I fluff up my long auburn waves, wipe a mascara smudge from under my hazel eyes, and head out. I'm planning on asking Linda to direct me to Grayson's room, but I don't have to venture that far.

Because as I step into the hall, the door right across from me opens, and there he is.

And for the first time since he walked through the front door of the inn, I actually have a moment to properly look at him.

It's been years since I last saw him in person, and those years have been more than kind. He's still tall and tan and blond—although the beard is new—with the kind of blue eyes often described in romance novels. Piercing and with the depths of the ocean and sapphires full of sunlight. But this Grayson carries himself differently than teenage Grayson did. Partly because it must be hard to lug around all those muscles every day. The man is regularly cast in action movies for a reason—he looks the part. But it's not just the physique, which is clearly visible underneath the thin fabric of his gray Henley. It's the confidence.

What I wouldn't give for just a smidge of that confidence. One pec's worth. Fuck, even one sliver of an ab's worth.

He closes his room door behind him, the sound jolting me out of my drool-filled compare and contrast.

"Hi," I say before he has the chance to turn down the hall and leave.

"So you do know the traditional greeting one normally bestows upon a colleague." He shoves his hands into his back pockets, causing the fabric of his shirt to pull even tighter across his sculpted chest and broad shoulders.

"Yeah. About that." I take another long breath, readying myself to swallow my pride. "I'm sorry about all of that." I wave my hand in the general direction of the lobby downstairs. "I didn't know you were coming. I hadn't heard about the last-minute replacement, and you caught me off guard."

He gives me a cocky grin—not that he has any other kind. "You're not the first woman to be flustered at the sight of me."

My nose wrinkles and I open my mouth to spar back, but then I remember why I'm here in the first place. To make a movie. *My* movie. With this man, if I must. "I wouldn't say flustered so much as surprised. But let's not argue semantics. I'm sorry if I was rude—"

"You were." He grins again, pushing up the long sleeves of his shirt to reveal his corded forearms before crossing them over his chest.

"Fine. I apologize for being rude." I turn to head down the hallway, not even sure where I want to go, but knowing I need to be not here.

"Then I guess I should apologize for not recognizing you."

His words stop me in my tracks. I spin back around, just in time to catch him giving me a long, slow look, those blue eyes tracing me from head to toe. The blatantly gross move ignites a spark of outrage in my chest. And a different kind of spark, somewhere farther down.

"Oh?" is the only witty retort I can manage.

"But in my defense, you have definitely changed since I last saw you." His eyes linger on my chest for several seconds too long.

"If you're done ogling me, I actually have somewhere I need to be." I'm praying Liz is in her room, because that's where I plan on stalking off to. As soon as I can make my feet move.

"Sure thing." He strides down the hallway, brushing past me, just close enough so the heat of him burns my cheeks. He pauses at the top of the steps. "I'm really looking forward to working with you again, Emmy." He tosses a wink—an actual wink—over his shoulder before bounding gracefully down the stairs.

Leaving me standing in the middle of the hallway like the idiot I must be.

CHAPTER

THREE

I FIND MY NAME AT THE LARGE OAK DINING ROOM table the following morning. A script is waiting at my place setting, with a small plate sitting off to the side. Pastries, a fruit platter, and a tray of bagels sit in the middle of the table. I'm too nervous to eat, but that doesn't stop me from grabbing a cinnamon roll and stashing it for later before they all disappear.

I slide into my chair, scooting in and sitting up straight, trying to maintain a look of professionalism. Which is unnecessary, as I am currently the only one in the room. Probably because I'm a half hour early. Wrapping my hands around the giant mug of coffee I snagged from the kitchen earlier this morning, I breathe in its familiar scent. My foot taps under the table, belying the nerves coursing through me. But from the waist up, I'm the picture of cool, calm confidence.

No one would ever know it's been more than a decade since I sat down to participate in an actual table read.

Of course, at my last table read, I fell head over heels into full-on teenage-girl crushdom. Grayson West walked into the room, flashed me a brilliant smile that lit up his aqua-blue eyes, and I completely melted. We flirted relentlessly during the first two weeks of rehearsal, my fifteen-year-old mind already seeing the movie of us as it would play out in the future: flirting would turn to showmance, showmance would turn to committed relationship, committed relationship would lead to engagement and marriage and the two of us running a moviemaking empire while also raising our gorgeous and perfectly behaved children. I didn't need to work too hard to picture the details—I assumed the story of Grayson and me would mirror that of my parents.

Ha.

All it took was one day of actual filming, one tiny little scene, one disastrous first kiss, and one nasty rumor to blow it all up. No showmance, no committed relationship, and sure as fuck no engagement or marriage or children. After that single day on set, Grayson and I didn't even speak to each other if the cameras weren't rolling.

And now here we are again. In another time and place at another table read. Something tells me this one will not be full of flirtatious banter and longing looks. Today's table read will be full of only one thing: judgment.

Today, I'm mentally preparing myself to be judged on my acting, not just my writing. Not only will the rest of the cast and production crew be taking stock of my performance but there's the added layer of knowing I wrote the words on the page. Normally, as a screenwriter, I don't have to attend these things. I usually don't hear my words read out loud by the cast until I'm watching the premiere. Sometimes what ends up on the screen sounds nothing like what I typed on the page, which is a reality I've learned to live with. But now, if an actor changes a line or Liz makes a correction, I'll be in the room when it happens, listening to them take liberties with my work while I attempt to stay in character. An extra dose of torture.

What the hell have I gotten myself into?

"Why am I not surprised to see you here early?" Liz blows into the room looking the picture of director chic, dressed in all black, pixie cut artfully tousled in the effortless way that takes most people an hour but really only takes her a few minutes.

I, on the other hand, spent an actual hour carefully applying my makeup so it looks like I'm not wearing any, followed by another hour curling my hair to achieve a naturally wavy look. And my skinny jeans and cable-knit sweater look casual and cozy, but in reality, the button of my pants digs into my stomach when I sit and the sweater is itchy. But comfort is not high on the list of priorities today.

Liz fills a coffee cup from the carafe set up on the large credenza in the corner of the dining room. "You ready for this?"

"No." I let my fake smile slip as I take another long sip of coffee.

She nabs a croissant and takes down half of it in one bite. "Well, you better get ready."

"I see I exhausted my supportive pep talk quota yesterday."

"I know how to get the best out of you, Harper." She flips through the huge binder sitting at the head of the table, not bothering to sit.

"Good morning!" A stunning Korean American woman breezes into the room, striding confidently up to Liz and wrapping her in a hug. "So good to see you again. I'm so excited for this!"

When I see her heading my way next, I push back my chair and stand, holding out my hand. "Hi, I'm—"

"Emmy!" She wraps me in a warm hug. "Thrilled to meet you in person! I'm Jenna. I'm playing your best friend Ashley, and I am a huge fan of your work."

Normally I would assume the compliment is a formality, but Jenna's voice is nothing but sincere. "Thank you so much."

She fills a coffee cup before sliding into the seat next to mine and leaning over to whisper to me. "And seriously, please don't hesitate to let me know if you have any questions during filming. I remember how nervous I was during my first movie shoot. I mean, of course, I'm sure you've been on set plenty—is it unprofessional to say how much I love your parents?—but it can feel different when you're performing."

"Oh, actually, this isn't my first time acting." I pick up my pen, clicking the top in rapid succession.

"Oh! I'm so sorry." Jenna fills her plate with fruit and pops a grape in her mouth. "I only know your work as a screenwriter."

That's more than a bit of a relief. "It's okay. It's been a long time, and I'm sure a lot has changed, so I'll definitely take you up on your offer." I quickly change the subject before she has the chance to ask me about that first movie.

The rest of the supporting cast—six other actors of various ages and genders—strolls in during the next few minutes. Everyone grabs coffee and breakfast, making introductions, finding their seats, and greeting me like I have every right to be there, even though I'm still not so sure myself. Liz opens her laptop to pull up a Zoom with the actor playing my father. He and I only interact over FaceTime in the movie, so he's back home in LA, shooting his scenes in the warmth and comfort of a studio.

Liz remains standing, lips pursed, eyes constantly darting to her phone to check the time. Only one seat sits empty. And it's the one directly across from mine, belonging to Grayson fucking West, of course.

The man himself saunters into the dining room at the exact minute the read-through is supposed to start. It takes him another two minutes to pour his coffee and take his seat.

Because I know Liz, I can tell how pissed she is by the set of her shoulders. But I also know she's not the kind of director to make a scene on the first day, in front of the whole cast.

"Thank you so much, everyone, for being on time." Passive aggression is more her style. At least, for the first offense. "I'm happy to see everyone made it safely. Hopefully, you've all familiarized yourselves with the schedule. Today is mostly for getting settled, feeling out the material, and then the real work begins tomorrow. So, let's get to it."

Before we turn to our scripts, we take a minute to go around the table and officially introduce ourselves and our characters. It's slightly less painful than a junior high class on the first day of school, but only slightly. Luckily, it's a small group, so it goes fast.

And then, we dive in.

The movie opens with me and Jenna in our characters' PR firm, lamenting how hard we've been working and discussing plans for my upcoming vacation. If friendship chemistry is a thing, we've got it, our lines zinging between the two of us like we've been buddies for years. When the scene changes to one with Grayson and the actor playing his brother, I let out a small sigh of relief. That wasn't so hard. Liz catches my eye and gives me a subtle wink.

"Nailed it," Jenna whispers, nudging my elbow.

I flash her a quick smile before turning my attention back to the script. I'm so dialed in I don't even hear how Grayson's first scene goes. What feels like mere seconds later, the pages flip and it's time for the all-important meet-cute. The first time Grayson and I will interact onscreen.

I deliver my line with perfect inflection.

Grayson delivers his with . . . nothing. Monotonous, completely flat, worse than those apps that try to talk you to sleep, nothing.

My eyes drift across the table, watching him read from the screenplay like it's the phone book. Practically of its own volition, my head turns slightly toward Liz. Not enough to be blatant about it, but enough so I can take in her reaction.

Her lips are pursed so tightly they've turned a soft shade of purple.

Jenna nudges me softly, and I realize it's my line again. I fumble this one, but my stumbling still has more emotion than anything coming out of Grayson fucking West's mouth.

The scene drags on interminably. It's only a few pages, but I swear it takes us an hour to read. Liz reads the setup for the next scene, between Grayson and the woman playing his mother, and it's like a damn switch flips. He suddenly sounds like a man who knows how to act.

This maddening, insulting, mortifying pattern continues. Every scene Grayson and I read together, he's robotic and stiff and nothing short of terrible. In the blessed few scenes he has with other actors, he sounds like an awards-season contender. The longer the read-through goes on, the more obvious it becomes. To the point where the rest of the cast makes it known—shifting in their seats and swapping WTF looks with one another whenever we start another scene together.

And oh, the flashbacks. It's like I'm right back on set all those years ago. Not in those blissful first two weeks of rehearsal when everything between us felt amazing and natural and like we were born to play opposite one another. But to all the scenes we shot after the disaster, where we could barely look at each other, let alone deliver our heartfelt lines with even a hint of emotion.

I assumed Grayson was enough of a professional by now to put aside the bullshit and focus on the work, but you know what they say about assuming.

By the time we make it to the end of the reading, my nerves are completely shot. I'm an anxiety trifecta: sweaty, nauseated, and unable to catch my breath. I push back my chair and bolt from the room, not caring how unprofessional I might seem—nothing short of burning down the inn could lower me to his level at this point. Taking the stairs two at a time, I sprint to my room, slamming the door closed behind me and collapsing into one of the armchairs.

But someone, presumably Linda, has been in to stoke the flames in the fireplace, and the heat is too much. I stumble over to the window seat, pressing my forehead to the cool glass. My skin burns with humiliation, so much so that I'm surprised I don't fog up the window.

Liz either knows I need a few minutes on my own or she's busy trying to salvage the travesty of the first read-through. In either case, by the time she pushes through the door and crosses over to me, I've at least regained my breath and have managed to settle the spinning teacups in my stomach.

She sits across from me on the bench seat, pulling her legs into her chest.

"Lizzie, I—"

"Nope." She holds up her hand to stop me from speaking. "You're not quitting. I'm not replacing you. This is going to be fine. He's being an ass, but it's just a read-through. It doesn't really matter."

"Except for the fact that he made me look like a complete idiot in front of the entire cast." I don't realize until that moment just how much the approval of my peers meant to me. That if they felt I could do this, I might actually believe it myself. I chance a glance up, meeting her big blue eyes. Big blue eyes full of resolve and maybe the slightest hint of pity.

"The only one who looked like an idiot was Grayson." She reaches over and squeezes my arm. "I know this is not how you wanted today to go. But you need to shake it off and do whatever you need to do to get in the right head-space for tomorrow."

I shove my hands into my hair, barely managing to keep from pulling it out. "Remind me what we're working on tomorrow?"

"You know what's on the schedule."

Right.

The meet-cute.

Of fucking course.

Liz stands, leaning down to give me a quick hug. "The best revenge is to show up tomorrow and knock everyone's socks off."

"Right."

"Should we grab dinner later?"

"Sure."

She hesitates for a second, like she wants to say something else to shake me out of my funk. But she knows me well enough to know I'm not there yet. So instead she heads to the door, closing it softly behind her, leaving me to sit alone and stare at the snow like some godforsaken lonely heroine who's been locked in the attic by her psycho husband.

All right, that might be pushing things a little far, but still. The snow outside my window is a blanket of silence, and no matter how lonely it might seem, I let the silence seep into me, calming me, stilling me.

TEN THINGS
WITH GRAYSON WEST

This week we're taking a look at one of our favorite action heroes and giving you ten facts about him you might not know!

1. Grayson West is his real name! It might sound like the perfect stage name for a guy who's made his fortune blowing up stuff, but lucky for Grayson, he was born with it.

2. His favorite color is blue.

3. He hails from a small town in Minnesota.

4. Grayson is an only child, although he has said before he considers his Hostile Hostages costars to be "like family."

5. In a previous interview, Grayson claimed he had no desire to ever act in a rom-com, saying love stories are "just not for me"—I wonder what made him change his mind!

6. In his spare time, Grayson likes to work out and listen to podcasts.

7. Even though he has been spotted out and about with many a hot Hollywood lady, Grayson has yet to have a serious relationship (or at least one that we know about).

8. He is one of only five men to be selected Sexiest Man Alive twice!

9. Grayson calls that achievement "one of the highest honors of my career."

10. His first acting role was in a tiny blip of a movie called My Love on Top (which was received terribly), costarring none other than his latest leading lady, Emmy Harper!

CHAPTER

FOUR

I'VE ALREADY BEEN IN THE HAIR AND MAKEUP CHAIR for two hours the next morning before Grayson comes sauntering in. We're filming in the local coffee shop, so we're set up in a trailer in the parking lot, and the entire energy of the decidedly small space shifts when the door opens, letting in cold air and a bad attitude. Any sliver of calm I might've achieved during all my deep breathing and staring at the snow soul-searching the evening before flies out the door and off on the wind.

Grayson plops into the chair next to me and greets our hair stylist Amanda with a charming grin. "Grayson West. Pleasure to meet you."

Amanda is a stunningly gorgeous white woman with a mane of red hair I would kill for. She shakes his hand, and I can tell by the glint in her green eyes that she is immediately swayed by that smile and those perfect lips.

Even though my eye makeup has already been applied, I close my eyes so I don't have to look at him. But even with my lids shut tightly, I can feel him looking at me.

Probably with a cocky-ass grin on his face. I peek out of the tiniest slit I can manage. Make that more of a smirk.

"Morning." His voice is all rumbly and gravel-like, as if he just rolled out of bed. Which he probably did because his call time is a whole two hours later than mine.

"Morning," I mumble back.

"Open up for me, sweetie," the makeup artist, Sam, instructs.

I do as I'm told, making sure my eyes don't stray at all to my right. Instead, I focus on Sam's smooth dark brown skin and his warm brown eyes.

Sam tilts up my chin, examining my face from every angle. "Perfection."

I give him a genuine smile because up until Grayson walked in the room, Sam was doing a great job of subtly soothing my nerves, filling the space with happy yet inane chatter. "Thanks, Sam." I start to push out of my chair.

"Hold up. I'm not done with you yet, Emmy." Amanda looks up from where she's currently tousling Grayson's hair with some kind of thick pomade. "Sit that fine ass back down."

My cheeks heat, either from her compliment or the way Grayson's eyes travel over to me, as if trying to catch a glimpse of said fine ass. I plop back down in my chair before he has the chance.

He catches my eye in the mirror in front of us. "Ready for today?"

I arch one perfectly stenciled eyebrow. "Are you?"

He has the wherewithal to look somewhat embarrassed. But he doesn't say anything about his abysmal performance the day before, instead turning his attention and charms fully on Amanda. The two of them make small talk without including me in the conversation. Sam excuses himself to go grab coffee while he waits for Grayson to be ready for makeup, leaving me to fend for myself.

Which is fine because it gives me a chance to go over my lines. Ones that, you know, I wrote and definitely already have memorized.

Luckily, Grayson's hair doesn't take too long, and once I'm back in Amanda's chair, she only needs a few minutes to touch me up before she sends me off to go get changed. I push out of the trailer without saying a word to Grayson, the tension thick between us. Which I'm sure bodes well for a great first day of filming.

After I'm dressed in a soft turtleneck sweater, designer jeans, heeled booties, and a gorgeous camel coat, and then decorated with gobs of stylish gold jewelry, I make my way into the coffee shop. Liz is consulting with her assistant, Deidre, but she pauses to throw me a smile and a thumbs-up.

The coffee shop is perfect, exactly as I envisioned it while writing. There's a butcher block counter at the front, along with a pastry case full of delicious-looking treats. Even though the shop is closed for business today, the smell of rich coffee and freshly baked cookies permeates the air. The space is small, so there aren't a ton of tables, but a few mismatched pieces of furniture are scattered throughout the room. If our shooting schedule ever allows for it, I'm certain to come back here for some writing time.

Grayson enters the shop a minute later, dressed in faded jeans and a blue sweater that perfectly matches those stupid eyes. Deidre hands him an apron and walks him over to the counter, pointing out the various props and presumably showing him how to fake make a latte.

Liz approaches me with a wide smile on her face. A smile I know to be false because Liz doesn't ever smile like that.

"What's wrong?" I ask before she can get a word out.

She links her arm through mine, being careful not to wrinkle any of my clothes. "Nothing is wrong. Why does something need to be wrong for me to come check on my best friend and star and make sure she is ready for her first day of filming in more than a decade?"

I shake my arm free and push back my shoulders. "I'm fine, Liz."

Her fake smile drops, comforted by the reassurance, and she turns all business. "Good. If Grayson starts to fuck around out there, don't lose your cool. Leave him to me."

"Would I ever lose my cool?"

"Not normally, no. But with Grayson West, all bets are off." She reaches out and squeezes my shoulder. "You got this, Em. Just stay out of your head, and you'll be fine." She gives me an air kiss on the cheek and then retreats to her command zone.

Deidre takes a few minutes to walk me through the blocking before heading back over to Grayson to presumably do the same with him.

"We're going in five!" Deidre calls, tying Grayson's apron strings around his waist for him before joining Liz.

I turn to face the corner, focusing on my breathing. I inhale for ten seconds and exhale for another ten, gathering my thoughts and steadying my nerves. Because despite what I told Liz, of course I'm not actually fine. And

Grayson is only one item on my long list of worries right now. As Liz so kindly pointed out, this is my first shoot in more than a decade. It feels melodramatic to act like everything is riding on today, on this movie in general, but really, a lot *is* riding on this movie, and today is what will set the tone for the whole production.

I channel myself back to my last first day on set, one of the few that actually went well. It was a few days before The Incident, my crush on Grayson still raging, my excitement about starring in my first movie overpowering any hint of anxiety. We were good together that first day, before filming actually started. So good I can't help but wonder how things might have gone differently for my career if Grayson hadn't turned out to be a total freaking douchebag. Maybe I would've been standing on that Oscar stage accepting an award for an entirely different purpose.

Not that it matters now. Or at least, that's what I tell myself as the seconds tick by and we get closer and closer to action.

I squeeze my eyes shut. I can do this. I know I can. Grayson may have ruined this for me before, but he sure as hell isn't going to get the chance to ruin it for me again. I *will* succeed, if only to spite him.

My eyes slowly slide open as I shake out my limbs. I turn to head to the front door for my cue, but when I spin around, I'm caught by Grayson's gaze. His eyes are on me, watching me. He's too far away for me to get a clear read on the emotion in them, but I'm sure that gaze is full of nothing but mocking. So I throw him an equally mocking smile and push through the front door.

I'll give him something to mock.

Wait. No.

Scratch that.

I will give him something he absolutely cannot mock, because it will be sheer and utter brilliance.

That's more like it.

My chest heaves with the long, slow breaths I force myself to take. The chilly air outside the coffee shop helps bring everything around me into sharper focus. I can be this character. I know this character. I *wrote* this character, for fuck's sake. And I've never written a character who shares so much in common with myself before. Not on the outside—Isobel is all rich New York City girl—but her fear of never being good enough. Her fear of opening herself to love. I know I can bring these traits to her because I took them directly from me.

Liz calls for action, and after one final deep breath, I push through the front door, letting the frazzled, outwardly snobby personality of Isobel wash over me. Delivering my first line with a toss of my hair over my shoulder, I turn expectantly to Grayson.

"Uh. Yeah. Yes. Definitely." The words are there, but this is not the sweet, bumbling Josh I pictured in my mind when I wrote him. "Coming right up." Grayson's words are cutting and sarcastic, and he's playing them the opposite of how they were intended.

Rolling back my shoulders, I continue on with the scene, trying not to let my frustration mount as Grayson takes the dialogue even sharper the further we go in the scene. Isobel and Josh are supposed to complement each other—her brash city girl tempered by his sweet small-town boy. Grayson is destroying the balance with every harsh line he delivers.

But Liz lets us play to the end before calling cut and coming over to join us.

I open my eyes as wide as possible, as if the irritation and ire can seep out of me more easily. Liz just gives me one of her patented shut-the-fuck-up looks and shoos me out of the way. She guides Grayson over to the far corner of the coffee shop, and her body language makes it clear that she is giving him a calm yet stern talking-to.

Good. Serves him right.

Liz suddenly slaps Grayson on the back like they're frat bros before striding back to her command zone, practically pushing me out the front door on her way.

Liz calls action again. I push through the front door again. Deliver my lines perfectly again.

And listen as Grayson totally butchers the intent of the scene. Again.

"Cut!" Liz calls, letting her frustration bleed into her voice. "Grayson. Come on, dude. We literally just had this conversation. Josh isn't mad at Isobel. Josh is bemused. Maybe a little flustered. But he is a happy guy. A nice guy."

Grayson merely nods before resetting himself in his original spot while I head back out to the freezing cold.

And we go again.

And again.

And again.

Finally, after what feels like hours, we break for lunch. I'm so done with the whole situation that as soon as

Deidre dismisses us, I storm out of the café, not even caring where I'm going. Stomping through the slushy snow covering the paved parking lot, I make my way to the back of the building, where there's a small, enclosed tent set up, a table laden with food on the right and a few seating areas and space heaters on the left.

A couple of production assistants and crew members sit at one of the tables, but the tent is otherwise empty. That is, except for the pair of broad shoulders currently taking up enough space to block the entire buffet.

"Excuse you." I elbow my way past his dumb blue sweater, grabbing a plate and practically throwing food on it without even looking at what I'm serving myself.

Grayson doesn't say anything. But he also stays firmly planted in my way, not moving an inch until I pivot on my heel and flounce over to an empty table. Or at least, it's empty until he slides into the chair across from me.

"Seriously?" I don't even bother to swallow the bite of turkey sandwich I just shoved into my mouth before snapping at him.

"Charming." His smile drips condescension as he takes a quite dainty bite of his own sandwich.

"Go sit somewhere else. Anywhere else. I was here first." Do I sound like a petulant child? Yes. Do I care at the moment? Fuck no.

He pops a chip in his mouth, crunching it loudly and excessively, like he knows it's my least favorite sound in the entire world. "I'm good here, thanks."

"So it's not enough for you to ruin my movie, you also have to ruin my lunch?"

"Is it your movie? Here I was, thinking filmmaking was a collaborative art."

"You know what I mean, asshole."

"Tsk tsk." He wags his finger. Legitimately wags his finger. "Such language is harmful and abusive and will not be tolerated on set."

I want to grab that finger and shove it up his ass, but he isn't wrong about the whole avoiding harmful and abusive language on set deal. And the union would probably really look down on actual physical violence between costars. "Your performance in there was harmful and abusive." Not my best comeback work, but it'll have to do.

"Just doing the best I can based on the quality of the material provided." He grins before chomping down on another chip.

Mother. Fucker.

Taking another aggressive bite of my sandwich, I let my eyes meet his and don't back down. After a swig of water without breaking eye contact, I shift my tone, hoping to catch him off guard. "Why are you here, Grayson? Did you really wait all these years, biding your time for another opportunity to torture me?"

His perfectly full and absurdly stupid lips turn down ever so slightly before he catches himself and rearranges them back into a smirk. "Not sure what you mean by that second question, but as for the first, if you must know, I saw your name on the screenplay and said yes before even reading the script."

I huff out a laugh, not surprised at the admission, but shocked he'd actually make it. "So this truly is about making me miserable," I mutter. At least now I know where we stand. I grab my plate and push back my chair, preferring to eat in the bathroom rather than across from Grayson fucking West.

Grayson's arm darts out to stop me from leaving. He hesitates for a second, not making contact with me, just creating an entirely unmovable barrier. "Wait. I didn't mean it like that." He sits up straight in his seat, bringing himself closer to my eye level. "Just that I saw your name and thought this would be something more along the lines of *Midnight Sunset*."

My brow furrows, and although I don't move back to retake my seat, I retreat a couple of steps. "You saw *Midnight Sunset*?"

"Of course. At Sundance. It was brilliant." He shrugs like he hasn't just detonated a bomb in my chest. "And so when I got the call from my agent, I thought that's what this would be. And my manager insisted it would be good for my career, so here I am."

Setting my plate down on the table, I slide back into my seat. "No offense, but low-budget-emotional-feminist-grief manifesto doesn't exactly seem like your kind of project any more than *No Reservations* does."

"It's not, which was kind of the point."

"Ah, ready to hang up the machine guns and try something different?" I ask the genuine question before I can catch myself. It's amazing how easily I'm distracted by a little flattery.

He hesitates for a half second, and if I didn't know any better, I'd think that might have been a burst of self-doubt darkening his eyes. "I'd like to start exploring some more serious roles, try something new." The words sound stiff, like he doesn't quite believe them.

I take a long swig of water. "Well, if you could cut the crappy attitude for a few minutes, you might realize that this project is, in fact, something new. For you, anyway."

He scoffs, any softness hinted at in the lines of his face fading. "This is not what I had in mind."

I purse my lips, wondering why I'm at all surprised by his condescending words. Grayson has made it very clear just who he is, and liking one of my movies sure as hell didn't give him a magical personality transplant. This time when I stand, I toss my plate in the trash. "I know this might come as a shock, but you're not exactly what I had in mind, either." I swipe his bag of chips right off his plate like the petty bitch I am and storm my way back into the coffee shop.

@DeniseWest53: OMG guys. I went and dug up that old Grayson West/Emmy Harper movie and Screen Scandals wasn't lying. It's terrible. 😭

@MrsJulieWest27: Is she just a really bad actress? How hard is it to pretend to be in love with GRAYSON WEST?!?!?!?!

@DeniseWest53: It's both of them, honestly. They just seem like they can't even stand to be in the same room as each other.

@OKAllison: Forget about the movie. I did some deep diving on the whole sitch, and he was such an asshole to her!

@RomComsWithRachel: What did he do to our girl?

@OKAllison: Apparently he was talking all this shit to the rest of the cast about how she's such a bad kisser (she was 15!!!) and then him or one of his dumbass buddies put it out all over social media. Can you imagine having to read that about yourself as a teenager? What a dick.

@MrsJulieWest27: He was a teenager, too! Teenagers say and do a lot of dumb things!

@OKAllison: Let's hope he's learned his lesson.

@RomComsWithRachel: I can't decide if this makes me more excited for this new movie or less . . .

CHAPTER

FIVE

THE NEXT THREE DAYS OF FILMING ARE JUST AS PAIN-
ful as the first. Maybe even more so. The only bright spot
is the one scene I shoot with Jenna. According to Liz, Grayson's scenes with the other cast members are going exactly
according to plan—better than expected, even. And yet,
every time the two of us are on-screen together, it feels as
if I'm acting opposite an angry robot.

He really does hate me that much, so much so that he's
willing to tank the entire movie, just to spite me.

Because it doesn't matter how good the writing might
be, or how strong the ensemble cast performs; if the two
leads in a rom-com want to throw each other off the Hollywood sign, the movie is going to bomb.

Day five of filming dawns colder than most we have
had so far. Luckily, the schedule only calls for one short
scene and some B-roll footage, which consists of those
montage-like shots everyone is so fond of.

And when Liz catches me in the dining room at breakfast and fills me in with her idea for the B-roll, it's the

happiest I've been since we arrived, before I ran smack dab into Grayson's idiotically chiseled chest. I don't even complain about the extra hours I spend sitting in the hair and makeup chairs. Today's scenes are all being filmed at or around the inn, so we're set up in one of the smaller rooms on the ground level and it's perfectly cozy. I even manage to smile at Grayson when he comes in.

After I'm beauty-cleared for takeoff, I head to another small room to collect my wardrobe for today, complete with a thick scarf, gloves, and a beanie. Amanda styled my long hair in loose curls, knowing the top of my head would be covered. I dress quickly, more excited than a kid on their way to Disneyland.

I'm so anxious to get to the B-roll portion of the schedule, I don't even notice how terribly Grayson botches his entire portrayal of Josh during the scene we film in the morning. Again.

I just wait for the signal from Liz.

"Okay!" she calls, trying and failing to fight back a knowing smile. "Time to shoot today's B-roll." She nods to the cameraman to keep filming.

"Anyone feel like cluing me in as to what exactly it is we're shooting?" Grayson rubs his hands together before tucking them into his jacket pockets.

Liz simply cocks her head in my direction.

I've taken up position behind a large mound of snow. But even with my hidden location, it's clear what my hands are busy doing as I cup snow in between my palms, shaping it into a perfectly round sphere.

"Oh hell no. This is not in my contract!" Grayson frantically searches for some kind of protective barrier, but the rest of the snow is flatly packed, covering the ground in a smooth blanket.

"Oh come on, action superstar. You mean to tell me you're afraid of a little snowball?" My arm rears back, and I pause to take aim.

He holds up a pleading hand as if that might stop me. "Emmy. Come on. You can't just throw a snowball at my face with no warning."

"Warning!" I call before letting my snowball fly.

It nails him square in the chest.

I'm not the only one who bursts into laughter at both the snow splattered over Grayson's wool coat and the look of outrage on his face.

"You're dead, Harper."

Within seconds, Grayson has an armload of snowballs. I've tossed three more his way, but none provide as perfect a hit as the first. I duck behind my snowbank, gathering more of the slushy stuff in my hands, shaping as many weapons as I can.

This whole time, I've heard the poorly stifled chuckles of the crew—everyone must be enjoying seeing Grayson get his due—but suddenly, everything around me falls completely quiet, as if the whole team has just packed up and left. As if Grayson realized he should give up the fight now and call it a day. Somehow, though, that doesn't seem like something he would do.

I cautiously rise up, peeking over my wall of snow. Only to be pummeled directly in the face.

I throw myself back behind the barrier, scooping as much ammunition as I can into my arms. Waiting for just the right moment, I pop up, launching three fast ones in the general direction of where I think Grayson is.

"Missed me," he taunts.

I don't have time to duck before I'm under assault again.

"Ready to give up?" His voice is as smug as the dumb smile I'm sure is spread over his dumb face.

"Never!" I search desperately for more good snow, but I seem to have depleted the limited supply within my hiding spot. "Fuck," I mutter under my breath, desperately trying to find anything I could launch at him.

"What was that?" His voice sounds closer than it did ten seconds ago.

And then I get an idea.

"Ow! Oh fuck!" I grab onto my ankle even though I know he can't see me.

There's a long pause.

"Emmy?"

"Shit. I think I rolled my ankle." I bite my lip, wondering how best to play him. "But I swear I'm not giving up! You're still going dow—ow, oh god, ow!" Scrunching my face as if I were in actual pain, I worry that I might have overdone it and blown my cover.

Until I see Grayson darting around the barrier, dropping to his knee in front of me, not a snowball in sight.

"Which ankle?" Concern laces his voice, and I'm surprised by how genuine it sounds.

"Um, the right." I watch him, surreptitiously checking his positioning, wondering how to best gain the upper hand here. No amount of probably fake concern is enough to thwart my plans.

He picks up my ankle, and I wince. Not because it

hurts, obviously, but because his touch is unexpectedly tender. He starts to unlace my wardrobe-provided hiking boots. "Does this hurt?"

I begin to shake my head before I remember that it *should* most definitely hurt. "A little."

His fingers stop toying with the laces. He cups my ankle in one hand, the other finding purchase on my calf. The heat of his fingers burns through the denim covering my skin and I suck in an involuntary breath.

"Sorry. I'll try to be gentle." He carefully turns my ankle from one side to the other.

My brain loses all function, so transfixed on the sensation of Grayson's strong fingers wrapped around my leg. But then his blue eyes meet mine, and I remember. I remember who he is and what he's done. "Maybe you could walk me back to the inn? I'm sure I just need to rest it for a bit and then it will be fine."

And of course the damsel in distress routine works on him. He slips one arm around my waist and practically lifts me off the ground. "This okay?"

I shift a little closer to him, getting a whiff of pine and charcoal. My nose wrinkles as I try to dispel the intoxicating scent, all while getting us into position. "This is great." I flash him an innocent, flirty, "thank you big, strong man for saving me" smile.

His fingers tighten on my waist.

I don't let myself think about how good the contact feels. I focus on the endgame.

It only takes a tiny little turn on my part, just a hint of tripping, and Grayson fucking West finds himself landing straight on top of my fluffy snow barrier, sinking into the cold, wet slush. His eyes widen as he realizes what I've done, how easily I fooled him.

And because I'm an idiot, I stand there for an extra second, enjoying the spoils of my victory. Which is just long enough for him to grab my wrist and yank me down into the snow next to him. The force of his pull is so strong, the more I try to dig myself out, the deeper into the snow I sink.

"You asshole." I scoop up a handful of snow and toss it in his direction.

"Me? I'm the one who was trying to help you." He sends a shower of snow back in my direction.

I turn my head, and suddenly he's there. Right there. His blue eyes and his chiseled jaw and his perfect lips just a few inches from my face. A snowflake is caught on his eyelashes, and I have to fight the urge to lean over and brush it off.

"Not my fault you fell for the oldest trick in the book." I have to purse my lips together to keep from laughing. And lace my fingers together to keep from reaching for him.

"You are a menace to society, Harper." His words lack bite. They might even be traced with an edge of humor. Grayson's breath catches, visibly stilling his chest.

"Back atcha, West."

A shadow falls over both of us.

"I think we got what we need for today." Liz offers me a hand, pulling me out of the snow and wiping my back clean. She offers Grayson a hand next, and I'm somewhat surprised when he takes it. Liz studies us both with an eyebrow arched. "What I just saw on my screen is exactly what's been missing this whole time. The chemistry is there." She claps Grayson on the shoulder and looks between us. "So let's get our heads out of our asses and start being professionals."

Color rises in his cheeks, and I imagine how much it must sting to be reprimanded in front of me. Any hint of lightness fades, and his jaw visibly tenses. "Yeah, well, if you don't like it, you're welcome to find someone to replace me." He stalks away, storming back through the front door of the inn. I turn my face away from Liz so she doesn't see how much it burns.

WHEN I PUSH THROUGH THE DOOR OF MY ROOM, I go directly for the bed, flopping on it face-first and burying my head in the mound of throw pillows.

For a minute out there, it seemed like Grayson and I actually might have had a moment. Not a romantic, sparks-flying moment, obviously, but more like an I-could-maybe-tolerate-you moment. At this point, even just tolerating each other feels like it might be the best-case scenario. But then almost instantly, our fragile snowball of a truce melted away as quickly as if it were dropped into hell. Which I'm pretty sure is where I must be currently located.

My suspicions are confirmed when the pesky ring of an incoming FaceTime call buzzes in the back pocket of my jeans. Somehow, I already know who it will be.

I swipe to accept the video call with a sigh. "How come you respect Liz's aversion to phone calls and yet you have no problem FaceTiming me without warning?"

"I birthed you and merely adopted Liz, so she has special

privileges." My mom's face fills my screen, her reading glasses low on her nose.

"That doesn't make any sense." I push myself up into a sitting position, leaning back on the mountain of throw pillows, settling in for what will surely be a longer call than I want it to be.

"Enough about you. Tell me everything. How's it going? What's the inn like? How's the rest of the cast? The idiot boy?"

I prop my phone on my knee so I can rub at both temples, attempting to dispel the sudden onslaught of a migraine. "It's going fine. The inn is gorgeous. The cast is awesome. The idiot boy is still an idiot."

She sighs loudly and dramatically. We should have put her in this movie instead of me. "Do I need to come up there and talk some sense into him?"

"That might be the only thing that could make the situation worse."

Frowning, she brings her face closer to the phone, as if that will somehow bring my own face closer. "What did he do?"

I let out my own long sigh. "He's not doing anything. That's the problem. I had more chemistry with my cardboard cutout of Zac Efron."

"To be fair, anyone could have chemistry with Zac Efron, even in 2D." She practically giggles.

"Mom. Gross." I pinch the bridge of my nose between my thumb and forefinger. "Anyway, he's just tanking the scenes he has with me, seemingly on purpose, which makes it impossible to film a romantic comedy, since he is neither romantic nor comedic."

"What a dick." She gives a sarcastic eyeroll.

I drop the phone and bury my face in my hands. "You. Are. Not. Helping."

"I'm sorry, I'm sorry. Take me out of the blankets." The sound of her voice is muffled, and I'm tempted to pretend the call was dropped.

But I'm a good daughter, so I fish her out of the covers. "Do you have any actual advice, or do you want to continue to make fun of this snow-covered hellhole you and my supposed best friend pushed me into? Did you ever have problems finding chemistry with your costars?"

"I had chemistry with everyone, baby." She winks, and I throw up a little in my mouth.

"I'm hanging up now."

"Don't go!" Her mouth purses like she's holding in another joke. But she takes a deep breath and resets her face, and when she speaks again, she's gone into problem-solving-mom mode, which is, frankly, the best mode. "Okay. Is he tanking all of his scenes, or just the ones with you?"

"I haven't been on set for his other scenes, but according to Liz, those have all been fine." I twist the tassels on one of the decorative pillows, trying to keep myself from ripping them out.

"Okay. So step one is to find out if this is just a him problem all around, or a him-and-you problem specifically."

"It's a *him* problem."

She doesn't seem to notice my correction. "Once you have the facts, then you can decide how you want to handle it."

"By handle it, do you mean punch him in his pretty little face?"

Her eyebrows shoot up. "So you think he's pretty?"

"What? No. It's just an expression." I bring a hand up to cover my face so she can't see my heated cheeks.

"Hmmm. Well, I think you should probably avoid punching him, no matter the circumstances. He may be a bad costar, but that's no reason for you to lose your professional cool."

"So then what should I do?"

"Have you tried talking to him? See if you can find out what the issue is." She says this as if having an honest and civil conversation with Grayson fucking West is a legitimate option.

I rub my forehead, closing my eyes in the hopes of relieving some of the tension. "I do know what the problem is. I'm just not sure he even remembers it."

"Then *you* see if you can resolve it. You're both adults now; you're not kids anymore. This is your job. Handle it like adults."

"Why do you make it sound so easy?" I flop back on the pillows once again, fully embracing my inner teenager.

"It doesn't have to be anything earth-shattering, sweetie. Just talk to him. Maybe his cockiness is a mask for his insecurity."

I choke on my laughter. "Trust me, that is not Grayson West's problem."

She shrugs. "You never know. I've certainly seen it plenty of times before."

We sit for a quiet minute.

"I guess I'll give it a shot."

"Good. Let me know how it goes. I love you, Emmy. I know you don't think you do, but you got this." She gives me a thumbs-up and blows a kiss through the screen.

"Love you, too, Mom." I end the call and toss my phone aside.

Then, taking my mom's advice about being a professional, I pick it right back up and pull up the shooting schedule. I have a scene with Jenna filming tomorrow afternoon, which means my morning is open. I scroll through until I find the breakdown for the entire day. Grayson is shooting with Brian, the actor who plays Josh's brother, during the first half of the day. Perfect. Instead of sleeping in, I'll head down to set early and see if I can catch him in the act.

And then we'll settle this. Once and for all.

Like adults.

CHAPTER

SIX

WHEN MY ALARM GOES OFF THE NEXT MORNING, I'M tempted to call off my whole *Harriet the Spy*–inspired plan and snuggle back under the covers until I actually need to get out of bed.

But then I think about being able to call out Grayson for his bad behavior and prove that it wasn't just me imagining things. He really is that much of an asshole. And being able to one-up Grayson fucking West is all the motivation I need to pop out of bed and into a hot shower. I slip into jeans and a sweatshirt, planning to stay mostly under the radar during my little detective mission.

Creeping into the dining room on overdramatic tiptoes probably doesn't help with that, but I am nothing if not committed to the bit. I peek around the corner to be sure the room is empty before I sneak in and grab a cup of coffee. Staying incognito probably means I should be avoiding public areas, but the need for caffeine trumps all other priorities.

According to the schedule, Grayson and Brian are shooting a scene in one of the open spaces in the back of the inn set up to look like an office. Grayson's character, Josh, is struggling to keep the inn open since his grandma died and left him ownership of the property. When I wrote this scene, I imagined my male lead deftly capturing this moment of vulnerability, something all of my heroes have to do at some point. It's the perfect time to catch Grayson in the act—the act of actually acting—because the scene requires him to be open and emotional, two things he hasn't been able to do whenever he and I are on set together.

Coffee in hand, I make my way—slowly and quietly—toward today's set. Thankfully, no one is paying attention to me because they're busy doing their actual jobs. I settle into a corner of the room where I'll be able to see the action but none of the actors should be able to spot me. I don't really care if anyone else knows I'm here—it's not like I'm forbidden from watching filming—I mostly just don't want Grayson to see me. In order for the spying to be authentic and all.

"What are you doing here?"

I jump at least a foot in the air, barely managing not to spill my coffee all over the place. "Jesus, Lizzie, you scared the shit out of me."

She shoves her hands in her back pockets and glares at me. "What are you doing here, Em? You know you're not on the schedule."

"Can't a girl just swing by set and see how the filming of her movie is coming along?"

"She can. But she very pointedly hasn't done so yet, so that's obviously not what's happening here."

Damn her for knowing me so well. Note to self: don't work with best friend on future projects.

I take an innocent sip of my coffee. "I merely wanted to see how the cast is doing in their scenes without me."

"And by the cast, do you mean Grayson?" She rubs at the furrowed lines on her forehead. I should feel bad for clearly causing her stress.

I should, but I don't. "Maybe."

She sighs, letting her hands fall to her hips in a way so alarmingly like my mother I almost recoil. "Do you promise to stay quiet and out of the way?"

"That's my whole plan. He'll never know I was here."

"Why do I not see that not coming to fruition?" she mutters under her breath, already turning away from me.

"Love you!" I whisper-shout the words to her retreating back and am slightly offended when she doesn't return the sentiment. "Rude."

Grayson and Brian take their places on set a minute later, huddled with Deidre as they go over notes for the scene. The three of them are smiling and laughing while Deidre walks them through the blocking, almost as if they enjoy working together. But surely no one can feel that way about Grayson after the performances he's been delivering.

But man. There is a lot of flannel, and a lot of forearms, happening on set today. Both men are dressed in worn jeans and plaid button-downs with the sleeves rolled up. Brian is a good-looking guy, but after a quick once-over, my eyes stray from him to Grayson and they can't seem to move after that, stuck on the corded muscles and dusting of golden hair covering his arms—and the grin on his face and lightness in his eyes. I take in all the foreign details, purely for research. Because he is my subject, and I am a super-stealth spy and all.

It doesn't take long for today's team to get everything ready for filming, and after a quick blocking run-through, Liz calls action and I perk up, pulling my attention away from the way Grayson's jeans hug his thighs and focusing instead on the scene as a whole.

And really, it's quite touching. I love writing male characters who share their emotions, not just with their love interests but also with their friends and families. And seeing it come to life, live and right in front of me, well, it makes my heart feel all squishy and warm.

That warmth could also be due to the burning rage currently coursing through my veins.

Because what the *fuck*.

Grayson is nailing this scene. Like, he is giving exactly what I imagined in my head when I wrote it, but somehow better? Even more perfect? He's taking my words and improving them with his performance. And it should be a gratifying thing to watch.

Instead, I'm fucking furious.

I don't even finish my coffee.

When the guys wrap for the day, Brian sticks around, chatting with Deidre about who even cares what. My attention is solely on Grayson fucking West. I stalk after him when he strides off set, super-stealth mode deactivated.

He ducks into the wardrobe room, and after furtively checking the hallway to be sure no one sees me, I barge in after him, closing and locking the door behind me.

"What the actual fu—" I spit out the words as I'm turning from the door, but the last syllable lodges itself in my throat.

Because by the time I turn, Grayson has already started

to change, his flannel shirt unbuttoned and hanging open, revealing the entirety of his ridiculous chest and abs.

"What the hell are you doing in here?" Grayson doesn't move to cover himself up, because why would you when you look like that. He does shoot a glare my way though.

A glare that makes my toes curl. In anger, obviously. Pure anger. "What the hell was that?" I gesture helplessly in the direction of the set, trying and failing to tear my eyes from the ripples of his stomach.

"What the hell was what?" He crosses his arms over his chest, partially blocking my view, but also enhancing the cords of his forearms.

"That. Out there. What was that?"

He smirks and takes a step in my direction. "That is called acting, Emmy. You might have heard of it, even if you don't seem to be familiar with the practice."

I let out an indignant squeak. "Excuse me? You are the one who has been phoning it in for our scenes." I strike a robot pose and affect a monotone voice. "Hello, my name is Grayson West. I do not know feelings. Must simply stand here and look pretty."

His smirk doesn't let up. In fact, it only grows when he homes in on the last two words of my stupid robot sentence. "You think I'm pretty?"

"Ugh. As if." I roll my eyes and make sure there's no drool on my chin.

"Okay then." Grayson shrugs out of the flannel shirt, leaving him bare-chested, wearing nothing but a pair of jeans. Jeans that look super soft, like they are begging to be touched. "So did you have something you wanted to talk to me about?" He reaches a hand behind his neck, like he desperately needs to smooth down his hair and striking this beefcake calendar pose is the only way to do it.

And I am not at all transfixed on the way the motion makes the muscles in his arm bulge and the ripples of his abs tighten. "Huh?"

He outright laughs at me before reaching for a blue Henley and tugging it over his head. As if that's going to help. "Did you have something you wanted to talk to me about? I can see you are at a loss for words, so let me help. Did you want to tell me how stellar my performance was today?"

"Yes."

He's as surprised by my admission as I am, his eyebrows shooting up.

"I mean, yes, your performance today was better than the bullshit you've been giving me." I pull myself up to my full height, trying to recall the anger that had been buzzing through me when I walked into the room. "So what gives? Why are you performing well in your scenes with Brian and not with me?"

He runs a hand over his beard like he actually has to think about it. "Well, let's see here. There's the fact that the first words out of Brian's mouth when he met me weren't 'What the fuck are you doing here?'"

I scoff, crossing my arms over my chest protectively. "I was surprised to see you. And if you'll recall, I apologized for that."

Grayson takes a step closer to me. "And there's the fact that Brian treats me with respect, like I'm a professional, and not some no-talent amateur."

"Respect has to be earned, and reciprocated."

Another step. "How about the fact that Brian doesn't look at me with nothing but disdain in his eyes?"

I take my own step forward, not wanting to give up any of my power. "I don't do that."

Grayson moves even closer, leaving just a foot of space between us. His charcoal and pine scent surrounds me, and a flush spreads over me. I find myself closing the gap even further, my body moving without my permission.

Grayson dips his head, his mouth landing just an inch from the shell of my ear. "Brian doesn't come to set smelling like vanilla and oranges."

My breath catches in my chest.

We're not touching, but I can feel him everywhere, his presence surrounding me, overwhelming me, and we're frozen in this bubble. A bubble I don't want to pop.

"Grayson . . ." His name rumbles out of me, hoarse and laden with something tense and charged.

And he steps away from me. The bubble collapses, breaking the spell.

He runs a hand through his hair, and I can't read the emotion in his eyes, but it's thick. "Brian—and the rest of this cast for that matter—doesn't treat me like I have no right to be here."

And with that, he pushes past me, letting the door slam behind him.

The sound is a jolt to my system, and I finally start breathing again.

What the fuck just happened?

My body is covered with goosebumps, yet I'm flushed

and a little bit sweaty under my hoodie. My breathing is ragged, like I just attempted more than five minutes of spin class.

And there's an emotion tugging at my core. An emotion I don't like, certainly not when it's due to Grayson fucking West.

But the guilt is easy to identify. Because he's not wrong.

I can't go so far as to admit he's right. But he's definitely not entirely wrong.

GRAYSON'S WORDS RUN ON A LOOP THROUGH MY mind for the rest of the day, and the night, and the following morning. The longer I let them simmer, the more I'm able to twist them like an LA yoga teacher. He was just trying to get in my head, make me feel like I'm the one who's doing the harm here, when really, he is the one to blame. He is the one putting in zero effort, from the moment we sat down for the first read-through. I don't have anything to feel guilty about. At all. In fact, the more I stew on the tension in the wardrobe room, the less responsible I feel.

He should be the one apologizing to *me*.

I take that energy with me during one of my rare afternoons off, deciding to hole up at the coffee shop from our first day and start work on my next project. For some reason, I'm really feeling an enemies-to-lovers storyline right now. Emphasis on the enemies. I order myself a latte and settle into one of the cozy chairs near the fireplace. Just an as outline starts to take shape in my mind, my phone dings with a text.

LIZ: Don't hate me.

LIZ: I know you're going to hate me.

LIZ: But you also have to trust me.

My brow scrunches in confusion as I wait for another set of blinking dots to appear, but Liz's ominous warning doesn't come with anything further. That is, until my email pings and I see there's been a change to the filming schedule. All of our scenes for the next two days have been cleared, making way for us to devote the next forty-eight hours to one tiny little five-minute blip in the movie. A tiny little five-minute blip that's actually quite pivotal. A tiny little five-minute blip I'm now kicking myself for including.

The sex scene.

Why the fuck did I write a sex scene?

Oh yeah, because when I wrote the screenplay for this movie, I had no intention of acting in it. And once I decided to take the role, I was planning on playing opposite an actor who I genuinely like and respect, not the egotistical asshole responsible for practically ruining my life.

Okay, that's dramatic even for me. The greatest struggles I've faced in life certainly have nothing to do with Grayson fucking West.

But still. He totally ruined it.

I pick up my phone and punch in my passcode to respond to Liz.

ME: Seriously? WTF.

LIZ: I know. But you're going to have to trust me.

LIZ: I've been watching the dailies and your scenes with Grayson . . . they're not good, Em.

ME: That's certainly not my fault.

There's a long pause before I see the typing dots appear.

LIZ: It's not entirely your fault, no.

Hmmm . . . is it just me, or does that make it seem like it's kind of my fault?

LIZ: But it doesn't matter who's to blame. The scenes aren't working, and if they don't work, the movie doesn't work.

LIZ: And so we have to try something different.

ME: Something different like making me get naked with GRAYSON FUCKING WEST?

LIZ: Yes.

LIZ: Trust me.

I throw my phone down on the table with a grunt. What the hell does she mean it's not entirely my fault? It's not my fault at all. I'm showing up every day and pretending to like his stupid, hot face, which, quite frankly, I deserve another Oscar for. He's the one who can't seem to find a single hint of emotion anywhere in his dialogue—perfectly written dialogue, I might add. Although that's not entirely true, because he seems fully capable of delivering the full range of emotions with the rest of the cast. And even if our terrible scenes were my fault—which they're not—how is forcing the two of us together in close proximity with no clothes on supposed to make anything better?

Liz is so lucky she doesn't live with me anymore, because

a move like this would have totally warranted Kool-Aid in the shampoo or hot sauce in the toothpaste in our younger days. Maybe even a demotion from best friend to casual acquaintance.

"Can I assume by the steam coming out of your ears that you saw the schedule change for the next couple of days?" Jenna approaches the table cautiously from the café counter, like I might jump up and bite her.

I bury my face in my hands. "Oh my god, this can't actually be my life right now, Jenna. How did I end up in this position?"

She slides into the chair across from me and takes a long sip from her mug. "Only one position? If I recall, the scene calls for several different positions. Him on top, then you on top, then you on your side . . . you're a very creative writer, Emmy."

I want to glare at her, but the teasing glint in her eye brings me close to a smile. "In my defense, I never imagined said scene would involve Grayson fucking West."

"Is that really what you want to call him right now?" She purses her lips like she's holding back laughter.

A giggle finally escapes me. "I've been calling him that in my head this whole time. I never really thought about that terribly coincidental context."

She laughs along with me, not at me. "Not going to lie, Emmy: most people who are attracted to men would not be mad at the prospect of cozying up to Grayson West."

My laugh sours in my stomach. "Yeah. Well, most people don't have our history."

She raises one perfect eyebrow. "Care to expand on that?"

I sigh, picking up my pen and tapping it on the table. "We did a movie together when we were teenagers. Barely anyone saw it, so I don't expect people to realize, but it was a disaster. We had this one big kiss scene, and it was my first kiss—ever. We had been flirting with each other on set, and I'd built up this huge crush on him and just couldn't wait to get to that moment."

"And he was a terrible kisser?"

"No." I shrug and drop the pen. "Or, well, I don't know really. I didn't have much to compare it to. But I kind of freaked out afterward because I was so nervous. I think I'd just built it all up in my head to be something much bigger than it was, so when he didn't immediately declare his love for me as soon as the director called cut, it felt like some kind of rejection. I bolted from the set the first chance I got. Later that day I heard him telling a bunch of the other cast members that *I* was a terrible kisser and that the only reason I'd gotten the job was because of my parents."

It was like he knew exactly where to stab to make me bleed the most. And—not that I'll ever admit this out loud to anyone ever—even with my limited experience, I knew our kiss was anything but terrible. To me, it had been nothing short of magical, and to learn that Grayson didn't feel the same way—in a public setting, no less—was soul-crushing. But I don't think it's that part that still smarts all these years later. It's more the knowledge that everyone on set believed my greatest fear—that I hadn't truly earned my role in the film, or lived up to the hype that came along with casting me.

"Ah. I might have read something about that on social media." Jenna buries her gaze in her coffee cup, as if she's embarrassed to admit she was looking at the gossip rags, even though we all do it.

"Yeah. It got picked up by some of the trashier sites, and the rumors sort of dominated filming. It was all anyone could talk about. Grayson completely shut me down after that. Wouldn't even talk to me, really." I hesitate for a second, not sure how completely vulnerable I want to get with someone I still don't know very well, no matter how awesome she seems to be. But I decide to trust my gut, and something tells me Jenna will keep my secrets. "It really got in my head, all the surrounding chatter and his rejection, plus the knowledge that no one thought I'd actually earned my role. I let it affect my performance. Critics ripped it apart, and I haven't acted since."

Jenna lets out a low whistle. "Sheesh. And here I was thinking this was all due to some unresolved sexual tension."

I laugh again, but this time it's humorless. "Oh god no. The opposite, in fact." Even though just the phrase "sexual tension" is enough to bring to mind the way Grayson's breath tickled my ear, how the smell of him invaded every one of my senses.

"So you're definitely not looking forward to tomorrow then? Not even a little bit?" Her gaze pierces me like an X-ray machine, even though her questions sound completely nonjudgmental.

"Not even a sliver of a little bit." I down the final dregs of my latte. "Have you ever shot a sex scene before?"

"Oh yeah. Never with anyone as hot as Grayson though." She laughs at my eye roll.

"Any advice?"

Her head tilts, and she scrunches up her nose in the most adorable way. "Really, you just have to approach it like you would any other scene. There's blocking to focus on, so think about the movements and how your character feels in the moment, all the usual stuff. Oh, and you need to trust your scene partner, of course."

I grimace, earning another laugh from Jenna. "Oh yes, just that one little final detail." I let my head flop onto the table. "Tomorrow is going to suck."

"Again, you might want to think about your phrasing there . . ."

I wad up a piece of scratch paper and throw it at her.

She pats my hand. "You'll be fine. I promise, the whole thing will feel so clinical and absolutely unsexy, you won't even care that your partner is your archnemesis."

I sit up straight. "I *have* always wanted an archnemesis."

"That's the spirit!" She pushes back her chair and stands. "Try not to think about it, and the whole thing will be over before you know it."

"Thanks, Jenna. I appreciate your support."

"Anytime." With a half wave and a smile, she's off, pushing through the front door of the café and letting in a cold wind.

I read through the schedule one more time, trying to think about the whole thing objectively. It's just another scene, nothing to worry or fret about. I will show up and be professional, just like I have with every other scene Grayson and I have filmed together.

And I'm sure he will show up and be a complete and utter ass, just like with every other scene we have filmed together.

I try to hold on to the sliver of positive vibes Jenna bestowed upon me as I shut down my laptop and pack up my stuff. But the more I imagine what's to come over the next couple of days, the more I can only see the negatives. I use the short drive back to the inn to mentally complain to an imaginary Liz about all the things I would never say to the actual Liz, because, of course, it is 100 percent her fault I'm in this position in the first place. If only she didn't make me take this stupid role. If only we pushed harder to find a different replacement for Jonathan. If only, if only. By the time I'm stomping up the stairs and back to my room, my vision is about as red as my cheeks undoubtedly are, judging by the angry flush I feel everywhere, all over my body.

And so when a pair of large hands lands on my shoulders, preventing me from running headlong into a stupid hard chest—again—I almost dropkick the owner of said hands. Probably would've were I not holding my laptop.

"Whoa. Easy there, tiger." Grayson must immediately realize his mistake in a) putting his hands on me and b) calling me tiger, because one look into my eyes and he's taking a giant step backward away from me. He shoves his hands in the pockets of his too-tight jeans. "I'll go ahead and assume from that laser beam glare that you saw the schedule change."

I don't bother responding, pushing past him and marching down the hallway toward my room. Even though I feel like I've made my desire to speak with him—which is hovering just below zero—pretty clear, I still feel him behind me as I unlock my door.

"I can see this is maybe not the best time."

"Ya think?" I push open the door and stride into my room, attempting to close the door behind me.

Grayson's hand jets out, stopping it before I can slam it in his face. "Just give me two minutes. Please?"

I don't let him in, but I stand in the doorway with my hands on my hips. "You already wasted ten seconds."

He sucks in a quick breath, running his hand through his hair. "Okay. I just . . . I get that things are not great between us, and to be completely honest, I don't quite know how we ended up in the place of hating each other—although to be clear, I don't hate you, not in the slightest—but you very clearly hate me, and I respect that, I guess. I just know tomorrow is going to be awkward, and I wanted to be sure you know that I'd never want you to feel uncomfortable or exposed in a way you aren't okay with, and I'm sure there are a million guys you'd rather have to do this with than me, but on my end, I promise to take it seriously and be respectful no matter what."

My mouth actually drops open. I want to hang on to the claim that he has no idea why I don't like him, because, seriously, what a crock of shit, but I'm too shocked by the rest of his speech, which not only sounds honest and genuine, but also incredibly thoughtful?

I obviously must have misheard the entire thing because *thoughtful* is not a word one could ever use to describe Grayson West.

"Did Liz put you up to that little speech?"

He runs a hand through his hair, which I'm learning is his nervous tic. "No, not exactly. I mean she did give me the whole 'it's essential to be respectful' lecture, but I was already going to be and I really do want to be sure you feel okay with everything that's going to happen."

"Hmm." I don't want to believe him, but unless his acting skills have markedly improved over the last few hours, I can't help but think he might be telling the truth.

He waits a few extra seconds for me to elaborate, and when I don't, he gives me a strained smile. "So yeah. I just know there's enough to worry about tomorrow without having to worry if your scene partner is going to be a total asshole, so I wanted to be sure you knew I'm not going to be a total asshole."

I purse my lips to keep in the smart-ass retort that's on the tip of my tongue. Instead, I nod and mutter, "Okay. Thanks, I guess."

With a small wave and another half smile, he turns and heads back to his room.

I stand frozen in my doorway for a solid minute before I regain motor function.

What the hell was that about? I shut my door, dropping my stuff on the small table in the corner of my room. Was that the closest I'll ever get to Grayson admitting he was a total douche canoe back when we were teenagers? If so, it was a pretty pathetic apology.

On the other hand, he definitely didn't need to come over here and say anything. He could've just showed up on set tomorrow, made out with me, and called it a day.

But no way in fuck does one nice sentiment overrule the past. And so I will show up tomorrow and do my job and make out with one of the hottest men on the planet.

But there will be no part of me that likes it. Zero. Zilch. Not one bit.

My Love on Top Is a Total Flop
BY GERALD WINGER

I understood when I walked into the theater that I was not the target audience for My Love on Top. The teenybopper rom-com is not the kind of film I would go out of my way to see, let alone review, and yet I found myself intrigued enough by the premise—and its young stars—to make my way over to a showing.

The story is nothing new—two teenagers experience first love and first heartbreak. It's a tale that's tough to make fresh, and yet we've seen it accomplished successfully time and time again. Unfortunately, this is not one of those times.

The script, penned by Elizabeth Walston, is the one high mark of the movie, and it's a shame the young actors couldn't manage the performance her words deserved.

So let's get to the writing on the wall. I would be lying if I didn't mention one of the major draws for me personally was witnessing the film debut of Tinseltown princess Emmy Harper. Daughter of Tom Harper and Diane Brenner, Emmy has grown up in front of the world's eyes. We've all been privy to her parents' ban on her working in films until she matured. Harper is sixteen now (although she was fifteen when filming), and I can't help but wonder if that ban should have been enforced for a few more years. Harper's performance is lackluster in her best moments and overwrought in her worst. I imagine living up to the family legacy brought a lot of pressure to the role, and every pound of it shows, weighing down her performance into something bordering on unwatchable.

Harper's counterpart is newcomer Grayson West. On paper, these two couldn't be more different—her hailing from one of

Hollywood's royal families and him a complete unknown from the Midwest. One thing they share is an apparent lack of acting skills.

What could have been a heartfelt and touching story of first love turned into a boring and painful slog. What could have been the launching pad for two storied careers is instead likely the first and last time we will ever see Emmy Harper and Grayson West on the big screen.

CHAPTER

SEVEN

I'M A LITTLE SURPRISED THE NEXT MORNING WHEN I
head into the dining room for emergency fuel, aka coffee,
and find Grayson, Liz, and a woman I don't know sitting
around the table, chatting casually like today isn't going to
be the worst day in the history of the world.

Liz catches my eye as I'm filling up my mug. "Oh good,
you're here. Em, this is Clare. Clare, this is Emmy."

The woman—white, late twenties, attractive—stands
and offers me her hand and a warm smile. "Nice to meet
you, Emmy."

For a second I wonder if she's my replacement. If she's
been brought in to act as my understudy in case I fuck it
all up today. If Liz is preparing for me to fuck it all up today.

"Clare is an intimacy coordinator, and she's going to be
working with you and Grayson for the next two days." Liz
gives me a pointed look, as if she already knew what I was
thinking.

"Oh. Great." And it *is* great. Intimacy coordinator is
a relatively new position in the world of movies and

television, but a much-needed one, even if the word *intimacy* paired with anything slightly touching Grayson fucking West still makes me want to hurl. But I won't lie; I definitely feel slightly more relaxed knowing Clare is going to be guiding every move we make. I slip into the seat next to Liz and across from Grayson, who I avoid looking at.

Clare wraps both hands around her mug. "We were just covering some of the basics in here, where we can chat comfortably before we head to the set. Have you filmed an intimate scene before, Emmy?"

I shake my head. "Can't say that I have."

"Wonderful!" She turns to Grayson as if she's sharing the best news she's ever heard. "So we have two first-timers."

I peek at him over the rim of my mug. I'm surprised this is his first sex scene, too, but as I think about it, I don't recall any of his action films ever containing more than a fade-to-black kiss. Not that I've seen all his movies or anything. Only one or two. Or ten.

Grayson raises his eyebrows, ever so slightly, as if challenging me to make some kind of snide remark.

Instead, I flash him an overly large, fake smile, like I want nothing more than to share the magical moment of popping our on-screen cherries together.

Clare asks a few more ground-level questions, mostly gathering information about how much we're willing to show (me: boobs, Grayson: butt), if there's anything we're concerned about or hesitant to do (two days wouldn't be enough time to fully answer that), and if we have any questions (do I really have to do this?).

Then Liz leads us to the room in the inn that will be the set for this travesty, tucked away on the lower level, near the back corner. It's actually one of the bigger rooms, which is necessary because more than half of the space is taken up by equipment and cameras.

And in the center of the room stands a bed. One single bed. I'll never look at one of my favorite tropes the same way again.

Liz walks us through some of the technical blocking, showing us specific marks we need to hit. And then Clare takes over.

"Okay." She clasps her hands together under her chin like this is going to be the highlight of her career. "So for today, clothes stay on. We're going to take those marks we need to hit from Liz and fill in the blanks. Every move you guys make tomorrow will be precisely choreographed so there are absolutely no surprises. Today is going to be all about the details."

And that actually relaxes me just a tad. Clothes on. Focus on the details. This part I can do.

Clare guides us to our starting mark, over near the fireplace, which, for today, sits dormant and cold. Like my soul.

I'm seriously rethinking writing another sex scene ever again.

Grayson and I find our places, standing as far away from each other as possible while both staying in the shot.

"Okay, so let's go ahead and move a little closer." Clare moves her hands, indicating the small amount of space that should be left between us.

We each take a grudging step forward.

I look anywhere but at him.

And yet I can feel his eyes boring into me.

He takes another step forward, and suddenly I have no choice but to look at him because he's everywhere. Heat radiates from his body, and his pine-and-charcoal scent envelops me. I stare at his chest, focusing on the closed button right below the peek of his throat.

"Good." Clare's voice breaks into my haze. "Now let's figure out where your hands are going to be. Grayson, why don't you put one hand on her cheek?"

He hesitates for a half second before he follows her instructions. His hands are surprisingly calloused, a little bit rough on the smooth skin of my cheek, but his touch is gentle. The span of his hand is so large, his fingers wrap around the back of my neck, tangling in my hair.

"And let's put your other hand on her waist."

This time there's no hesitation. Grayson's other hand settles on my hip, grasping lightly.

"Emmy, let's start with both your hands on Grayson's hips."

Okay. Hips. I can do that.

I settle my hands, one on each side, just below his ribs.

He lets out a soft puff of a breath, and I realize I've been holding my own. I let it out slowly.

Clare steps back. "Good. Hold that for a sec while I check in with Liz."

She disappears, and even though I know she hasn't gone more than a few feet, it feels like the two of us are suddenly alone, standing in the middle of a cozy hotel room, mere inches separating our faces, our bodies touching in at least ten different spots.

"I guess it's kind of fitting that my first kiss is also going to be my first on-screen lover." Grayson mutters the words close to my ear.

The word *lover* dances across my skin, and I shiver.

"You mean your first on-screen kiss?" My eyes are still focused on that blasted button, even though now the space between us is so slim, all I can think about is popping it open and seeing what's underneath.

He chuckles, and it's husky, and I feel not just the breath of it on my skin, but the rumble of it pressed against my chest. "No, I meant actual first."

I inhale sharply. "So you do remember."

He pauses for a second, like he's been caught. "Of course I remember, Emmy."

My head tilts up, almost of its own volition. His eyes are waiting for mine, the blue as bright as a glittery snow-flake.

"Emmy, I . . ."

"Okay, this works on camera. Let's move on to the next mark."

For a half second I think about telling Clare to go away because I need to hear what Grayson was going to tell me. And I'm not exactly hating how it feels to be pressed up against him. But she's already guiding us to the next spot.

Grayson squeezes my hip before dropping his hands and moving away.

"SO THAT COULD'VE BEEN WORSE." LIZ PLOPS DOWN at my lunch table with a sandwich and an apple on her paper plate. "Frankly, I didn't think we would escape the day without one of you sustaining some kind of life-threatening injury."

I spear a bite of melon on my fork and shove it in my mouth. "The day is still young."

Liz takes a huge bite of her sandwich, giving us both a minute of silence. "But seriously. How are you feeling about everything that just happened in there?"

My skin is smoldering like the ashes left in a fireplace. My heart is pounding like I just ran a full marathon, not that I would ever do that. And my brain is whirling like a cocktail in a martini shaker. Being shaken. Repeatedly.

"I'm fine."

The look she gives me. I swear, I regret each and every day the closeness between her and my mother. Liz is channeling her flawlessly, and that is definitely not a compliment.

I sigh, dropping my fork and abandoning my plate, even though I've barely eaten more than a few bites. "What do you want me to say, Liz?"

She takes a crunch out of her apple and shrugs. "You don't need to say anything. I just wanted to check on you because I know that couldn't have been easy."

Too bad the real problem is how easy it was. How I don't think I'm going to have to pretend to be attracted to Grayson fucking West. How the only part I didn't like about the whole rehearsal was when it ended and we jumped apart like we'd been shaken awake from a nightmare.

But I sure as hell can't voice that thought, can't put those dangerous words out into the universe. "I'm a professional, and for today at least, Grayson seems to be pretending to be a professional, too. So, we'll be fine."

I know my words won't convince her, because they don't even convince me. But it's the best I've got for now.

AFTER LUNCH, WE ALL MEET BACK IN THE STAGED hotel room. Liz has excused everyone besides me, Grayson, and Clare, so the room is quiet and still.

And heavy.

During the first part of the day, we had the luxury of having choreography to focus on—Clare directing our every move, Liz stopping her to adjust us as needed, lighting guys and sound techs chiming in whenever a problem arose.

But now Liz and Clare step to the back of the room, completely out of our line of vision. It's just me and Grayson, standing in the middle of the set, getting ready to rehearse our blocking. Clothes on, but everything else full out.

In other words, I'm about two minutes away from my second kiss with Grayson West. And the first one didn't really work out all that well. At least, not for me.

I wonder if he's also thinking about that first time, way back when I was fifteen and he was seventeen. I wonder if he felt that spark when our lips brushed all those years ago. I wonder if he's thinking about what came after. If he knows what a monumental effect his stupid, immature words had not just on teenage me but on my career.

I don't have to wonder if he's as anxious as I am right now, though, because I can tell he is. His eyes are tight and his lips are pressed together as we both take our places for the start of the scene.

The beginning part is easy, and we move through the

lines quickly. Today isn't about focusing on emotion, just about nailing the movements.

And then there we are. Right next to the only one damn bed.

"Yes," I say, and the word comes out breathless.

I am Isobel. He is Josh. I am Isobel. He is Josh.

I keep the mantra running through my head as Grayson's hands find their places on my cheek and my waist.

I am Isobel. He is Josh. I am Isobel. He is Josh.

My hands float up, seemingly of their own volition, landing on his hips.

I am Isobel. He is Josh. I am Isobel. He is Josh.

For a second, our eyes meet.

All I see before me is Grayson fucking West.

And then his lips are on mine and heat spreads through me like someone just poured warm maple syrup over my head, only slightly less sticky. Our mouths stay closed because that's what we blocked, but that doesn't stop his lips from moving softly against mine. It doesn't stop my fingers from digging into his hips. It doesn't stop his own from knotting themselves in my hair, pulling ever so slightly in a way that makes me have to press my thighs together.

I think there are steps we should be taking, blocking we should be following. I know there must be, because we ran through it a million times. But none of the other times involved Grayson's lips on mine, and it doesn't even matter that I wrote the whole damn thing, because I can't for the life of me remember my next line.

Luckily, Grayson seems to have retained some amount of brain function, because he leads me closer to the bed, just like we practiced. He breaks the kiss because tomorrow we—and by that I mean Isobel and Josh—will be using this time to remove each other's clothes.

When we part, our eyes lock. The blue of his has darkened, his pupils expanded. There's a look of soft surprise on his face that I'm pretty sure is reflected on mine.

But we still go through the motions. I mime unbuttoning his shirt. He pretends to lift my sweater over my head before his fingers land back on my face, both of my cheeks cupped in his strong hands.

I choose a different mantra this time.

This is all pretend. None of this is real. This is all pretend. None of this is real.

And yet, when Grayson's lips lightly graze my neck, I have to fight the instinct to yank them back to my own and thrust my tongue inside his mouth.

Because that's not in the script. Or the blocking.

And this is all pretend. None of this is real. *This is all pretend. None of this is real.*

When his mouth does make its way back to mine, the kiss is still chaste, but it sure as fuck doesn't feel innocent. This time my hands are the ones lacing into his hair, and I don't recall Liz asking for the soft grunt he releases when I tangle my fingers in the longish waves at the nape of his neck.

And oh god. That tiny sound I'm only somewhat sure only I could hear does something to my insides. My lips become a little more enthusiastic, and when I feel the slightest brush of the tip of his tongue at the seam of my lips, they part involuntarily.

He pulls back, putting some much-needed space between us.

But I'm happy to see he's breathing just as heavily as
I am.

*This is all pretend. None of this is real. This is all pretend.
None of this is real.*

I fall back onto the bed, pulling Grayson down on top
of me.

Tomorrow we'll be bare chest to bare chest, but today,
even with layers of fabric between us, my heart pounds
out an accelerated rhythm his matches. Somewhere in the
back of my brain I know Liz and Clare are watching us,
making note of every move we make.

But I focus only on Grayson. On the lightning blue of
his eyes. On the slight tilt of a smile he flashes before lowering his head and kissing me again. On the heat of his
fingers as they trail over my chest, discernible even through
the cotton of my shirt and the padding of my bra.

"Okay, and we'll go ahead and stop there." Liz's voice
echoes in the empty room.

Grayson and I part immediately.

He hops off the bed like the mattress just caught fire.

And in the meantime, I'm left lying there like a dead-
brained zombie.

Liz offers me her hand, pulling me up, the smirkiest of
smirks on her face.

By the time I make it back to standing, Grayson is across
the room, as far away from me as he could possibly be.

And suddenly the heat rushes out of my body and I'm
so cold I legitimately shiver.

I'm fifteen and starring in my first movie and scared and awkward and intimidated by my incredibly good-looking costar who I've had a crush on from the beginning; I'm feeling every emotion when he gives me my first kiss—on-screen or otherwise—and I'm mortified when he pulls away from me like my breath is rancid and I have BO.

"Hey." Liz's hands grip my forearms. "You okay?"

I nod, not because I am, but because I need to pretend to be.

She bends her knees a little so we're eye to eye. "Em. Are you okay?"

I clear my throat and shake off her hands. Grayson might have bolted across the room to get away from me, but he can still see me, can still hear our conversation. "I'm fine. Should we go again?"

Grayson grimaces, running a hand through his hair and over his beard.

Like the thought of running the scene again makes him ill.

Liz studies me for a second. "No, I think we're good for today."

He races from the room the second we're dismissed.

Liz looks like she wants to keep me there, probably to ask me if I'm okay for the third time.

But I don't give her the chance. I pull myself together for approximately ten seconds, saying polite goodbyes to both Clare and Liz before calmly walking out of the room.

As soon as I'm clear of the set, I speed up the stairs and down the hall, needing to be in the comfort and security and silence of my own room. But when I turn the corner, he's there, standing in front of his door across the hall from my own.

I take a deep breath and keep walking, turning my back to him and inserting my key.

"Emmy . . ."

"Please, don't. I can't continue to do my job if you're going to mock me, and I need to continue to do my job." My voice is as small as he's made me feel.

His steps thud on the polished wood floor, and I can feel him behind me. "I'm not going to mock you. I would never."

I spin around, desperate to catch the lie in his eyes. "Well, you already did."

His face scrunches up like he has no idea what I'm talking about.

I roll my eyes. "I heard you, you know. After filming that scene for *My Love on Top*." He still looks bewildered and so I barrel on. "You told our entire cast that I was a nepo baby who kissed like a dead fish, Grayson, and then one of them—or maybe even you—put it all over social media."

The moment of realization washes over him, I can practically see the memory popping back into his head. His confused face morphs into an "oh shit" expression before transforming into pure annoyance. "Are you seriously telling me you're still pissed off about something I said more than fifteen years ago? A dumb throwaway comment made by a stupid, immature kid? That's why you hate me?"

I cross my arms over my chest defiantly because there's no way I'm letting him spin this. "A throwaway comment that haunted me every time I logged on to my social media accounts for months! That ran through my head every time the director called action. Yes, that's why I hate you. Jesus, Grayson. I was fifteen! I was halfway in love with you and delusional enough to think you might feel the same. Hearing you say that shit about me, calling me out on one of my biggest insecurities, it destroyed what little confidence I had. It affected my performance, which affected my reviews. I stopped acting because of you!"

A flash of sympathy darts through his eyes for a half second before it's clouded over with anger. "I was seventeen—and an idiot. I'm sorry I said what I did, but I'm not going to take the blame for you giving up on something you loved after one bad experience."

"Of course not. Why would you take responsibility when everything turned out just fine for you?" I pull myself up to my full height, although it doesn't bring me anywhere near his eye level.

He turns away, striding the few steps across the hall toward his room. He stops but doesn't turn back to face me. "I was just as scared and insecure as you were. And maybe you've conveniently forgotten this part of the story, but you ran away from me as soon as they called cut, Emmy. And I thought I was alone. In what I felt. In what we'd shared. So yeah, I said something dumb, and I am sorry that I hurt you. But don't you dare blame your insecurity on me. I've never once blamed mine on you."

I watch in silence, mouth hanging open in shock, as he pushes into his room and shuts the door behind him.

CHAPTER

EIGHT

I DON'T SLEEP AT ALL THAT NIGHT, THE DAY'S EVENTS running through my brain in a constant loop of confusion and arousal. That, coupled with crippling anxiety because I realize I still have to *film* a sex scene with Grayson fucking West, doesn't exactly lend itself to restful slumber. When it becomes clear I'm not going to be able to catch even a wink, I head down to the dining room early, needing to fuel up on caffeine sooner rather than later.

And of course he's already there, early for the first time since we started filming. Neither of us says anything as I cross to the sideboard and fill my mug. Grayson is stirring sugar into his own cup and wordlessly hands me the creamer. I wonder if it's some sort of peace offering. I don't know what to do with the words he threw at me yesterday, with the emotions they riled up. What I do know is that I want nothing less than to have to bare myself to this man, quite literally, within the next couple of hours.

I shake off the proffered creamer. "No dairy today." I pat my stomach. "Don't want to be bloated."

He sets down the small pitcher and looks me over from head to toe. "You're always gorgeous, Emmy."

And before I can formulate a response to that—was that sarcasm?—he's pushed through the swinging door to the kitchen and disappeared.

I head into hair and makeup, desperately needing a distraction and some humor, otherwise the dread pooling in my stomach might actually devour me from the inside out.

Sam and Amanda both come at me at once, tools and brushes flying, and I've never been more grateful to have to sit still and be gussied.

"How are you feeling about, you know, all of this?" Sam gestures wildly to the room at large, his eyes twinkling with something like glee, although he tries to hide it behind a veil of forced sympathy.

"Fine. I'm totally fine. It's going to be fine."

Sam and Amanda exchange a look that is laden with something I don't want to parse out.

Amanda wraps a strand of hair around a thick curling iron. "'Fine' is one way to describe a naked Grayson West."

My nose wrinkles, forcing Sam to pause his concealer application. "Ew. No, thank you."

Sam gives me a pointed look. "My friend, I know the two of you aren't exactly besties, but you cannot deny the man is gorgeous."

Sam's right, and of course we all know he's right, but I'm not going to tell him that. "He's okay, I guess."

They exchange another look, lips pursed and eyes knowing. It's clear they've had many a conversation about the topic when I'm not in the room. I burrow down into myself, determined to not think about Grayson again until

I absolutely have to. Sam and Amanda seem to catch on to my bad mood, leaving me to fester alone in silence until they pronounce me camera ready.

Wardrobe takes a surprisingly long time given I'll be half naked for most of the day. Not only do I have my actual clothing for the start of the scene, but I also have a matching panty and bra set and, of course, the nude-colored bikini bottoms that I'll be wearing once we get to the nitty-gritty.

After I'm dressed and primped and shaved and moisturized, I make my way to the back-corner room of the inn. It feels like I'm quite literally walking the plank. Or perhaps making my way to the guillotine.

Liz and Clare are already stationed in their director's chairs, and the room is full of crew members, even though we'll go down to as small a crew as possible when we actually get going. I hang by the doorway, wanting to wait until the very last second before making my way inside. Focusing on my breathing, I let my steady inhales and exhales calm my nerves.

I feel him before I see him, and any hint of calm flies out the window, but he doesn't stop to acknowledge me hovering by the door. He just strides into the room like he does this every day. And he probably does. Not the filming part, I mean, but I can't imagine Grayson fucking West isn't out there getting laid whenever he damn well pleases.

Liz sees me, hops out of her chair, and gestures me over, forcing me away from my perch and into the center of the room. I trudge over, leaving as much space between me and Grayson as humanly possible.

Liz claps her hands together and looks at us both, eyes moving from one to the other. "Look. I'm just going to be straight with you. I get that today is going to be weird and uncomfortable for everyone. But we are all professionals here, and I know we can push through and get this done. Yes?"

I nod.

Grayson mutters his assent.

"Good. Today is going to involve a lot more stopping and starting than yesterday so we can adjust lighting and sound and wardrobe as needed, so please be patient with us." She takes one of each of our hands in hers. "And please, for the love of all that is holy, if you forget everything else today, remember this."

I wait for her to bestow some life-changing acting wisdom upon us.

"Your characters like each other. So for today, you need to like each other." She gives my hand an extra squeeze before heading back to her chair. "All right, everyone, let's take places."

We shoot our entrance into the room in one take—the first time we've gotten anything done that quickly throughout the entirety of filming so far. Because, of course, we're suddenly able to manage the one thing standing between us and getting naked.

Before I'm fully ready, we're back in front of the fire, mere feet from the bed. I do my best to erase my total disdain for Grayson from my face, and honestly, once he's in my space and his hands are on me, I don't have to try very hard. It's like his touch completely wipes out all my rational bordering-on-hatred feelings toward him, which is as annoying as it is arousing.

Our eyes meet for a half second, and there's a question in his, like he needs me to be okay with what's going to happen between us during the next few hours. I don't have time to give him a real answer—or even figure out one in my head—before our lips meet and my body once again feels like it's been drenched in lava.

His mouth is even more gentle today—at least, that is, until I dig my fingers into his hips. He lets out a nearly silent grunt, but I feel the vibration of it as his lips move against mine, his pressure increasing as my fingers tighten.

We kiss for longer than needed, and I give myself over to it. Fuck the mantras. Today I'm letting myself feel it because focusing on the pleasure of Grayson's kiss, of his hands, of his body pressed against mine, might be the only way I get through this without completely losing it. It basically goes against everything Clare instilled in us yesterday, which was to focus on the process and procedure of it all, but I don't really care.

Grayson walks me back toward the bed, and when we hit our mark, Liz calls for us to pause.

We part. Breathless. Grayson's cheeks are flushed, and I can tell by the heat I feel that mine are, too. His pupils are completely dilated. So if nothing else, I know his body is as into this as mine is, whether his brain is on board or not.

The few remaining crew members bustle around, measuring lighting and adjusting booms. Sam comes over to touch up my makeup, his eyes wide and his mouth tight like he's holding back a grin.

And strangely enough, we don't break our position. Grayson's arms are still wrapped around my waist, while mine stay fisted in his flannel shirt. Hardly any space separates us and yet, after Sam heads off, Grayson lowers his head so his question stays between us. "Are you okay?"

I don't think I can form words, so I nod. The movement causes my lips to graze the golden beard covering his chin, and I have to fight the urge to nibble my way along his chiseled jaw.

He pulls out of the embrace, just enough to be able to look me in the eye. "I promise that you can trust me with this, Emmy."

And despite everything, I believe him. I wasn't lying just then when I said I was okay, but I realize that added reassurance was exactly what I needed.

Because despite the intensity of the kiss we just shared, we're still about to take off our clothes on camera. We're about to touch each other, move with each other, feel each other in the most intimate of ways, pretend or not. I'm about to be more vulnerable with Grayson fucking West than I've been with my last five boyfriends. Combined.

"You can trust me, too." And despite everything, I mean it. I lean in just the slightest bit. Our height difference means he can rest his chin on the top of my head, which he does. But first he brushes a single kiss across my forehead. And my heart pitter-pats.

"Okay, we're ready to move on," Liz calls from her perch behind the monitor. "Action when you're ready."

Grayson doesn't hesitate. He takes my face in his hands

and kisses me once again, slowly and gently. My fingers find their way to the buttons of his flannel shirt.

I break the kiss to deliver one of my few lines. "Is this okay?"

"God, yes," Grayson says as Josh. He helps me shuck off his shirt.

My hands come to rest on his bare chest. I'm surprised by the smattering of golden hair spread across his pecs and down the center of his ridiculous abs. I had him pegged for a waxer, but I'm delighted by the tickle of his hair on my palms. He sucks in a breath as my hands trace the edges of each of his cut muscles, and I don't know if he's reacting as Grayson or as Josh. I find that I don't care.

Grayson's hands skim the bottom hem of my sweater. "Is this okay?"

"Fuck, yes." My response is most definitely Isobel's, although I certainly share the sentiment.

Grayson lifts the soft cotton over my head, tossing it off to the side. He steps back for a moment, his eyes lingering on my chest, wrapped up in periwinkle lace thanks to the wardrobe department.

And it's a strange sensation. Because I know exactly what he is going to do, what he is going to say, what move comes next. But the heat in his eyes and the small curve of his smile catch me off guard.

He pulls me into his arms, and his hands snake around my back to unhook my bra. It's attached with Velcro so it comes apart easily, the familiar sound to be removed in post. I let the straps slide down my arms before I toss it off to the side.

Grayson swallows thickly, giving me an appreciative

once-over before he pulls me into his embrace. And holy fuck. My nipples graze his chest, and a jolt of electricity shoots through me. My gasp is unplanned, and he swallows it like he's hungry for more. He lowers me gently to the bed, our bodies staying pressed close together. He holds his weight off me until I wrap my arms around the taut muscles of his back and pull him down.

"Okay, we're going to cut here for wardrobe adjustments." Liz's voice shocks me back into reality.

Our lips part, and this time there's no heavy breathing, just an absolute stillness as we both come back to ourselves. Grayson stays covering me until someone from wardrobe tosses us both robes. He hands me mine before hopping up and waits until I've tied it before he offers me his hand to help me stand.

For a second we just stand there, hand in hand, nothing and everything between us.

Clare clears her throat.

Grayson drops my hand, and we both turn to face her.

"So, slight change. We're going to go right to under the covers. Liz is happy with what we have so far, so we'll skip the awkward trying-to-get-out-of-our-pants dance and go right to the main event." She gestures to the bathroom. "Take a few minutes to get ready if you need it."

"Go ahead," I tell him. "I can do what I need to do under my robe."

He nods tightly and strides across the room to the bathroom.

Sam and Amanda both rush over to me. Brushes and cotton swabs and mascara wands are suddenly flying at my face.

I'm dying to ask them how everything is looking, but I know they haven't been part of the closed set while we're actually shooting. I'm also not sure I want to know. I want to get through this next part—the most intimate part—before I can even start to process what has really been happening in this room.

"You look gorgeous," Sam tells me with one final swipe of powder. "Knock him dead." He blows me a kiss before he and Amanda exit the room and head out to the camp they've set up in the hallway.

When they're done with me, I remove my jeans, leaving my robe still tied around my waist.

I pace around the room a little while I wait for Grayson. My eyes meet Liz's for a second. She raises her eyebrows, but I give her a tight smile in response. If something were majorly wrong, she would've told me by now, so I'd prefer not to get distracted by any comments just yet.

Grayson emerges from the bathroom a minute later, avoiding the eyes of everyone in the room as he makes his way over to the bed.

Clare stands between us and the four other crew members in the room—a lighting technician, a sound operator, a camerawoman, and Liz. She gives me a warm smile. "When you're ready, Emmy."

I don't hesitate. I've been topless for quite some time now, so by this point, it isn't a huge change. I remove my robe, which leaves me just in the nude pair of panties, and climb into the bed, adjusting my hair on the pillow.

I turn my head to the side so Grayson can disrobe without me looking at him. Because he's doing a butt shot, all he'll be wearing is a flesh-colored fabric jockstrap. I haven't ever actually seen one in person, but Liz described it to me, and I know if I were in his shoes, I wouldn't want my costar staring directly at my junk.

And so even though I really want to see his junk, I keep my gaze respectfully averted until he settles himself on top of me.

This time I do the check-in. "You okay?"

His smile is tight, almost pained, and he won't meet my eyes. "Yeah."

I pull away as much as I can considering my head is resting on a pillow right beneath him. "Grayson, if you're uncomfortable, we don't have to do this." I shift on the bed so I can gesture for Clare.

But he blocks me, finally bringing his eyes to mine. "I'm okay." He lowers his forehead until it's resting on mine. "I want to do this."

I don't know if I'm imagining the added layer of meaning in his words.

"And action when you're ready," Liz calls.

I waggle my eyebrows at him in the hopes of loosening the tension. "No turning back now."

He chuckles, although it's clearly a pity laugh. "You ready?"

I bring up one hand to cup his cheek. "I'm ready. And I trust you."

"I trust you, too." He turns his head and kisses my palm. Which is most definitely not part of our original blocking.

And it's the simple gesture that kicks my heartrate into high gear. I pull his lips down to mine, and we kiss. It's soft and sweet and as close-mouthed as all of our others. He sinks down to his elbows, and his hips start to move. It's the slowest of simulations, one I knew was coming, and yet I was not prepared.

Yes, there are two layers of fabric separating our nether regions, but they don't do enough. My hands are supposed to clutch Grayson's back, as if I were pulling him deeper into me, but I have to scratch that in the moment because oh god this does not feel pretend.

Grayson West is on top of me and between my legs and his mouth is on mine, and it's not enough. The aching urge to feel him inside of me is almost overwhelming.

I can't hold back the hint of a groan that escapes me. Grayson pulls his lips from mine, burying his head in the crook of my neck, his mouth getting lost in the waves of my hair.

"Fuck," he breathes. It's a hint of a whisper I know only I can hear.

I take his face in my hands. "You okay?" I brush the words faintly across his lips.

He increases the pressure of the kiss in response before muttering, "I'm sorry," without ever breaking contact.

I have no idea what he's apologizing for at first. But then his weight shifts and the hard length of him presses against my thigh.

Fuck.

I might be new to actually participating in one of these rather than just writing them, but I do know one thing: dudes usually do *not* get hard when filming sex scenes. Everything I've ever heard on the subject claims there's no way to get fully aroused when under the pressure of filming with the crew all over the place, and yet here we are.

And Grayson looks mortified.

But if we're being honest, I'm just as turned on as he is. I'm just able to hide it.

"Okay, cut. Pause here for a minute. You guys can get up if you want to."

The color drains from Grayson's face at the thought of having to climb out of this bed right now.

I turn my head away from him, aiming toward Liz. "Actually, can we stay here? I don't want to have to get my robe on and off again." It's a flimsy excuse, but it's the best I've got on the fly.

"Sure," she responds with a knowing tone.

I grit my teeth because I'm going to pay for that with an interrogation later.

I reach down as best I can, pulling the sheet up so it covers both of us. Grayson shifts his weight off me, his hip resting on the mattress right near mine. It gives us some space down there but leaves our legs tangled and our torsos pressed together.

"Thank you." The words are a soft rumble, vibrating against my chest.

"You're welcome."

The sheet is covering just about everything from the collarbone down and yet I've never felt more exposed. My hands rest on my stomach as if to provide some sort of cover. One of Grayson's hands still cups the nape of my neck. The other is resting on his thigh. But as we lay there in silence, a thin piece of fabric shielding us from the eyes of the crew, his hand travels, lightly tracing up my bare leg to my elbow. It makes its way down my forearm to my hand, and before I know what's happened, our fingers are laced together.

I tilt my head up. He's perched over me, his blue eyes locked on mine.

And this feels more intimate than anything else we've experienced today.

Liz puts us into our final position—me on top, sitting in Grayson's lap, his arms wrapped around my bare back and my hands tangled in his hair—and when our lips finally meet again, it feels like breathing. Like oxygen. Like air.

And when she calls cut and we separate and don our robes and don't say a word to each other as we head back to our rooms like the whole world didn't just shatter, my heart stops.

Grayson West Doesn't Kiss and Tell!
by Kaylee Simmons

You know him, you love him, and if you've ever encountered any interviews with him, you know there's one line of questioning Grayson West hates more than any other. So of course we sat down with the star to try to finally uncover the secret love life of Hollywood's hottest heartthrob!

KAYLEE: *You are notoriously tight-lipped about your love life, but our readers are dying to know one thing in particular: Are you single?*

GRAYSON: *I am single at the moment, yes.*

KAYLEE: *I know that just made a lot of fans very happy! Can you tell us what you look for in a partner?*

GRAYSON: *Mostly someone who can make me laugh. Someone I feel comfortable with, the person I want to be around more than any other and come home to at the end of a long day.*

KAYLEE: *I can think of a few volunteers!*

GRAYSON: *I'm sure the right person will come along when they're meant to.*

KAYLEE: *Care to share any details on any of your past relationships?*

GRAYSON: *Not really. I like to keep my private life private.*

KAYLEE: *Okay, how about an innocent one then. Tell us about your first kiss!*

GRAYSON: *My first kiss was . . . it was perfect in some ways, messy in others. But I mostly think it was the right person but the wrong time.*

KAYLEE: *Intriguing! Any chance we can find out who the lucky girl is?*

GRAYSON: *Not on your life.*

KAYLEE: *It was worth a shot.*

I ROLL OVER IN MY BED, STRETCHING MY ARM OUT TO
the opposite side, searching for something. Something—
someone—should be there, but when my hand grazes the
cool, empty sheet, I remember that I'm no longer Isobel. I
didn't actually have sex with a super-hot man the day before. And he certainly didn't spend the night tucked under
the covers with me. In fact, as seems to be Grayson fucking
West's MO, he bolted as far away from me as possible as
soon as he was able.

It's the very definition of a rude awakening.

I reach over to the nightstand, grabbing my phone and
turning off the alarm that hasn't rung yet. Something tells
me I won't be falling back asleep. I flop over onto my back,
stretching my limbs as wide as they'll go until I make a
star worthy of the night sky you can actually see out here
in the middle of nowhere.

Flashes of moments from the day before play on a loop
in my mind like a super-sexy montage—minus the sketchy
porn background music. Normally, I'm all about a super-
sexy montage, but this one is leaving me with nothing but

a dull throbbing behind my eyes—and maybe an equally dull throbbing somewhere in the nether regions, but I can neither confirm nor deny.

I'm honestly not certain what I was expecting from a kiss with Grayson West, but a not-so-small part of me was hoping whatever spark I felt when I was fifteen would have been snuffed out by now. After yesterday, I think it's safe to say the spark is thriving, mere moments away from setting me and all of my carefully constructed walls aflame.

Luckily, in just a few more weeks, I'll be safe and back home in LA, sex scenes and cold sheets and irritating costars no longer a part of my daily life. The thought should make me happy; instead, I just find that dull throbbing traveling upward and making itself at home right in my chest.

I tell myself that's at the thought of leaving the inn, which really has started to feel like home lately. It definitely has *nothing* to do with being away from Grayson. I will have no problem leaving him behind. No matter how sparky his kisses might be.

Although, I can't help but hope that we bridged some sort of gap yesterday. I feel like there must be a sex pun in there somewhere, even if we didn't physically bridge the actual gap.

For all of filming so far, Grayson's been stilted and rude and downright horrible. But yesterday he was kind and supportive and professional. We connected, and we let ourselves be vulnerable with each other. He held my hand.

And we also both got turned on as fuck.

I roll back over, burying my face in the pillow. I've never been more thankful for my ability to keep my arousal deftly hidden between my legs. Although I'm sure he had to have known. The whole room had to have known.

Ugh. Whatever. If anyone says anything—which thankfully they won't because we all had to take sexual harassment training—then I'll just chalk it all up to my amazing acting skills.

Yes. It was all acting. Even those oh-so-tender unscripted moments that no one could see or hear but us.

I slither my way out of bed and into a very cold shower because even the slightest hints of a callback to yesterday are enough to set my blood singing. I don't bother doing anything with my hair or my face because I've got three hours in the chair ahead of me.

When I push my way into the dining room, I'm happy to find it empty. At least Grayson has returned to his regularly scheduled programming, where he can saunter in for his call time two hours later, the lucky bastard. I'm back to normal wardrobe that covers me up, so I dump extra creamer in my coffee and grab a cinnamon roll for the road. Not only are Linda's pastries delicious, they're also excellent conversation deflectors. Every time Amanda or Sam nudge me for details from yesterday, I can shove a bite in my mouth and delay having to answer.

They eventually give up the interrogation, switching the topic to the latest episodes of *Real Housewives*, which is a dialogue I'm always happy to partake in.

And speaking of interrogations, I'm still expecting one from Liz. We haven't talked since we wrapped yesterday. As soon as we were dismissed and it became clear Grayson was putting a marathon's distance between us, I beelined straight to my room, and she knew well enough to leave me alone. I know today I won't get off so easily. There will be no getting off today, pun clearly intended.

When I get the all clear from the team, I slowly walk to the door, planning to make my journey from hair, makeup, and wardrobe to the set take as long as humanly possible. Anything to avoid seeing Liz. Double goes for seeing Grayson.

My hand reaches out to wrap around the doorknob, twisting it back and forth a few times before I actually attempt to open it. But as soon as it unlatches, the door flies forward, directly toward my face. I just barely manage to get out of the way before it fully swings out, banging into the wall.

"You are lucky I have lightning-fast reflexes! I don't think Sam would take too kindly to having to cover up a black eye for the next week." I aim my words at the culprit while I'm still half crouched on the floor and unable to see who's responsible for my almost demise, although I've got a sinking suspicion.

Grayson grunts, pushing past me without so much as a hello, let alone an apology for nearly maiming me.

"Good morning to you, too," I mutter, righting myself with a grunt of my own. Now that one of the people I'm trying to avoid is here, I pick up the pace, pushing out of the room and letting the door fall closed behind me with a thud.

So much for bridging a gap.

I head to the set, knowing Grayson still has prep work ahead of him. If I have to face Liz, I'd rather do it without the full cast and crew there to witness my humiliation.

But when I arrive in the kitchen, where we'll be filming

the morning-after scene (where Josh makes Isobel pancakes like a gentleman and not an imbecilic asshole who can't even say hello), Liz is tucked behind a monitor, headphones covering her ears. I wave to her, but whatever she's watching is so engrossing she doesn't even acknowledge me.

Which seems to be happening a lot lately.

I mosey over to the craft services table and help myself to some more coffee. Watching Liz over the rim of my cup, I wait for her to see me and for the Spanish Sexquisition to begin. But she never once looks up from her screen. If I hadn't just had my face painted and hair curled and body dressed, I might start to think I'd swallowed some kind of invisibility pill, which on a normal day would be fucking awesome.

But today, not so much. Today I need someone to see me. I know Liz and I had that talk about boundaries between our friendship and our professional lives, but today I could really use her in the role of best friend instead of in the role of intrepid director.

The moment Grayson steps onto set, the energy shifts, like everyone was in some kind of cloudy haze until he blessed us with his majesty and now we are all ready to kick it into high gear.

Deidre guides him into position behind the large kitchen island, which is already set with a series of bowls and flour, eggs, and spatulas.

Liz finally comes over, giving me a quick hug before getting right down to business. She walks both of us through the blocking for the scene, and we mark it a few times. Grayson doesn't look at me once.

I'm well aware that we didn't actually sleep together the day before, but honestly, in a lot of ways, it felt like more than that. I told him I trusted him—and I meant it. I covered for him when he needed it most, and he thanked me, genuinely.

He held my fucking hand.

And so, no, I can't pretend like this behavior doesn't sting. Not only are things not magically better between us, it feels like we've taken ten steps back. The rejection is a stark reminder not only of who Grayson is now but also of who he was in the past, and I can't help the flood of negative feelings his rebuff stirs.

I don't like it.

At the very least, when the cameras start rolling and we're both in character—a couple who are actually happy they shared an intimate experience with each other—he'll have to look me in the eye. Maybe even give me some sort of smile.

Wishful fucking thinking. When Liz calls action, we're right back at day one. Grayson mutters his lines with zero inflection, as if he literally can't be bothered to put in the bare minimum level of performance. And instead of pushing through and trying my best, I succumb to the anger pulsing inside of me. Anger always has been easier for me to handle than sadness, and so I sink into it, not willing to admit Grayson has the power to make me feel sad.

And all of a sudden, Josh and Isobel seem really pissed about the mind-blowing sex they shared the night before.

Liz calls cut and redirects us so many times that I lose track of what number take we're on. All I know is that the number is high—as high as the tension mounting in the room the longer the day drags on. This is meant to be a short scene that we should have finished in only a couple of hours, and yet, we work through the evening, shooting the same dialogue and motions over and over again until I hate the very words I wrote on the page.

Finally, Liz calls a wrap for the day and the room exhales a sigh of relief. Except for me, because she's stalking in my direction, and I can't remember the last time I saw my best friend look angry enough to put someone in a choke hold and WrestleMania them to the ground.

I take a few steps back, forgetting that Grayson is behind me until my butt bumps into his hip. He moves away from me like I burned him. I turn and give him my best icy-cold glare, but he still won't even look at me. Shock of shocks.

Liz doesn't stop until she is two inches outside my bubble, and I have never regretted more being the same height. Great for sharing clothes, not so fun when she's staring me down with venom in her eyes.

"You two will meet me in my room tomorrow morning at ten a.m., where we will spend however long it takes to figure this shit out. The jig is up. I get that things were weird in the beginning, and I think I've been very understanding about that. I've given you eight entire days of this production's time to pull your heads out of your asses, assuming you could get over yourselves, but I can see now it was eight days too many." She turns her menacing glare on Grayson, and I'm happy to see him shrink back. "Enjoy tonight, because starting tomorrow, you are mine. The games are done. We're putting on our big girl panties and making a fucking movie." She spins on her heel and storms off, calling over shoulder, "Don't even think about being late!"

Grayson and I share a quick glance, like siblings who just got in trouble for fighting and share a brief moment of unity against Mom.

I ruin it first. "Try to dig up some of those acting skills you claim to have before tomorrow, yeah?"

"Even the best acting skills can't turn shit writing into a good movie, sweetheart." He crosses his arms over his chest and stares at me defiantly.

I mimic his pose. "You suck, West."

He leans in just enough for me to get a good whiff of pine and charcoal. "You wish, Harper."

He doesn't even get to see the outrage and horror—and, yes, maybe a hint of lust—on my face, because he's already striding across the room and pushing out through the kitchen door.

I SHOW UP TO LIZ'S ROOM EARLY THE NEXT MORNING, determined to arrive first. Not that I necessarily needed to, because Grayson clearly doesn't seem to keep the same time as the rest of us, but I also want to squeeze in a moment alone with Liz. I know we're maintaining professional boundaries, but I owe her a best friend check-in. I rap softly on her door and keep my head down when she lets me in, like the chastised child I am.

She gestures for me to sit in one of the armchairs arranged in front of her TV.

"Lizzie, I—"

"Nope. No talking."

My mouth stays open, frozen in position. Okay then. I guess I'll put a pin in that check-in.

Grayson knocks on the door a few minutes later, on time for once. He folds himself into the chair next to me without a word of greeting.

Liz perches on the low top of her dresser, arms crossed, managing to stare down both of us at the same time. "I've been exceedingly patient with the two of you. To be honest, I probably let this go on for longer than I should have, but I let myself believe you would come to your senses without my intervention."

I open my mouth to protest because I am clearly an innocent party in all of this and certainly don't require any patience or intervention from Liz. But she shuts me down with one tight stare before I can even squeak out a single word.

"I get that this is not the situation we hoped for or planned for. Please trust me when I say I tried everything to make sure we didn't end up here. But here we are." She turns her attention to Grayson, who shifts uncomfortably in his seat. "I know this movie is out of your wheelhouse, West. But you knew what you were signing up for. And you knew who you were signing up with. I'm not going to let your shitty attitude kill a movie that literally hundreds of people have a stake in. Be a professional, or get out."

I purse my lips together, trying for a half second to hide my smug smile before I give in and let it take over my face. I turn it full force to my left, thrilled to see Grayson sinking as low as possible in his chair, chastened and humbled as he should be.

"And you."

My blood freezes as Liz turns her wrath toward me. Which is not how this conversation was supposed to go at all.

"You are my best friend, and I love you. But you begged me to take on this project because it's so personal to you, and I did, and now I need you to pull your weight. I get that circumstances are not ideal, but some actual acting needs to happen here, Em. I won't allow you to tank our movie either."

My mouth drops open, and I'm not sure whether I should be shocked or angry. Both? Nope, angry it is. Definitely angry. "You mean *my* movie?"

Unsurprisingly, she doesn't back down from my unflinching gaze. "You may have written it, but it belongs to all of us now. Investors, producers, your fellow castmates, your crew." Her eyes start to ping-pong back and forth between me and Grayson. "This is not about the two of you. You're actors. If you don't like each other, pretend." She turns around to grab the remote and flips on the TV. "Now, here's the plan. The two of you are going to sit and watch. You are going to come to some sort of agreement about how you would like to proceed. And then tomorrow, you will show up on set and make a goddamn adorable romantic comedy. Where you convince people you actually like each other."

I shoot Grayson a look out of the corner of my eye. He's still sulking, hunched in on himself and practically curled up in his chair.

Liz's voice softens the tiniest bit. "I know you both are capable of turning in amazing performances." She hits play on the remote. "Just get over your bullshit already."

And with that, she strides out of the room, letting the door thud shut behind her.

I sneak another peek at Grayson, but he's still pretending like I'm not here, so I do the same, turning my eyes to the screen in front of us.

The moment the image pops up, it becomes clear what

Liz is doing. I watch myself push open the door of the coffee shop, full Isobel attitude in place. I watch Grayson fumble with making a latte, zero Josh characterization evident.

And my smug smile comes back. Liz might have come down equally hard on both of us, but clearly she is still Team Emmy. I understand her goal here: make Grayson watch the footage of himself, see how terrible a job he's doing, and hope that finally brings him around.

By the end of the meet-cute scene, my smile is so wide I probably look like a scary jack-o'-lantern. I nailed that first scene, and Grayson bombed it. I sit up a little straighter in my seat as the next scene plays. It's one where Josh and Isobel are starting to realize their feelings for each other, where Isobel is supposed to be softening toward him.

But nothing about my performance is soft. Grayson still plays the scene with no emotion or inflection, but I just sound mean. Like I hate him. Which, to be fair, I do. But Isobel doesn't hate Josh, not at this point, anyway.

By the third scene, which is meant to be another romantic moment, I sink back into my chair, smug smile completely wiped from my face. It's more of the same. Nothing from Grayson; anger from me.

By the fourth, I've pulled my legs up to my chest, arms wrapped around them to make myself as small as possible, my chin tucked behind my knees so I can watch and hide at the same time.

I don't dare watch Grayson watch this footage.

Because I've been blaming him this whole time, but in reality, my performance is just as bad. And yeah, I could blame my anger on his total lack of participation, but if I were truly doing my job as an actor, I would still be turning in good work. And this work sucks. On both our parts.

Grayson clears his throat, drawing my full attention back to the screen.

Where we're suddenly locked together in a passionate kiss.

Oh god.

What's more mortifying than realizing you're a terrible actor? Watching your terrible sex scene.

Except . . .

It's not terrible.

Not at all.

My head slowly creeps out from behind the shelter of my knees, but I keep my legs pressed firmly together.

Because this is hot.

Nipples peaked and panties damp hot.

Grayson clears his throat again, and I catch him adjusting his jeans. So I'm not the only one who thinks so.

And as the scene continues, as we take off each other's clothes and fall into bed, I realize it's not just that the scene is steamy—which it most definitely is—but it also feels sweet and genuine, like our characters are connected and actually have feelings for each other. I watch Grayson kiss my palm, and I suck in an audible breath.

This right here is movie magic.

The scene fades out a minute later, replaced by a blank black screen.

Neither of us says anything for a solid minute.

What is there to say?

Finally, Grayson pushes himself out of his chair and heads toward the door.

"Wait." I untangle my limbs, falling gracelessly out of my seat. "Liz said we needed to talk and figure things out."

His voice comes out gravelly and rough, like he just choked on something. "I need some time to myself. I'll come find you later." And he pushes out the door, letting it fall shut gently behind him.

I stare in shock at the closed door for thirty seconds before I start to move. If Liz comes back and finds me in here alone, there is going to be hell to pay, and clearly, I will not be spared. After double-checking the hallway to be sure it's clear, I dart back to my room, sagging with relief when I get the door closed without being caught. Like I'm back in high school, aka the last time Grayson fucking West ruined one of my performances.

All right, maybe it's not totally fair to lay the blame for my shitty acting at his feet. At least, not entirely. Yes, Grayson is an asshole who has a way of getting in my head, but the truth of the matter is, I let him. I've been walking around this set feeling oh-so-superior, and I've been just as bad as he's been. And at least he knows he's turning in a lackluster performance—he's even been doing it intentionally. I'm the one who's deluded herself into thinking I was Oscar worthy.

I finally push off from the door, slipping out of my shoes and pacing around my room.

All right. Time to find a solution. I can't imagine Grayson will actually take Liz up on her offer to leave. Quitting a movie this far into production is not a good look, and his pride won't let him be the bad guy here, I'm sure. So that means we have to find a way to work together. What is it that's been making it so hard for us to connect? Other than him being a total asshole.

There's our messy past, of course.

But honestly, I feel far removed from that at this point. Once I got over the shock of seeing him, I didn't need that past anger, because I had present frustrations to focus on.

There's his total disregard of me.

That definitely stings, especially after we made some progress while shooting the sex scene.

And there's the tension.

Which never seems to go away.

Except for when it did.

It went away when we were naked and kissing and vulnerable with each other. The one time Grayson and I have been able to put something on film that doesn't put us up for Razzies contention was when we were being physically intimate. Our best work came when we were both naked and tangled up together, when we were connecting on a physical level. Chemistry is the one thing we've always had, despite all the bad feelings.

I stop in my tracks. The chemistry. The physical connection. The only thing we do well together.

Do we?

Can we?

Should we?

My head shakes back and forth, vehemently, but then I pause to consider. I feel like I'm the kombucha girl: Is this the best idea I've ever had, or am I a total idiot?

A thumping on my door puts a pin in my thoughts.

I open it, worried I'll find Liz on the other side, although she probably would have just barged in. Instead, it's the second-worst option.

Grayson fucking West.

He's still wearing the faded jeans and long-sleeved T-shirt from before, but it's only now that I notice how both are clinging in all the right places. His hair is tousled, not in the purposeful way, but like he's been running his hands through it. "Can I come in?"

I push open the door and he brushes by me, leaving me with a whiff of pine and charcoal. Just the faintest touch of his fully clothed skin to mine solidifies my decision.

He stops in the middle of the room. I turn to close the door and walk slowly toward him like he's an animal that might spook.

"I've been thinking about what Liz said." He scrubs a hand over his beard.

"So have I."

We both take a deep breath.

"I think I should quit," he says.

"I think we should have sex," I say.

Heat rushes to my face. His words came out jumbled, but not so jumbled that I didn't catch what he said. And judging from his wide eyes and open mouth, he heard exactly what I said, too.

Mortification floods through every single one of my veins. I can't believe I just said that out loud. And not only that, but he wants the exact opposite of what I just offered—which was, quite literally, myself. Just end me now.

"Shit." I spin away, not wanting him to see the flush creeping over every inch of my skin.

He takes a few steps closer to me, and I can feel the heat of him at my back. "What did you say?"

"Nothing." I cross my arms over my chest. "It's—I—I would never want you to do something you don't want to do. This is silly. You don't want me, obviously, that's been pretty clear from the beginning. I didn't mean—" My words catch as one of his arms snakes around my waist, tugging gently until I spin around to face him.

He doesn't let me go, his head lowering until our mouths are inches apart. "You think I don't want you?"

"It was a stupid idea. I just figured maybe it would help with the tension, since *that* scene was the one thing we did well together. But again, it was a colossally dumb idea. Like the dumbest, I should never have suggested—"

My words are cut off by the crush of his mouth on mine.

For a moment I'm too stunned to react, but then I sink into his kiss, looping my arms around his neck, pulling myself closer into his embrace. And there is nothing closed-mouth or PG-13 happening here. Grayson's one hand tightens on my waist while the other cups my neck, his fingers threading into my hair. It might mimic the position we took on set, but as he pulls me into him, his tongue sweeping into my mouth, this is nothing like what we did on camera. Heat pools in my belly as our lips and tongues collide.

I whimper. I legitimately whimper.

And he growls.

I push him out of my space for a half second, just long enough to tug my sweater over my head. "One time only. No strings. There's clearly some tension here. Let's just cut it and save the movie. Yes?"

"One time. No strings. Got it." His voice is hoarse and raspy, but his eyes stay locked on mine. "Are you sure about this?"

I nod, biting my lip and hoping he doesn't back out now. Because I'm realizing just how badly I want him, how much I need this. "I'm sure. Are you sure?"

He grunts his assent, his eyes finally drifting down to my chest. He moves in to kiss me again, but I shove him back. Gently.

"Shirt off. Now."

He grins, and it's nothing short of salacious. He reaches behind his head, grabbing the back of his shirt and yanking it off in that way only guys seem to do.

Today's bra isn't a costume piece and so it has real hooks, but that doesn't stop him from releasing it in one quick snap.

This time I move back into his space and he's the one who puts up a hand to stop me. His eyes trace me, from the tangled waves of my hair to the curves of my breasts. "You're fucking gorgeous, Harper."

I let my hands run over the ridges of his chest and stomach. "You're not so bad yourself, West."

He grunts again, yanking me back into his arms, the skin-to-skin contact making me sigh. His mouth finds mine but doesn't linger there long before his lips move down to my jaw. When he reaches my neck, his teeth graze along my skin, and I thread my fingers through his hair, bringing him back to me for another searing kiss.

His hands travel up and down my bare back before they land on my ass, cupping me, pulling me into his hips. He's hard as a rock, and I'm hungry for him. As I abandon his golden waves, I let my hands slide down the ripples of his stomach until I'm stroking him through the denim of his jeans. He thrusts into my hand, groaning as I squeeze.

"Fuck, Harper." His fingers dig into my butt, lifting me and literally tossing me onto the bed.

"Wait." I push myself up onto my elbows before he can cover me with his body.

Something like anguish flashes in his eyes, but he doesn't come any closer to me.

"Condoms are in the bathroom." I give him a wicked smile. "Top drawer."

He disappears for a minute, and while he's gone I shimmy out of my leggings, thankful I put on semidecent underwear this morning. They're plain black briefs, but when Grayson comes back into the room, his eyes darken like I'm wearing the sexiest of lingerie. He tucks the foil packet under the pillow, unbuttons his jeans, and pushes them down over the thick muscles of his thighs, his eyes never straying from me.

The outline of his cock is rigid through the thin fabric of his boxer briefs, and I want him in me. Now. I reach my hand under the pillow and pull out the condom.

He wraps my fingers around it, closing it in my fist. "Not yet."

And then he lowers himself over me, and he's hard and hot everywhere, yet his lips turn soft and gentle, licking at my neck, nibbling along my collarbone. His mouth travels down to my breasts, letting out a soft puff of air that makes me squirm.

"Grayson . . ." I wiggle beneath him as if that will force him to give me what I want. But that was stupid of me.

He lifts his head, meeting my gaze with an evil smile. "Did you need something?"

"You know what I need." I glare at him, arching my back so my breasts press into his chest.

Shifting his weight off of me, he props himself on one elbow, perching above me. He trails a single finger over the curve of my breast. "This?"

Even though I shudder from his touch, I manage to maintain my glare. "No."

He traces his blasted finger to my peaked nipple, giving it the softest of pinches. "This?"

My breath catches, but it's still not enough and he knows it. "No."

Lowering his head, he swirls his tongue around the tip of the bud. "This?"

"No." My protest comes out breathless and not at all convincing.

"Hmmm." Without warning, his light, teasing lick turns into a gentle but firm bite.

I gasp, my hips arching off the bed.

Grayson quits the teasing almost as quickly as he started, his mouth licking, sucking, and nibbling one nipple before turning his attention to the other, until I'm writhing beneath him. I shove my hand down the front of his boxer briefs, and he groans. I feel the vibrations of it on my skin as I wrap my hand around the hard length of him.

He pulls his mouth from my breast with a muttered, "Fuck. You're going to end me before I've even gotten started with you."

And that might be the hottest thing a man's ever said to me. So hot I wiggle out of my panties, kicking them off to the side. Grayson shucks his boxer briefs, and I finally get a good look at him. Although I think we can all agree that penises are not the most attractive of body parts, Grayson West has maybe the sexiest penis I've ever seen. He's on his knees, perched in between my wide-open thighs, and I don't even care that I am literally baring myself to him in this moment.

I want him, consequences be damned. I don't care if this makes things better or worse on set. Fuck, I don't care if the whole movie gets canned.

I fish out the condom once more, and he doesn't stop me this time. Instead, he brings his teasing finger down to where I'm aching most, skimming over me as lightly as possible when all I want is pressure and thrusting. I rip at the condom wrapper, and he increases his pressure when he sees me struggling, distracting me from my end goal. Like he's enjoying torturing me. Which I'm sure he is.

I finally manage to get the condom out of the wrapper, and as I move to slip it over him, his finger finally finds my clit, circling until I can hardly see straight, let alone get his cock covered in some latex.

"You're making this very difficult," I pant.

He brings his head down, his tongue flicking over my nipple. "That's the plan." He sucks the bud, pulling it into his mouth as his finger slips inside me, his thumb providing the much-needed pressure on my clit.

And that's all it takes. I come apart underneath him, and I cry out his name as release rips through me.

It takes me a couple of seconds to come back to myself, and when I do, the first thing I notice is the shit-eating grin on his face. The second thing I notice is his hand, slowly stroking himself. He's got the condom in his other hand.

I take it from him, slipping it over his hard length, replacing his hand with mine. "Why are you not inside me right now?"

He stills for a second, losing the grin, and I worry he's changed his mind, which might literally kill me at this point. "Just want to be sure you still want to do this."

I grab his hips, guiding him to my entrance.

"Say it, Emmy." He shifts back the tiniest bit, leaving a small space between us. And there's something hidden in the shadows of his darkened eyes. Something like uncertainty. Like insecurity.

I swallow the sarcastic retort on the tip of my tongue and cup his cheek in my hand. "I still want to do this, Grayson. I want you."

His eyes lighten the tiniest bit, and he leans down, placing a soft kiss on my lips. He pushes into me, slowly, stretching me right to the borderline of pain. Stilling once he's fully seated inside me, he kisses me again, deeper this time, until my body relaxes around him. One of his hands finds its way back to my hair. I let mine roam everywhere, over the muscles of his shoulders and back, down to his rock-hard ass.

"You feel even better than I ever imagined," he mutters into my ear.

And something ignites inside me, not just because his thrusts are growing stronger and deeper, but because he's thought about this before.

Because yes, maybe I also have thought about this. Once or twice. But it doesn't dampen the thrill of knowing he's done the same.

"Have you ever touched yourself while thinking about me?" The question slips out in a whisper before I have time to think about it.

He puts just enough space between us so he can look into my eyes. He has his usual wicked glint, but I also know now that he'll give me an honest answer. Maybe because he's currently buried deep inside me, but whatever the reason, I'm not picky.

"I jerked off in the shower last night thinking about you." His hand travels back to my breast, pinching my nipple before leaning down to lick it. "Have you ever touched yourself while thinking about me?"

"No." I'm not going to lie to him, but I thrust my hips up to meet his. "But I'm sure I will after today."

His hand slips down between our bodies, landing on the perfect spot, as if he wants to give me one more vision to add to my spank bank. "I want to make you come, Emmy."

I roll my hips up to meet his, increasing our pace as his fingers continue to work over me. I'm close, frustratingly close, but I can tell by the way his rhythm falters that he is, too.

"Kiss me, Grayson."

His lips crash down on mine without hesitation, and a second later my whole body tightens beneath him. I cry out another release, but his mouth never leaves mine, not until he shudders out his own release a minute later.

Our kisses turn soft and slow until we finally both

come down. Grayson pulls out of me, immediately hopping out of bed and heading to the bathroom to dispose of the condom. He hesitates in the doorway for a half second before moving to his clothes, getting dressed while I cover myself with the sheet.

Part of me—maybe a not small part of me—wants to ask him to stay, but that's not what this was. It was a one-time offer for earth-shattering sex so we can cut the tension and focus on the work. And so even though I'm tempted to tell him to stay naked and get his ass back in bed, instead I watch as he silently pulls on his jeans and shirt.

When he's fully clothed, he hesitates again, just for a second. Then he crosses over to me in two long strides. He leans down and kisses me once. "That was amazing."

I nod, unable to stop myself from fisting my hand in his shirt and bringing him back to me for one more kiss. "See you tomorrow."

"See you tomorrow."

He lets himself out of my room, closing the door softly behind him. Judging by the light outside my window, it's still only midafternoon, but I can't bring myself to get out of bed. So I don't, instead spending the rest of the day wrapped up in sheets that smell like Grayson fucking West. Emphasis on the fucking.

CHAPTER
ELEVEN

FOR THE SECOND TIME IN AS MANY DAYS, I WAKE UP reaching out for the invisible man next to me, only to find cool sheets and empty space. This time, when visions from the day before flash in my mind, they're real ones. Grayson licking my neck and biting my nipple. Grayson pushing into me. Grayson's fingers threading through my hair. Grayson kissing me like I have never been kissed before.

I groan, pressing my thighs together and burying my head in the pillow.

While ruminating in the very cold shower I need after a few more minutes of reminiscing, I play out the two possible scenarios for today. One, yesterday's idiotic, libido-based decision totally ruins everything and the entire movie falls to shambles. Two, banging Grayson West has the desired effect and we both get over our bullshit and turn out some good work.

Scenario two also means you could screw him again, an impish little devil says from her perch on my shoulder.

An involuntary moan escapes me at the mere thought. But no. That is absolutely not an option. Even if we both turn in the performances of our lives today, yesterday was a one-time-only affair. Grayson and I will not be sleeping together again. Ever.

Mind resolved, I step out of the shower and throw on some lounge clothes before I head downstairs for coffee and hair and makeup.

Sam and Amanda exchange a look when I enter the hair and makeup room, sipping at my coffee as I hop into the chair. I wonder how much the rest of the cast and crew know about our meeting with Liz yesterday. Hopefully about as much as they know about what happened after: nothing.

Sam studies me while Amanda starts to blow out my hair, but I don't pay attention to his unwavering gaze, instead focusing my attention on the much-needed caffeine in front of me.

He's harder to ignore, however, when he's smack-dab in front of my face, smoothing creams and lotions and paint over my skin. His brow furrows. "Did you do something new yesterday?"

Had I still been drinking coffee, I would've choked on it. "Something new? Nope. Not a thing. Yesterday was like all other days. Nothing out of the ordinary."

His perfectly sculpted eyebrows rise up, practically to his hairline. "All right then. Nothing new. It's just your skin is glowing. And your eyes are brighter."

I purse my lips together tightly. "Oh. Um. Well, I might have tried a new moisturizer?"

He doesn't even try to hide his disbelief as he sneaks a look at Amanda. "Sure. That was probably it. New moisturizers can do wonders for the skin."

"I always love when I try out a new moisturizer," Amanda adds as she wraps a long strand of hair around a curling wand. "It just brightens up the whole day."

"When I try a new moisturizer, I always feel so invigorated afterward." Sam can barely contain his giggles.

I glare at both of them. "Why do I get the feeling we're not actually talking about moisturizers?"

Which is, of course, exactly when the door to the room opens. I know it's him before I see him, like I've developed some kind of special Graydar. Also, Sam's lips purse so tightly I don't know that he'll ever be able to pry them apart. I very purposefully avoid any and all eye contact with Grayson, even when he plops down in the chair next to mine.

"Good morning, Emmy."

It's by far the nicest, friendliest thing he's said to me on set that wasn't scripted. Both Amanda and Sam pause in their ministrations, eyes going wide.

Shit.

The only thing worse than the fact that I had mind-blowing sex with Grayson fucking West would be everyone finding out I had mind-blowing sex with Grayson fucking West.

"Ready to not totally suck at acting today?" I throw the barb his way, but I know it lacks its usual venom.

Sam and Amanda exchange another knowing glance.

"Hmm. I'm not sure I've done enough sucking yet. I've got a quota to meet." His eyes meet mine in the mirror in front of us, and he licks his lips slowly and purposefully.

My mouth drops open, and I swear a little drool escapes.

He quirks up one eyebrow.

Oh. Fuck.

Sam swipes a gloss over my lips and flashes me a quick wink. "And . . . that's that for today! All set, Em."

God bless Sam. Forgiveness for ruining the word *moisturizer* is granted.

I bolt from the room before my blood has a chance to boil over and burst into flames. I head to wardrobe next, where the sheer act of removing my clothing and stepping into my costume only further stokes the fire one freaking sentence and a little lip licking from Grayson West ignited.

Liz catches me on my walk from wardrobe to the kitchen set, where we'll be filming today. "Everything go okay yesterday?"

I steadfastly avoid eye contact. Liz is not only my best friend, but she's also perceptive as hell. The second I open my mouth she'll know something happened. And frankly, I have no idea how she would react to yesterday's shenanigans—in a way, we *did* deal with the issue, like she asked us to, but something tells me our course of action wasn't what she had in mind. It's practically impossible for me to keep something of this magnitude from her, but I know I have to, for now at least. Boundaries and all that. So I summon all my acting skills—the real ones, not the terrible shit I've been pulling out for this movie so far.

"Everything went great! I think today is going to go really well! It's all sorted!" Instantly, I know that was way too upbeat, but I force a fake grin and practically run away from her as soon as the kitchen is in sight, scurrying behind the counter where Deidre waits to explain how to fake bake cookies.

Grayson joins us a few moments later, and damn, he looks good. He's wearing worn jeans and that blue sweater that's the exact color of his eyes. And the apron Deidre hands him should make him look ridiculous, but instead, it's the cutest fucking thing I've ever seen.

Deidre gives us a quick rundown before heading back to her perch behind the camera next to Liz.

"Hi." The word dances from his lips over the shell of my ear, and given the way my body responds, you'd think he just recited a goddamn sonnet.

"Hi."

He grabs the spatula, drumming it on the counter while we wait. "You feeling okay? About yesterday?"

I want to yank the spatula out of his hand, but I stymie the urge after realizing the drumming sound is loud and distracting and the perfect cover for this conversation. "Yeah. I'm good." I chance a glance at him. There's nothing weird or creepy in his gaze. I let out a breath. "I just really want today to go well, you know?"

He leans in just a smidge, and his hand, hidden by the counter, slips underneath my sweater to trace along the small of my back. "It will."

And god help me, I believe him.

From the moment Liz calls, "Action!" it becomes clear that he was right. Nothing pisses me off more than Grayson West being right, but in this case, I'd happily shout it from the rooftops.

I feel the difference immediately. Grayson delivers his lines with these weird things called feelings and emotions. And those feelings and emotions allow me to also express feelings and emotions, ones other than anger and frustration. The chemistry zings between us, and by the looks on the crew members' faces when Liz calls cut, the shift is clearly noticeable.

We do a few takes, but for once, it's not because we're screwing up and are attempting to turn out something bordering on salvageable. Instead, we get to do several to be sure we get the best possible iteration of the scene. And then Liz lets us loose to shoot some more B-roll, and the air around us lightens to pure champagne bubbles.

At one point Grayson leans over and licks a drop of frosting from the tip of my finger, and I almost have a spontaneous orgasm. The heat in his brilliant blue eyes lets me know he's just as affected as I am, and I curse myself for limiting us to just one time.

But even though the experiment clearly worked, I still feel good about my decision. We can't risk it again. Having sex once with no strings is totally doable; more than once veers into the danger zone of someone developing feelings. And although I clearly could never develop feelings for one Grayson West, I don't know that the same can be said for him. Then he'll end up with a broken heart, which might have sounded appealing at one time, but now just makes me feel kind of sad, actually.

So instead I have fun with him—smearing flour on his cheek and stealing the cookies Linda prebaked for us—but when we are dismissed for the day, all I offer is a small smile and a wave goodbye.

I duck out of the kitchen quickly, not needing to be trapped with Grayson and most definitely needing to avoid Liz and the questions I know she has for me. As much as she was delighted by our performances today, I could tell from the look in her eye that she knew something more was up than colleagues finally acting cordially. I shuck my costume quickly and practically sprint to my room.

Which I soon realize was a mistake. Because as lovely as my room is, the big four-poster elephant in the room is the bed where yesterday Grayson fucking West gave me an orgasm to end all orgasms. Two, if you want to get technical. And although the fireplace is lovely, it is not nearly lovely enough to distract me from replaying yesterday's events in my mind. Over and over and over.

My skin suddenly feels too tight for my body, and I know I need to get out of this room fast, before I make a dumb decision. A big dumb naked decision.

I grab my purse and throw open the door, intending to march right down the hallway and out the front door of the inn to spend the afternoon somewhere else, anywhere else.

What actually happens is that I throw open the door and march two paces across the hall and knock on the door of one Grayson West.

Before I can fully formulate what I want to say to him, he's standing in front of me. Leaning against the doorjamb. Wearing jeans. Wearing only jeans.

Words escape me, so I simply place a hand on his bare-naked, rock-hard chest, shove him back inside the room, and jump into his arms like we're on *The Bachelor*.

"Hi," I say as I work my fingers into his hair.

"Hi," he says as he walks us over to an armchair, his arms firmly latched under my butt and holding me up. "I thought we agreed on only one time?" The question rings false because he pairs it with a searing kiss.

"Two times. We're doing this two times." I gently yank on his golden waves so I can nibble on his neck. "And only for the sake of the movie."

"Whatever you say, Harper." He sinks into the armchair, simultaneously removing my sweater, which is a smooth move, even for him.

I kiss a trail up his throat, brushing my lips over his. "Say that again."

"Not a chance." His hand slides up my back, grasping onto the nape of my neck and bringing my mouth to his.

I pout against his lips. "You're no fun."

He sucks my lower lip before giving it a gentle bite. "That's not what you said yesterday."

I can't help the laugh that escapes me. "You're lucky you're good in bed."

He snaps the release on my bra, palming my breasts in his hands with a wide grin. "Actually, I think *you're* lucky I'm good in bed."

I roll my hips, noting he's already hard beneath me. "Hey, West?"

He grunts.

"How about you stop talking and fuck me?" I pair the words with a smile but freeze when I notice his has dropped.

He stills for just a second before he laughs. "Whatever you say, Harper." And then he kisses me senseless.

@OKAllison: So are we taking bets on whether or not Grayson West and Emmy Harper are going to find themselves in an enemies-to-lovers situation?

@DeniseWest53: I sure as fuck hope not. I can't compete with her!

@RomComsWithRachel: Because the only thing keeping you and Grayson West apart is the fact that he's never met you, right?

@DeniseWest53: Obviously.

@OKAllison: I for one hope they remain costars. She's too good for him.

@MrsJulieWest27: What the hell are you talking about? No one is too good for Grayson West. He's too good for her.

@RomComsWithRachel: Please. Emmy is an Oscar-winning writer, and Grayson West is the epitome of a himbo.

@RomComsWithRachel: And don't get me wrong, I love a himbo, but I don't see Emmy falling for someone like him.

@DeniseWest53: She should be so lucky.

CHAPTER

TWELVE

WAKING UP THE MORNING AFTER ROUND TWO, IT'S like Groundhog Day. My arm skates over empty, cool sheets. I take a cold shower. Grayson flirts with me in hair and makeup. I pretend not to see him. Amanda and Sam shoot us knowing looks. We turn in another performance that hits the perfect mix of steamy and sweet.

And as soon as we're dismissed, I bolt from the set, discarding my costume and heading straight up to my room.

Despite my lightning-fast exit, Grayson still manages to beat me. I find him leaning casually in the doorway of his room when I come up the stairs and arrive in our shared hallway. He strides a few steps across the way, meeting me in front of my door.

"We can't do this again," I say, even as I move closer into his personal bubble.

He wraps his fingers around my wrist, slowly stroking the thin skin, cluing me in to the fact that wrists are an erogenous zone. "Can't do what?"

I check up and down the hall to be sure we're still alone. "We can't keep sleeping together. It's too dangerous."

He brings my wrist up to his mouth, placing a single kiss at my pulse point. "Dangerous how?"

I want to pull away from him, really I do, but then his kiss turns into a suck and I couldn't move my wrist even if I tried. "Sex once is a fluke. Twice is dumb but still recoverable."

"And sex three times?" He doesn't move his mouth from my skin, his beard and his lips equal parts tickling and arousing.

"Sex three times means feelings." And it's that thought, finally saying it out loud, that brings me back to myself. Enough at least to take a step away from him, freeing my wrist in the process.

I miss his lips the second they're gone.

"Do you have feelings for me, Emmy?" He leans one hand against the doorjamb, towering over me. Gone is the usually wicked glint from his lightning-blue eyes. They search mine, as if by locking in they can peer inside my head—and my heart.

"I—uh—um—I . . . Do you have feelings for me?" Returning the question is easier than answering it for myself. Which is ridiculous because clearly I do not have feelings for Grayson fucking West.

He pauses for a minute. A minute charged with tension and wanting and chemistry. "No. I don't have feelings for you."

It's the answer I expected. And wanted. Of course he doesn't have feelings for me. How could he? *Why* would he? Aside from the two times we've had universe-imploding sex, we've done nothing but bicker and tear each other down.

"But I do like you, Emmy. I never hated you, despite what you seemed to think. And I didn't come here to mess up this movie for you." He closes the space between us and threads his fingers through mine. "I think we should be friends." He lowers his head and places a single kiss on the side of my neck. "And I sure as hell wouldn't say no to continuing our sexual relationship."

He sounds so calm, so even-keeled. Like we're making dinner plans or a grocery list.

In the meantime, just one brush of his lips on my neck and I'm practically salivating. I swallow thickly. Scratch that, I'm actually salivating.

"Just friends then." I meet his eyes, and they flash with something shadowed. "Friends who have sex. Grown-ups who have a sexual relationship and also a working relationship, because we are adults and we can separate feelings from sex."

"Are you trying to convince me or yourself?" A slow smile spreads across his face, and his free hand snakes around my lower back, drawing me closer.

"No convincing needed." I slip my hand under his shirt, tracing my fingers along the edge of his waistband. "My room or yours?"

He presses my back against the door. "Yours has the fireplace."

I pull my room key from the back pocket of my jeans. "Sex in front of a roaring fire? How very cliché of you, Mr. West."

He takes the key from my hand, unlocking the door

while still keeping me pressed close. "How about going down on you in front of a roaring fire? Is that too cliché?" He kicks the door closed behind us and wastes no time leading me over to the cushy rug in front of the fireplace.

"I write romance movies for a living. I love a cliché."

THREE DELICIOUS ORGASMS LATER, I COLLAPSE ON top of Grayson's bare, slightly sweaty chest. "That was incredible."

I wait for him to shift me aside and move out from underneath me as he's done previously, but instead, he wraps his arms around me, hands stroking up and down my bare back in a soothing and sleep-inducing motion. A contented sigh escapes my lips, but as soon as I start to get comfortable, I force myself to sit up, clambering off him in a move that is part drunken stumble, part toddler gymnastics.

The second he's free of me, he jumps up and heads for the bathroom.

That doesn't mean I can't check him out, though, because asking me to keep my eyes off his Greek god naked statue body would be cruel.

"Why are you staring at me?" He beelines out of the bathroom to collect his various items of clothing.

"Because you're naked and gorgeous?" Pretty sure the "duh" is implied.

He turns away from me as he steps into his boxers and yanks on his jeans. As he tugs his shirt over his head, he spins back my way. He doesn't school his face before it's clear of his shirt, which means I catch the flush on his cheeks and the hint of doubt in his eyes.

But it can't actually be doubt hidden in those deep pools of blue. Grayson West is one of the cockiest, most confident men on the planet.

The look is gone before I can really puzzle it out. He strides over to me, offering me a hand and pulling me up with enough force I land squarely in his arms. He lowers his head and gives me a blistering kiss. My still naked body automatically responds to him.

I'm a second away from asking him to stay for another round when he plants a final close-mouthed kiss on my upturned lips.

"See you tomorrow, Harper."

The door has already closed behind him by the time I'm able to make my brain and mouth connect enough to form words.

And so it begins. For the next several days, I have nothing but Groundhog Days. Possibly the world's greatest Groundhog Days, but Groundhog Days nonetheless. Grayson and I continue to deliver performances worthy of my script and our own individual talents. The mood on set lightens noticeably, everyone else's performances bolstered by the fact that the stars of the movie no longer seem to want to kill each other. I walk off set each day happy and proud of the work I'm turning in.

Liz still hasn't asked about what happened between Grayson and me. She's my best friend, and I know she knows, but I think we both assume that by not talking about it, it means we can continue making movie magic, and for both of us, that's priority number one. At least for the time being. As long as Grayson and I don't pop this fragile bubble of perfection, we don't have to discuss why I'm sleeping with the man I've referred to as a skull-numbing, fart-fragranced dickbag for half of my life.

And I don't want to discuss with Liz why I'm sleeping with Grayson, because that would require *me* to examine why I'm sleeping with Grayson, and really all I want to be doing is sleeping with Grayson. It's easy and hot and satisfying and sexy, and it makes me feel good. And so every day when we're both dismissed, we pick a room. We each get an orgasm—I usually get two or three—and then we part ways and do it all again the next day.

I keep waiting for the excitement of it to wear off. Surely, part of our explosive chemistry has to be due to the almost forbidden nature of our relationship. Eventually we'll get bored, the urges satisfied, the tension well and truly managed.

Instead, the opposite happens. We grow more comfortable with each other, and instead of making the sex boring, it actually makes it better. With Grayson, I'm not afraid to ask for what I want, and so far, he's willing to try anything, do anything I ask him to. And it's hot as fuck.

Sometimes that talking, that asking for what I want, turns into more conversation. I've never been big on talking during sex, aside from the occasional harder/faster/more-type instructions, but with Grayson, it's somehow easier to chat when he's buried deep inside me.

And you know what they say: if it ain't broke, don't fix it. So I'm not fixing it. I'm not doing anything to disrupt this precarious work-life-sex balance-beam act we've got going on.

Between all the sex and actually working, I haven't had nearly as much time to explore the town of Pine Springs as I would've liked. As a born and bred Angeleno, I have a fascination with small towns, and even though this is the first time I've set a movie in a picturesque village, I've always harbored a secret fantasy of living in one. Maybe not full-time—I don't think I could live without ready access to live theater and fine dining and Target—but just for a little pocket of escape.

So when I find myself with an afternoon off, an afternoon when Grayson will be on set filming, I hop in my car and drive downtown. The main street is small, consisting of a pub, a diner, the café where we filmed our first week, and a couple of quaint little shops. I wander through most of them, spending the longest in the tiny bookstore that's stuffed to the brim with both new and used books.

Hmmm. Maybe I should write a screenplay set in a bookstore. I take an extra lap around the shop before I make my purchases, just to see if any sort of inspiration strikes.

The stack of new-to-me books I leave with can be chalked up purely to research. I haul them with me to the wine bar next door—say what you will about it, but any town with a bookstore and a wine bar next door to each other is okay with me—settling down into a leather club chair. After I order a glass of local pinot noir, I open one of my new books and lose myself in the pages.

I don't look up from the small-town romance I purchased—it felt too fitting to pass up—until the door to the wine bar opens, a gust of cold wind fluttering the pages of my book.

An automatic smile spreads across my face when I take in the tall hunk of a man shaking off a chill and hanging up his coat.

It might be the first time in history I'm genuinely happy to see Grayson West. At least in a moment when there's no chance of ripping off his clothes.

"Hi," he says when he catches sight of me, and I'd like to think he's fighting off a smile of his own.

"Hi." I mark my place in my book. "Fancy meeting you here."

He holds up a book of his own. "Great minds and all that."

There's an awkward moment where we both just sit in silence, staring and smiling slightly at each other.

"Um, did you want to sit down?" I gesture to the chair across from me. "You don't have to, of course, but you can if you want."

Grayson folds himself gracefully into the seat. "Thanks." He orders a glass of wine for himself and another for me, the server's eyes widening in recognition before she darts away to fill our orders, and then we're both awkwardly staring at each other again.

I clear my throat. "How was filming today?"

"Good. It was good. Really good."

"Good. That's good."

This time the silence is short, broken when we both bust up laughing.

Grayson runs a hand through his hair. "God. This is awful. I swear I know how to make conversation."

"Well, this might be the first civil conversation we've had that's not scripted or naked, so . . ." I smile widely, accepting a second glass of wine from the server.

Grayson takes his own glass, gulping down a large swallow.

My eyes get caught on his throat, watching the muscles of his neck work. I take a long drink of my own wine, which is certainly the cause of the flush heating my cheeks.

He sets his wine down on the low table between us. "What are you reading?"

I hold up the cover, not at all ashamed of the scandalous clinch featured on the front. I love a good clinch. "I'd like to pass this off as research or some kind of career-related reading, but mostly I just can't get enough of small-town romances right now. What about you?"

He chuckles, holding up his own book so I can see the cover. "I won't even pretend this is career-related. I just can't seem to get enough of this series."

It's one of those books I jokingly (sort of) refer to as "men's fiction." There's a Vin Diesel wannabe pictured on the front, with explosions and cars and all those stereotypical masculine images in the background. Chances are, if the book were turned into a movie, Grayson would be in the running to take on the lead role.

"I'm a firm believer in everyone reading what they love."

He raises one eyebrow in an almost maddeningly picture-perfect arch. "You're not going to give me shit about being a reader?"

I swirl my wine around in its glass. "Why would I do that?"

He shrugs, setting down his book and picking up his

wine. "Mostly because you seem to live to give me shit, and this one's an easy target."

"Okay, I do enjoy giving you shit, not going to argue that point. But why would you reading a book be an easy target?" I'm not playing dumb. I don't actually understand what point he's trying to make.

"I just expected some kind of 'Wow, Grayson, I didn't know you could read' kind of comment." He stares into the depths of his richly colored wine.

"I know you can read, thanks to a little thing called a read-through." I throw him a snarky smile, but he doesn't return it. "Did you really think I was going to make fun of you for liking books? Writing is basically my entire life, West."

"No, not make fun of me. More like be incredulous that it's one of my hobbies." He chuckles a little, like he's trying to pass off the sentiment as a joke.

"Wow. So I guess all of our sleeping together hasn't changed your opinion of me. You still think I'm a huge asshole?" I try to inject some humor of my own into the words, but I don't think I hide the sting very well. And maybe I deserve it, his low opinion of me, but despite all my best intentions, I was actually starting to like Grayson. As a friend, I mean. And it doesn't feel great that the feeling isn't reciprocated.

I chug the rest of my wine and signal to the server to bring me my check.

"Emmy. I didn't mean it like that." Grayson leans forward, his elbows resting on his knees.

There's still a fair amount of space between us, but it

doesn't stop his pine and charcoal scent from filling my nose. "It's fine."

Our server heads over to the table and I pull out my credit card to hand it over, only to find Grayson has beat me to it.

I glare at him because if he's going to think the worst of me, I might as well earn it. "I was going to do that."

He shrugs. "You can get the next time."

I shove out of my seat and gather my stuff. "There isn't going to be a next time. I think we had the right idea from the beginning. We're good together in bed, and now we're good together on set. We probably shouldn't push our luck and try to be okay together anywhere else." I slip my arms into my coat. "Costars with benefits. That's all this is. We certainly don't need to be friends."

Strutting out of the wine bar doesn't go quite as smoothly as I'd like because, as per usual, I bought too many books, and carrying them all while in the midst of a dramatic exit throws me off-balance. I manage to right myself as I push out of the front door and onto the sidewalk, but just barely, and the delay gives Grayson enough time to catch up with me.

"Let me help you with those." He reaches for the stack of books, but I pull them close to my chest. Sighing, he runs a hand through his hair. "I didn't mean for all that to come out the way it did, Harper." He gestures in the general direction of the wine bar. "I wasn't trying to insult you, and I don't think you're an asshole. At least, not anymore." He nudges me with his elbow, a small smile pulling on his perfect lips.

I shift the heavy weight of the books in my arms, halfway wishing I'd let him take them off my hands but not willing to give in that easily. "We don't have to be friends, but I would like to think we at least have mutual respect."

He reaches for the books again, and this time I let him take them. "Of course I respect you, Ems. I think you're brilliant, and honestly, I'm just worried you think I'm a himbo like the rest of the world."

A real smile spreads across my face. "A himbo? Really? People have actually called you that?"

He gives me a sheepish smile. "Not to my face. But, as we've already determined, I do, in fact, know how to read."

I nudge him in the direction of my car, and we start walking, slowly because the sidewalk is icy and slick. "If it makes you feel any better, in my world, being a himbo is a good thing."

"How so?"

"Himbos are gorgeous and sweet and kind and lovable and just want to make everyone happy."

"So essentially I'm a golden retriever?"

I laugh, and the genuineness of it startles me. "I mean, yes? But in a good way, I promise."

Another silence falls between us, but this one is comfortable. We reach my car, and Grayson carefully places my books in the backseat before joining me on the sidewalk.

"Did you drive?" I shove my hands in the pockets of my coat because I'm faced with the sudden urge to reach for him. But we're not safely stored in one of our rooms, and I don't quite know what to do with that feeling when it's not an immediate prelude to sex.

"I walked." He cocks his head in the direction of the inn. "I should be getting back before it gets any colder."

"Why don't I just drive you?" I blurt out the words before I really consider the ramifications of sitting in a car alone with Grayson, even if it is just for a few minutes.

"You don't mind?"

I swallow thickly, realizing I can't take back the offer. "Of course not."

We climb into our respective seats and buckle up, and why did I buy such a small car, and god, he is sitting so close to me. Which is a ridiculous thing to be freaking out about, because the man literally has been inside me, but here we are.

It's only five minutes. I can do this. I'm not going to be overcome with the sudden urge to bang Grayson West in five minutes.

Even though it's not the urge to bang him that I'm really concerned about.

It's these other weird, kind of warm, and not totally hateful feelings that may or may not be sprouting like mistletoe—the poisonous kind, not the one with magical kissing powers. If I'm honest with myself, I know these not-hateful feelings have been growing for a while now, but having a real conversation with him with our clothes on seems to have acted as some kind of magical plant food, and the worst thing that could happen would be for those sprouts to grow roots. Also, I need to possibly lay off the plant metaphors.

We don't say much on the drive, but it doesn't feel awkward or uncomfortable. When I park back at the inn, Grayson automatically grabs my books from the backseat, carrying them inside without me even having to ask.

We stop in front of the door to my room. The natural progression of things would be to invite him in for our nightly fuck-fest, but before I can extend the offer, Grayson clears his throat.

"If you don't mind, I'm feeling a little wiped tonight. I was going to head back to my room and get to bed early."

"Oh." I unlock the door to my room and push it open. "Yeah, of course." I reach for the stack of books.

He nudges me aside, crossing into my room and setting them down on the small table in the corner.

I stand in the doorway, and all the awkwardness we dispelled earlier flows into the room like an avalanche.

Grayson stops just outside the bubble of my personal space on his way out. "I enjoyed hanging out with you today, at least the parts where I wasn't making a total ass of myself."

"Enjoyed it so much you have to run away?" I nail the inflections, the question coming out clearly as a joke, but I don't think it masks the tinge of disappointment in my voice.

He runs a hand over his beard. "Will it make it worse if I say it's not you, it's me?"

"Yes. God. Never say that, please." I roll my eyes and punch him lightly on the arm.

He captures my hand in his, pulling me closer so our hips are flush.

My breath catches in my throat.

He takes my face in his hands, lowering his head until our lips brush. Once, twice. Then his mouth captures mine for a full kiss. I open to him, and he doesn't hesitate, exploring me with his lips and his tongue, until our breaths are mingled, our bodies cemented together.

When he breaks the kiss, I instantly miss the heat of him.

His forehead falls to mine. "It's not that I don't want to, Ems." He subtly shifts his hips until I feel all the evidence of his want. "I just think I need a little space. Yeah?"

Everything in me is screaming no, but how can I say that when he so clearly needs me to agree. I simply nod. "Yeah."

He puts some of that stupid space between us, leaning down to give me a chaste, close-mouthed peck. "I'll see you tomorrow."

"Tomorrow." I seem to have lost all ability to form my own complete sentences.

"Good night, Harper."

"Good night."

I close the door behind him, locking it and letting my back fall against it. My fingers float up to my mouth, tracing my lips. Lips that I can tell are swollen and still bear the mark of him. Lips that are aching to be back on his.

But he was right to put some distance between us. Because today we almost felt like friends. And friends with benefits is completely different from enemies with benefits, or even costars with benefits. Friends with benefits is just a detour on the road to friends to lovers, and it is literally my job to know how that trope turns out.

So space is good. I'm here for the space. All about that space.

There's a knock on the door—the door I'm still using to keep myself upright.

I open it without checking the peephole, assuming it must be Liz or one of the production assistants.

Instead, I find Grayson with his forearm propped against the doorjamb, breathing heavily, like he must have just paced back and forth between our rooms a few hundred times. "You know what I just realized? Space is overrated."

I grab his sweater, yanking him into the room and slamming the door behind him. "Fuck space."

CHAPTER

THIRTEEN

WHEN I MEET LIZ IN THE DINING ROOM THE FOLLOW-ing morning, she gives me a wicked grin. "Ready for this?"

I groan, pouring myself the largest cup of coffee I can manage. "You know I'm not. If I'm ever manipulated into acting in one of my own movies again, please remind me not to make my character do all the things I hate."

She raises her eyebrows as she takes a long sip from her own mug. "Oh, is that so? I think you're quite enjoying 'doing' one of those things you claim to hate."

I spin away from her, busying myself with pouring heaps of milk and sugar into my black liquid gold, hiding my burning cheeks from her all-too-knowing gaze. "I have no idea what you're talking about."

"Emmy. How long have we been friends?"

"More years than I care to think about." My cheeks feel like they have returned to a normal temperature, so I angle myself back in her direction, although I still avoid her gaze.

"And have you ever once successfully in those many, many years lied to me about anything?"

"Not that I know of."

She leans across me, grabbing a cinnamon roll. "So why would you ever think you could keep a Grayson West–sized secret from me?"

I snatch the cinnamon roll from her hand, taking a huge bite and speaking around the gooey deliciousness. "How long have you known?"

"Since about five minutes after it happened."

I swallow my bite and wash it down with half of my coffee. "Seriously? I thought we were pretty stealthy."

"You thought I wouldn't notice how both of you suddenly found the acting skills not to apparently hate each other every second of every frame?" There's just a hint of smugness in her expression, enough to make me wonder if she planned this all along.

"It's just sex."

"I told you not to lie to me." She takes an apple from the fruit bowl and swaps it for her cinnamon roll, pushing the fruit on me. "You're going to need some real sustenance for today."

"Yeah, yeah." I crunch into the apple, holding it between my teeth while I refill my coffee, completely ignoring her implication that whatever this is between me and Grayson isn't just sex. Because it definitely is.

"Shall we?" Liz holds out her arm, and I link mine through it.

"Do I have a choice?"

"Not really, no."

"You're driving."

We pull up to the town's ice rink a few minutes later. Like everything else in Pine Springs, it's idyllic and picture-perfect, a frozen pond surrounded by trees with a gingerbread-cottage skate-rental booth that doubles as a hot chocolate stand. Even though we're a hop, skip, and jump away from spring, the air outside is still bitingly cold.

A trailer is set up in the parking lot for hair and makeup, and as I make my way to it, I notice we aren't the first to arrive on set.

My steps lead me in the opposite direction of the trailer, toward the ice, like there's some kind of magnetic pull drawing me closer. Chances are, it's not the ice I'm attracted to, but the man skating around on it.

Grayson is dressed in jeans and a hoodie, with a navy blue beanie pulled over his golden hair. His feet are strapped into heavy-looking black skates, the kind hockey players wear. He flies up and down the ice, skirting the edges of the oval pond, coming to sudden and complete stops before switching directions and skating backward. He moves like he doesn't even have to think about it, like skating comes as naturally as breathing, his movements quick and sharp and oddly graceful.

I can't take my eyes off him.

"Emmy! Let's go!"

My eyes are only pulled away from Grayson when Sam hollers my name from the trailer. I've no doubt my little detour has already put everyone behind schedule, probably not for the last time on this cursed day.

Grayson looks up when he hears my name. I'm too far away to see his eyes, but he as soon as he realizes he's not alone, he spins around and exits the mini rink, plopping down on one of the benches circling the pond.

WHEN I'M HAIR-AND-MAKEUP READY, DRESSED IN MY ice-skating best (which is sadly not a sparkly miniskirt, but jeans and a thick sweater), I head over to the ice, taking my sweet-ass time as if the extra two minutes will make any sort of difference in delaying the inevitable.

Liz hands me a pair of pristine white figure skates with a gleeful smile. She's lucky I love her because these blades are sharp and I'm not above cutting a bitch.

Plodding along through the snow, I make my way to one of the benches, slip off my UGGs, and attempt to shove my feet into the stiff leather of the skates. When my feet are actually in, I'm faced with the daunting process of doing up the laces.

"'Write an ice-skating scene,' she said. 'It will be so cute and full of rom-com magic,' she said," I mutter, no one but myself to be mad at.

A low chuckle from behind me does nothing to improve my mood.

Then a warm hand picks up my foot, setting it on top of a muscled thigh. Strong fingers adjust my skate before setting to work on the laces, looping them and tying them in a fraction of the time it would've taken me.

"Thanks," I say, when the second lace is tied and Grayson has returned my now be-skated feet to the ground.

"First time?" The glint in his eye is impish and sexy. The bastard.

"You do know if I go down I'm taking you with me, right?"

A grin splits his gorgeous face. "You can try."

I cock my head in the direction of the ice. "You looked pretty comfortable out there."

"I'm from Minnesota," he says with a shrug, like that's the answer to all of life's questions.

I raise one eyebrow.

"I could skate before I could walk. It's kind of our thing." He rises and holds out a hand to help me up.

I take it, but only because I'm pretty sure I would fall flat on my ass without his support.

Liz comes over and claps her hands together in sheer and utter delight. "Okay. So I should probably tell you to take this seriously and remember to deliver your lines and blah blah blah, but honestly, you can improv a bit. It doesn't matter what you say in this scene. It's going to be comedy gold."

I glare at her. "You are out of the will after this."

She gives me a fake pout. "Right. Well. Try to call each other by your characters' names because we'll be continuously filming, although we can always dub things in post if we need to. And Emmy? Try not to kill Grayson." She strides back to the command center without a backward glance.

My mouth drops open in not entirely mock outrage.

Grayson purses his lips and at least attempts to hold in his laughter. It doesn't work, but at least he tries.

I glare at him, too. "If I break myself, there will be no more sex, West."

"I promise I won't let you break yourself." He slips an arm around my waist. "Nothing vital for the sex, anyway."

I swat his arm and then immediately grab onto it with a death grip because he's steadily walking us toward the ice.

"Have you really never skated before? Not even at the mall?"

"I grew up in LA."

"LA does have ice rinks, you know."

"We also have earthquakes. Doesn't mean I'm a fan." My fingers dig into the soft flannel he changed into during his transition from Grayson to Josh.

As we reach the edge of the ice, Grayson turns around so he's facing me. He takes my elbows in his hands, allowing me to clutch his forearms as he gracefully steps backward out onto the frozen pond.

"First thing to remember: eyes on me." He lets go of one elbow just long enough to tilt up my chin.

I drag my eyes away from the ice. "But shouldn't I see what I'm doing?"

"Looking down just throws off your balance." He gives me a gentle tug, pulling me closer to the slick surface. "I promise I'm not going to let you fall."

I take a tentative step forward.

"At least not yet."

My second foot joins the first on the ice just as I catch the meaning of his words. I wobble literally the second both skates hit the ice, but true to his word, Grayson doesn't let me fall. Although he does flash me a cocky grin.

"Good. That wasn't so hard, was it?"

"I'm literally just standing here."

"Standing is the first step." He tugs on my arms just a tad, and because I'm standing stiff as a board, I glide closer to him. "Bend your knees a little."

I follow his directions, my hands hanging on to his perfect, flannel-clad forearms.

"I'm going to skate you around a bit, just so you get comfortable on the ice, okay?"

"Do I have a choice?"

He smiles, and it's a wide, genuine grin. "You're the one who wrote the scene, Harper."

"Yes, well, I wrote a lot of things in this movie that I'm coming to regret."

He leans into me, his mouth brushing the shell of my ear. "In all the times I've made you come, you never once seemed to regret it."

I throw him a look dripping with disdain. "Really?"

He shrugs. "You set me up for that one."

"I think I would rather skate than listen to junior high-level sex jokes."

"All right then."

Before I can protest, Grayson effortlessly pushes off, skating backward and pulling me along for the ride whether I want to go or not.

And once I get over the initial shock of the burst of cold air on my cheeks, it's not so bad. I mean, it's not fun or anything, waltzing around on the ice, but with Grayson's strong arms supporting me, it's maybe not as terrible as I made it out to be in my head.

There might even be a sincere smile on my face as we glide around, and I'm sure it has nothing to do with the way Grayson's eyes stay locked on mine.

We do a couple of laps before he guides us to a gentle stop.

"Good." He pulls away from me a bit. "Now, keep your knees bent. We're going to practice moving."

"Or—another option—we just stick to gliding for a

while. I'm sure that's all the scene really needs, and I am the writer of said scene so I'm pretty sure we can just cut now and call it a day."

"What are you afraid of, Emmy?"

"Falling on my ass and breaking all my bones?"

"Didn't I already promise you wouldn't break anything essential?"

"I think I'm more worried about an ankle or an arm than breaking my vagina, West."

He pulls me into him, close enough so our hips are pressed together. "You're going to have to trust me, Harper."

I let out a long-suffering sigh, which only makes him smile. "Fine. Impart your vast knowledge and wisdom, Obi-Wan."

He leans down and presses a quick peck to my lips. It's the definition of short and sweet, and yet both our eyes widen the second we part.

"Shit. Probably shouldn't have done that."

I shrug, biting my lip so a scary, clown-like grin doesn't overtake my whole face. "Liz already knows."

His brow furrows. "You told her?"

"She figured it out." I spare a quick glance over my shoulder at the rest of the crew. "I wouldn't be surprised if they have, too."

"Any day now!" Liz's voice echoes around the frozen pond.

Grayson clears his throat. "Right. Where were we?"

"You were just about to tell me how I've done a stand-up job for my first time ever ice-skating and there's no need to go any further with my impromptu lesson."

"Sure." He spins around effortlessly so we're standing

next to each other. His arm is wrapped firmly around my waist.

I lean into the solid weight of him, drawing no small amount of comfort from his presence next to me.

"So first thing is to angle your feet like this."

"I thought I wasn't allowed to look down?"

"Has anyone ever told you you're a terrible student?"

"Literally never. My teachers loved me."

"I bet they did." He bumps his hip into mine, just enough to wobble me a tad.

I study his skates for a second before moving my feet into position.

"Good. Now, you don't want to approach this like walking. You want to push off with your back leg and glide forward on your front leg."

I bend my knees a little more, basically doing anything I can to delay having to actually skate.

"You got this, Ems. I know you can do it."

I tilt up my head and meet Grayson's gaze. His blue eyes are bright in the afternoon sunshine, and he's wearing an encouraging smile. And suddenly, I don't want to disappoint him. I want to show him that I can, in fact, do this.

"I trust you," I tell him. And it's not lost on me that the last time I said those words to him, I was in an equally vulnerable position. Somehow, Grayson has become a safe place. The realization sends a burst of warmth through my frozen limbs. "Right." I bend my knees and push off my back leg. I'm as wobbly as a sleepy toddler, but I manage to glide for a half second before I stumble.

Grayson's arms lock around me, holding me upright

before I can even come close to falling. "That was actually really good."

"Why do you sound so surprised?" I get my feet back into position, ready to try again.

"You surprise me all the time, Harper."

I push off again, gliding forward for a full second this time before coming to a shaky halt. "Is that a good thing?"

"Most definitely." His fingers tighten, squeezing my waist. "Let's try again."

I don't even know how much time passes, but by the time Liz tells us we can wrap it up, I'm actually skating. I probably look like a baby giraffe while doing so, but I'm actually skating. And Grayson never once let me fall. No broken ankles, arms, or vaginas to be found.

We come to a halt in the center of the ice, hands intertwined, although Grayson no longer has to hold me upright.

"You did really well today, Ems." The smile on his face borders on proud, and it sends a jolt of heat straight through me.

"Thanks." I rise up on my toes, pressing my lips to his and not really caring who sees it. I lose my balance after a hot second, but I let myself stumble, knowing he'll be there to catch me.

And he does, his strong arms wrapping around me as he lifts me off the ice completely. The kiss deepens and I open myself to him, lost in the sensation of his warm lips and strong hands.

"Isobel and Josh haven't had their first kiss yet!" Liz's voice booms once again, this time like she's being amplified.

Which she is. We break the kiss, and I look over to see Liz shouting into a megaphone and wonder just how long she was trying to get our attention.

Grayson sets me gently back down on the ice. "We should probably head in."

I place a halting hand on his chest. "Thank you for everything today. You were a brilliant teacher."

He runs a hand through his hair and shrugs. "It was nothing."

"It wasn't nothing. You were patient and kind, even when I didn't quite deserve it. Plus, you were breathtaking to watch when you were skating. I couldn't take my eyes off you." I fist my hands in the flannel of his shirt, tugging him closer. "Not going to lie, watching you out there, seeing how talented you are, it was super sexy." I lean in, nuzzling into the warm skin of his neck.

He abruptly pulls himself out of my embrace, and for a second, I think he's going to skate off and leave me to fend for myself. But he hesitates for only a second before he starts to slowly guide me back to the edge of the pond. "Yeah, well, like I said, everyone does it back home."

"Seriously Grayson, you could have been an Olympian or something." I gesture back toward the empty ice. "I find it hard to believe everyone in Minnesota can do that."

"Well, they can. I don't have any kind of unique talent, okay? It's just skating." His words are sharp and as biting as the cold air around us. "It's nothing special. Not that big of a deal." He helps me make the transition from the frozen pond to the waiting bench, practically dumping me on the wooden surface before stalking away in the direction of the trailer.

"It was pretty special to me," I say to his back, although I don't know if he hears me.

I stare at his retreating figure, wondering what the hell just happened. How did we go from a full-on make-out session to me getting unceremoniously tossed onto a bench? I thought I was complimenting him and yet there he is storming off like we're back to our old ways.

Whatever. I bend over to unlace my skates and, for maybe the first time ever, wish Grayson was still here.

CHAPTER

FOURTEEN

WHILE I WAIT FOR GRAYSON TO COME TO MY ROOM that evening, I run the events of the day on a loop through my brain. I keep landing on how infinitely kind he was. How much fun we actually had together. How Grayson was patient, and gentle, and a good teacher; how he never once let me fall.

How that kiss reached down and punched me in the gut.

And how annoyed and angry he looked as he stalked away from me.

With Grayson, it's always been easy—ever since we started hooking up anyway. No strings and no fuss. There are no feelings involved, and it's made the whole thing complication-free. Until today.

Enough time passes without a knock on my door that I realize he isn't going to come by tonight. And that's okay, I guess. I mean, sure, we've been meeting at least once a day for our sex sessions, but it's not like we have a set schedule or anything. And it's just one night. I'm pretty sure I can live without Grayson West's dick for one night. But I can't shake the feeling that something might actually be wrong. Grayson's absence, coupled with the way he stormed out earlier, could mean he's really going through something.

I don't want to care about his feelings and yet I find myself marching across the hall and banging on the door.

"It's open."

I can barely make out the words, but I push through his door anyway, ready to throw him some attitude and throw off my clothes, preferably at the same time.

Except when I enter the room, closing and locking the door behind me, I find Grayson sitting on the edge of his bed, his elbows resting on his knees, his head hanging as low as it could possibly reach. Suddenly sex is the last thing I'm thinking about, which likely hasn't happened since the first time he kissed me. Even in our few fully clothed conversations, the wanting has always been there.

"Hey." I cross the room in a few strides, landing right in front of him. "What's wrong?"

"Nothing." Grayson's voice is barely a whisper. He doesn't lift his head even a fraction of an inch, but he does pull his hands back so he doesn't have to touch me.

"Well, that was super convincing." I'm not at all offended by his clear and present desire to make zero contact with me whatsoever.

He looks up at me, cheeks flushed and eyes flashing. "I wasn't aware I owed you any sort of convincing."

I raise both eyebrows, not about to let his pissy behavior go unchecked. "You don't. I just wanted to check on you."

"Because I didn't come begging for you right away?" His words are a quick stab in the gut, laced with real hurt and not at all like the playful jabs we normally throw.

It doesn't take a therapist to deduce that I'm not the one who's really hurting in this situation. I push myself farther into his space, forcing him to sit up straight and drop his hands so I can wedge myself between his thighs. "Why don't you spare us both this 'I'm fine' bullshit song and dance and just tell me what's wrong."

"I'm sorry I don't feel like fucking you tonight, Emmy."

I shrug, placing both my hands on his shoulders and wiggling even farther into his space because I need to be closer to him, to feel him, and to understand what's turned his normally shining eyes a shade as dark as the twilight sky. "That's fine. But I'm not going to leave until you tell me why you're so upset."

"I don't want to talk to you about my problems. We're not friends."

My lungs seize. "Okay." I take a step back, hoping that little flutter I feel in my eyes is not a tear. There is no way in hell I'm going to let him see me cry. There is no way a few words from Grayson West are going to make me cry.

Noticing my reaction, Grayson reaches for my hand and grasps it with a sigh. "I didn't mean that."

"It's okay if you did," I lie, my voice small and choked.

He scrubs his free hand over his beard. "It's not okay, and I didn't mean it."

There's a minute of heavy silence during which I work my way back between his knees.

"I thought we had a good day today, Grayson." I keep my voice quiet, and although I still keep some space between us, all I really want to do is crawl into his lap and wrap him up in my arms.

"We did."

"And yet here we are with all our clothes on." I brush his hair out of his eyes, letting my fingers linger, working themselves into his golden waves.

He gives me a small half smile. "I haven't skated since I moved to LA." He tilts up his head, meeting my gaze. "Today was the first time in more than fifteen years."

"How come?" I ask, genuinely interested in his answer.

His hand settles on my waist, subtly pulling me an inch or two closer. "I was supposed to go pro, in hockey. It was my entire life from the time I was four years old. I had a full ride waiting for me, scouts already poking around. It was all determined for me before I was even old enough to vote."

I already have so many questions I don't even know where to start, but I keep my mouth shut, not wanting to interrupt him, and I focus instead on smoothing back his hair.

His fingers tighten on my waist. "My dad had been my coach since my very first team. Before that, he trained me: running drills, skating every morning, shooting pucks every evening. I was only in kindergarten." He huffs out the last words with a laugh, although there's no trace of humor in his voice.

"So then what happened?"

He gently tugs me down to his lap. "My junior year, I was failing my theater arts elective and the teacher told me I could get extra credit if I'd audition for the school play." He shrugs, his eyes drifting down to my chest. For once it's not in a salacious way; rather, it's simply at eye level, a resting spot as I see his gaze focus in and out. "Even with a scholarship waiting for me, I had to graduate high school first. So I auditioned."

"And you got the lead?" I loop my arms loosely around his neck.

He laughs again, but this time it's genuine. "Hardly. It was only a small speaking part, but from the moment I stepped onto that stage opening night, I was hooked."

"It'll do that to you."

"At first, my dad didn't seem to care too much, as long as I kept up with hockey practices and drills, but it didn't take long for my focus to slide and shift. When I told him I wanted to audition for the next play, even after I'd already passed the class and finished my required elective, he told me I had to choose: acting or hockey."

"I imagine that choice didn't go over very well." I rest my hands on his shoulders, which are tense beneath my fingers.

"That's putting it mildly. He was never one to heap praise, even when I did exactly what he wanted. When I went against his prescribed life plan for me, he basically cut me off." His arm tightens around my waist. "I auditioned for *My Love on Top* in secret, moved to LA with the money I made from it, and I haven't heard from him since."

"Wait. Are you fucking kidding me?" My voice is louder than I intended, and definitely louder than it should be given the seriousness of the moment, but I can't control my volume any more than I can control the anger humming through my veins.

The corner of his lips rises just a touch. "No, I'm not fucking kidding you."

"Jesus, Grayson. That is beyond shitty." Grayson and I haven't spoken about my dad yet, and I don't want to bring it up now, because this sure as hell isn't about me, but father relationships are a touchy subject for me. It's been the big elephant in nearly every room I've walked into for the past four years, feeling lost without him. I can't imagine what it must be like for Grayson. Even if my dad didn't always agree with my decisions—like giving up acting after only one failed attempt—I know with every fiber of my being that there is nothing I could've done to push him out of my life completely. At the end of the day, he always, always supported me. And my heart hurts for Grayson, knowing he didn't get to experience that. "I'm so sorry you had to go through that, are still going through it."

"It's not your fault." He tugs me a little bit closer, letting his head droop and press against my shoulder. "A lot of times I wonder if I should've just listened to him. I could've gotten a free education, gone pro, probably done all right for myself."

"Did playing hockey make you happy?"

"Sometimes." He raises his head. "I think it could've made me happy. Probably more so if he wasn't always there telling me to push harder, go further. I was always waiting for the moment when I would be enough, when he'd be satisfied. But now I'm just a mediocre actor, making mediocre movies, and he'll never be proud of me." His voice catches on the last words, as if he's thought them a million times but never before voiced them out loud.

I cup his cheeks in my hands and bring my face right

up to his. "Hey. You are not mediocre. I would not cast a mediocre actor in my sure-as-fuck-not-mediocre movie."

"You didn't cast me, remember?" He pairs the remark with a snarky half smile.

"Well, I should have. There is nothing mediocre about you, Grayson West. Come on now, you've been voted Sexiest Man Alive! Twice!"

"All that means is I'm not bad-looking."

"Not bad-looking . . . I cannot even with you. You have the face of an angel and the body of a Greek god, the smile of a toothpaste commercial and the eyes of a Disney prince." I squeeze his cheeks between my palms. "Do you know how hard it is for me to give you that many compliments in a row?"

His smile is quick to fade. "It's still just surface-level bullshit."

And suddenly a lot of things about Grayson West make a lot more sense. "Is that why you wanted to do a serious movie? Why you jumped on this one when you thought that's what it would be? You think your dad would be more accepting of your career if you were in the kind of movie that makes people cry?" I thread my fingers through the hair at the nape of his neck, pulling gently so he's forced to meet my gaze.

"Yes?"

"Fuck that, Grayson. Do you like what you do? Do you enjoy being in movies where everything blows up and you're all sweaty and shirtless and the dialogue sometimes sucks but it's entertaining and audiences love it?"

"Yes?" A smile tugs on his lips again.

I lean down and press my lips to his. "Then let that be

enough. You get to do what you love. And you're damn good at it."

"Simple as that?"

"Well, no. I also highly recommend therapy. For real, it'll change your life."

He rolls his eyes, his hands slipping around my lower back and pulling me close. "You're a piece of work, Emmy Harper."

"I have been told that before." I take his face in my hands again. "All the bullshit between us aside, Grayson, you *are* a talented actor. And more importantly than that, you're a good person. You've been a caretaker, and today you were a brilliant teacher. Above everything else, you made me feel safe and comfortable in the moments when I've doubted myself most. You should be proud of yourself." I press my lips to his again before he can argue with me. When I feel I've sufficiently stymied his natural inclination to refute everything I say, I put some space between us. "Now, I seem to recall you mentioning you have no interest in fucking me tonight?" I layer the question with just the right amount of humor and seduction.

"Is that okay?" He pulls me in for a hug, cutting off our eye contact.

Thank god for that because I don't think my eyes can hide my shock. Now that we've talked out our feelings, it should be time for the sex. And yet I find myself snuggling deeper into his embrace.

I force myself to pull away before I can sink too deep. "Of course that's okay. I'll see you tomorrow then?"

He doesn't let me go. "You don't have to leave. We could just hang out here for a bit."

"Oh. Sure." I freeze, halfway between his lap and standing.

Grayson shifts, laying back on the bed and holding out his arm for me to tuck myself into his chest. And fuck if it doesn't tempt me. It's a really good chest.

Instead I lay next to him, leaving a couple of inches of space in between us and pretending I don't see the flash of hurt in his eyes when I don't cuddle up to him.

But we've never done cuddling unless it's of the naked variety, and seeing as how we are both still fully dressed, there will be no cuddle action happening here.

"Can I ask you something?" He directs the words toward the ceiling, but I assume they're meant for me.

"Sure," I say, having no intention of answering his question if it veers in the direction of feelings. There already have been more than enough feelings for one night, and I feel like we're on the verge of swerving into dangerous territory I don't know if we can come back from.

"What was it like winning that Oscar? How did it feel to achieve the culmination of everything you've been working for your whole career?"

"Oh." It's one of the few questions I wasn't expecting. "Honestly, I don't quite know how to answer. I never thought I'd even be in the Oscar conversation, so I never really dreamt about it."

"Really?" He turns his head, and I feel his eyes studying me. "Even with both your parents winning?"

I shrug, turning on my side to face him. "I never had any delusions that I'd be doing what they do. I always set out to write rom-coms, a genre that's as good as invisible when it comes to awards committees."

He turns on his side, mirroring my position, and all of the sudden we're very close together. Not naked close, but close enough that his breath tickles my cheek. "And that never bothered you? That you wouldn't get critical recognition for your work?"

"Not really. I want to write movies that make people happy—and they do. I don't really need anything more than that." I tilt up my chin, bringing our lips within an inch of each other. "Is winning an award something you're aiming for?"

His lips purse, and his eyes drift away from mine. "I never thought so, but Kevin, my manager, lately he's been pushing me to go for more serious roles. He's been with me since the beginning, and he's never steered me wrong before, so . . ."

There's a whole lot of misgivings wrapped up in that *so*. Grayson, who doesn't feel accepted by his dad. Grayson, who has trusted the same manager for his entire career, almost half of his life. Grayson, who is signing up for projects he doesn't really want to be involved with.

"If it doesn't feel right to you, then don't do it, Grayson."

He reaches for me again, and this time I let him pull me into his embrace. He tucks my head under his chin, and it's alarming just how perfectly we fit together. "I admire the way you don't need anyone else's approval."

"Well, I wouldn't say that. I guess I just didn't need *that* kind of approval." I stiffen as I realize just how much I've melted into the warmth of his chest. What happened to not cuddling? Why does just laying here and talking feel just as good as all the sex we should be having? I wiggle to put a few more inches of space in between us.

Grayson tilts his head down toward mine. "Everything okay?"

"Yup. Great. Totally fine." I make the mistake of meeting his gaze.

A smile tugs on his lips. "Very convincing." He reaches out and cups my cheek in his hand before leaning in to brush a soft kiss against my lips. "This doesn't have to be anything more than it is, Ems."

I lean into the kiss, letting him pull me closer, hoping it very well may turn into more than just a kiss. I need to get back on solid ground.

Because this relationship we have is just sex. Good sex. Mind-blowing sex. But just sex. It can never be more than sex, not just because he's Grayson West and that's not what we do. But because he's Grayson West, and if I ever truly open myself up to him, to the possibility of not just him but us, I don't think I can ever come back from it.

The couple of guys I've dated since losing my dad were chosen carefully, with the intentional knowledge that none of them were ever quite right, knowing that when we inevitably ended, it wouldn't break me. Because I knew my heart couldn't sustain any more cracks without completely shattering.

At the beginning of all of this, I might have put Grayson in that category—a hot fuck with no potential for emotional destruction. But I've been lying to myself. Clearly. Grayson is so much more than I ever would've given him credit for, but it goes beyond that. It's the way he makes me feel about myself, like I'm capable of anything and everything. No man has made me feel like that in a long time. If we were to continue to grow closer, make this something more than what happens between the sheets, Grayson could destroy me. Losing him could destroy me.

Grayson breaks the kiss and moves to wrap his arm around me once again, to pull me further into him. "Do you want to stay here tonight?"

Neither of us has ever stayed the night before. Just the thought of waking up next to him sends a wave of warmth over me, and I know I need to get out before it burns. Instead of answering him, I push up off the bed. I lean over and press a quick peck to his lips, ignoring the questions and the hurt in those stupid blue eyes.

I shut his door behind me and cross the hall to my own room. I should shower, but instead I climb into my own bed, burrow down under my comforter, and let myself breathe in the scent of Grayson that seems to now be permanently embedded in my skin.

IN A MIRACLE OF GOOD TIMING, I'M NOT SCHEDULED to film with Grayson the day after . . . whatever the hell that was. Jenna and I have a scene together in the morning, and despite being distracted by the events of last night, we actually manage to finish ahead of our scheduled end time.

"I was going to run down to Main Street and grab lunch at the diner, if you want to join me?" Jenna offers as we both head to wardrobe to change back into our own clothes.

My mouth opens to tell her thanks, but no thanks, but then I think about what's waiting for me here at the inn. A whole lot of thinking about Grayson fucking West. "Sure, that sounds great." I tug my sweater over my head. "Let me just run upstairs to get my coat. I'll meet you in the lobby?"

"Sounds good."

And I make sure the running is literal, aiming to put as much distance as possible between me and the prep rooms because Grayson is on the schedule this afternoon and I'm not ready for a run-in just yet.

The hallway is clear, and I pop into my room and quickly grab my coat.

But I apparently have impeccably bad timing because as soon as I open my door to head back downstairs, I hear his voice in the hallway. I freeze, hoping he didn't see or hear my door open and can't tell I'm currently hiding behind it.

"I told you I'm working on it, Kevin. Why can't you just let me do my thing and trust that I know what I'm doing?" Grayson's voice is laden with frustration. His manager, Kevin, has been out in LA this whole time, so I figure they must be on a call.

And yes, I know I shouldn't be eavesdropping on Grayson's conversation, especially not after I ran out on him the night before. But to be fair to myself, I wasn't trying to listen in, I just got stuck here. If I close the door, he might notice me, so really I have no choice but to stand here with it ajar until he leaves.

"I really want that audition, and I know they're seeing people soon. I spoke to James, and he's already got one on the books." Several seconds of silence follow.

I wonder what kind of audition he's looking to get. And which James he's talking about. I can't imagine Grayson having an issue booking an audition for anything requiring a sexy leading man. Did our conversation the night before spur this on? Is Grayson pressing Kevin to get back to his action roots, and is Kevin giving Grayson pushback?

"Whatever, Kevin. I'm doing my part here; I need you to do your part, too."

Silence falls over the hallway, and a quick peek through the peephole lets me know Grayson hung up the phone, although he's still got it clenched in his grip like he might throw it at the wall.

My phone vibrates with a text.

JENNA: Hey, where'd ya go? Are we still going for lunch?

Shit.

ME: Sorry, got sidetracked for a second, be right down!

I keep an eye on Grayson, but he's still pacing in front of his door. Fuck it. I push my door all the way open, loud enough so he knows I'm here. "Hey." Closing and locking my door behind me, I shove my room key in the pocket of my coat.

"Hey." He freezes, and for a second, an almost guilty look crosses his face, as if he's been caught doing something illicit, but then he relaxes and gives me a tight smile. "Going out?"

"Yeah, Jenna and I wrapped early so we're going to go grab some lunch."

"Cool. Have fun." He turns away from me and starts down the hallway.

"Will I see you later tonight?" I regret the question the

moment I ask it. Not because of embarrassment, but because I know I shouldn't want the answer to be yes as badly as I do.

Stopping and spinning, Grayson gives me a searching look. "Do you want to see me later tonight?"

I cross the few steps separating us. "I do. If you want to, that is." I reach out a hand and smooth an invisible wrinkle from his thin cashmere sweater, letting my fingers linger on his pecs.

He picks up my hand and pulls me closer. "If you want me there, then I'm there."

It's a simple declaration, yet the searing look in his bright blue eyes leaves me with nothing but questions.

I clear my throat. "I should go. Jenna's waiting for me."

Grayson brings my hand to his mouth, kissing my palm before letting it go. "Until tonight, then." He gives me a wicked, knowing grin before bounding down the stairs.

I wait a few seconds before I stumble down behind him, needing the time to attempt to clear my head.

Jenna is waiting for me in the lobby, and the look she gives me is like Santa catching a kid in the midst of being naughty. "You okay?" she asks with a teasing smile. "You look a little flushed."

"I'm fine." I push open the front door of the inn. "You okay with walking? I could use the fresh air."

"I bet you could," she chuckles under her breath.

"Ha ha."

We avoid any serious topics of conversation until we've arrived at the diner and slide into a booth near the front window. The restaurant is small but has a warm and cozy atmosphere. Everything is pastel and plush, and I order a grilled cheese with tomato soup because comfort food sounds pretty amazing right now.

"Want to talk about it?" Jenna sips from her mug of hot chocolate, and her smile is knowing but not judgmental.

"Is it that obvious?"

"That you're sleeping with Grayson West or that you're developing feelings for Grayson West?"

I rub at my temples, letting out a groan. "I can't even admit that to myself. How do other people already know?"

"Maybe not all other people. But definitely me." She shrugs. "And probably most other people."

"Stop being so perceptive."

She flashes me a wide grin. "It's part of my charm."

"It's stupid, isn't it? All of it? Sleeping with him. Definitely the feelings, which may or may not exist. I'm an idiot." I signal for our server and order a milkshake. I have a feeling this conversation is going to require the big guns.

"Why? Because you guys have some sort of messy history from when you were teenagers? Who doesn't?" Jenna accepts her soup from the server and digs in with gusto.

I take a cautious spoonful of my own soup, letting the heat trickle through me and warm my core. "It's not just that. I mean, it started out as that. But now it's more a question of if we even make sense together."

She opens a packet of crackers and dumps them into her bowl. "Do you guys have anything in common, aside from being in the industry?"

Spooning another bite into my mouth, I take a second to think about it. "We both like to read."

She nods. "Okay, that's good. Anything else?"

"To be totally honest, there isn't a lot of deep conversation involved. Usually." I smile sheepishly as I feel my cheeks flush.

She laughs and gives me wiggly eyebrows. "No one can fault you for that, my friend."

I giggle along with her, but my laugh fades as I start to really consider Jenna's question. Thinking through my encounters with Grayson, they're sexy as fuck, obviously, and aside from the night before, our conversations might feel surface-level, but that doesn't mean I don't know him. "He's the kind of person who always makes sure everyone else around him feels comfortable. He's a caretaker, and when he looks at you, you know he's really listening. He's kind, and thoughtful, and funny." I dunk my grilled cheese in my soup. "He's a good man."

Jenna sets down her spoon. "All that and a six-pack?"

I take a bite of my soup-soaked sandwich. "Eight-pack, actually."

She levels me with a piercing glare. "Then what the hell is the issue?"

I stare into my bowl like it holds the answers to all of life's problems. "We agreed to a costars-with-benefits kind of a deal. It wouldn't be right to try to change that. Especially not when we're so close to wrapping."

Jenna accepts the milkshake our server delivers, scooping out a big bite of ice cream before handing it to me. "So what you really mean is that you like him and you're afraid he doesn't like you?"

"God, you really are perceptive." I bite the cherry from the milkshake, pulling it off the stem. "Are you certain you and my mother have never met?"

"Are you kidding? I wish!" She gives me a sweet smile.

"But I will take that compliment and let you in on a secret: he likes you, too."

"I feel like I'm back in junior high." I take down half of my sandwich in one bite.

"I'm just saying. Maybe you should tell him how you feel."

"I don't even know how I feel." I'm also a lying liar who lies.

She rolls her eyes at me and steals another spoonful of my milkshake.

"Okay. Enough about me and my silly boy problems. Tell me what's going on with you. What's next after shooting wraps?"

Jenna's eyes light up as she details her next project, one she helped develop with one of her best friends. We spend the rest of lunch talking about everything but Grayson West, and it's comforting how well we click and mesh, how she reads me easily enough to know I can't let the conversation linger on him.

Too bad that doesn't keep him out of my head.

WHEN I GET BACK TO THE INN, I'M SURPRISED TO spot Liz lounging in one of the armchairs in front of the fire in the sitting room. I don't think I've seen her look so relaxed in months, and a little stab of guilt gets me right in the stomach.

"Everything already done for the day?" I ask, flopping into the empty chair next to her.

"Yup." She tilts her head back and closes her eyes as if she is totally at peace.

We sit in the quiet for a minute.

"Liz, I'm really sorry."

One eye pops open as she gazes at me warily. "What did you do now?"

"Ha ha." I straighten in my chair, leaning my elbows on my knees. "I'm sorry it took me so long to pull myself together. I know I put us behind schedule, and that must have been really stressful for you, maybe even more stressful than the shit show that was the casting process."

She sighs and sits up, mirroring my position. "It certainly wasn't the greatest of starts, but we're in a good spot now." She pats my knee. "You're doing great work, Em. And you wrote another beautiful script."

"Thank you. And thank you for doing this. I couldn't trust anyone else with this project."

She smiles, and it's nice to see some lightness back in her eyes. "You know I'd do anything for you."

"I know. And I'll try to abuse the privilege a little less after all this." I stand, offering her my hand and pulling her out of her seat. "Come on. I'll treat you to a glass of wine."

"A glass of wine from one of the bottles you demanded production pay for?"

"Yup, one of those." I sling my arm around her shoulder as we make our way upstairs. "Free wine is free wine, baby."

She laughs. "You got me there."

CHAPTER

FIFTEEN

I CAN TELL BY THE SMIRK ON LIZ'S FACE THAT WHAT-
ever bomb she's about to drop is going to be a big one.
Despite things feeling weird between me and Grayson the
past few days—even though we went back to our usual
hooking-up schedule after that one-off night—it feels like
things have shifted. But we made it through today's filming with our chemistry still intact, so I figure that whatever it is that has Liz grinning like a gleeful clown, it has
nothing to do with our performance. Which only makes it
all the more terrifying.

She claps her hands together as she approaches Grayson and me, stopping us on our way back to wardrobe,
where we were headed to change out of today's costumes.
"So. A delightful opportunity has presented itself, and I, of
course, have already accepted on your behalf."

Knowing Liz, a "delightful opportunity" could be anything from volunteering at an animal shelter to studying
the origins of silent film through the medium of mime. My
money is on something that doesn't involve cuddling cute
puppies.

Before either of us can ask questions, Liz gestures to an attractive woman in her midtwenties who's been following along behind her. Thank god filming's almost done, because I swear this woman is drop-dead gorgeous and could replace me, or any of us in this movie, in a heartbeat.

And you can bet I take notice of how Grayson reacts to this inhumanly stunning woman. She offers him a blinding smile along with her hand, which he shakes for the required half second before dropping it. The smile he gives her is small and insincere, although I doubt anyone other than me would pick up on that fact. My own smile is just a tad bigger than usual.

Of course, none of this really matters because Grayson is certainly allowed to flirt with whomever he chooses, but it still warms my frigid heart, just a smidge, when his eyes don't even linger on her impressive chest.

I mentally rejoin the conversation just as Liz is explaining why the mystery woman has blessed us with her presence. "The marketing department is starting to kick things into high gear and so we thought it'd be fun if the two of you did your own little version of *The Newlywed Game*— you know, as a cute little promo." Liz hates the word *cute*, so I know she's hamming it up because she knows this is my nightmare. One of the best parts of being strictly behind the scenes as a writer is not having to participate in stilted, cheesy games like this one. Being comfortable on camera in character is one thing; being comfortable on camera as myself is a whole other beast.

I'm trying to figure out a way to politely say "absolutely the fuck not" when Grayson throws his arm around my neck, pulling me in like he's about to give me a noogie.

"Sounds like a fun way to get people excited about the movie. Doesn't it, Emmy?"

I glare at him, and if this is payback for dipping out the other night, then I think the scales have been unfairly tipped. "Sure. Great. Sounds like fun."

Liz shuffles us off into a quiet room where three chairs already have been set up. The woman—whom I finally learn is Crystal, a member of the PR team assigned to *No Reservations*—sits across from us and hands each of us a whiteboard. While she's securing her camera on a tripod, she explains the rules of the game. "Okay, so I'll take turns asking you questions about each other. You'll write down your answers and then reveal them together and see how many matches you can get."

"What does the winner get?" Grayson asks with a smile, although he directs the question to me and not to Crystal.

She laughs anyway. "No prizes, at least not today. This is just for fun."

"And for promo. Don't forget that part." I don't mean to sound like a cynical bitch, but sometimes I just can't help it.

Crystal jumps up from her chair. "Just one second. Let me grab an extra charger, just in case."

Grayson takes advantage of her absence, leaning over to nudge me in the ribs. "Care to make a little side bet here, Ems?"

I glare at him again, but my competitive side is stoked. If there's one thing I hate more than my emerging feelings for Grayson West, it's losing. "You're on. What do I get when I win?"

He drops his voice lower, the rumbling of it tickling my skin. "Whatever you want, Harper."

I raise my eyebrows. "That's a lot of leeway, West. I'm not prepared to offer the same. Name your prize."

He turns his head ever so slightly, his lips brushing along the curve of my neck. "When I win, I get you. For a whole night. No interruptions, and no rushing out the door."

The heat of his words and the warmth of his breath on my skin make it seem like a mostly sexual request, but I can't help but feel like what Grayson is really asking for is a lot more than just that.

More than I'm prepared to give.

Because I definitely don't want this to be more than what it is. I can't want that.

But that won't deter me from accepting his challenge. I know I can win this. "You're going down, West."

He winks at me. "I usually do."

Crystal pops back in, messing with the camera for another second before turning to us with a bright grin. "Ready to get started?"

"I was born ready," Grayson says.

I nod, already with my game face on.

"Great. First question should be an easy one. Each of you write down where the other is from."

Grayson and I both immediately start scribbling on our whiteboards, and even though it's not a race, it's important to note that I finish first. Crystal asks us to reveal our answers, and of course, we both come up with the correct responses.

The first few questions are softballs—first movie roles

(which earns a round of good-natured groans), favorite colors, biggest accomplishments. Although I'm not entirely shocked when we each get them all right, it is a little surprising to see the evidence of our relationship, outside the bedroom, on clear display. If Crystal asked for all of my favorite sexual positions, I'd expect Grayson to come up with the correct responses, but it's a little startling when he remembers the name of my favorite stuffed animal from when I was a kid.

Crystal flips through her notecards after we each correctly identify the other's childhood celebrity crush. "I have to say, I did not expect you guys to be getting all of these right. Let's make things a bit tougher, shall we?"

"Bring it." I shoot Grayson a cocky grin.

"It's on," he responds, with a flex of his arms, and if he thinks I'm going to be distracted, he's only partially right.

Crystal clears her throat. "All right, let's get to it then. What is the biggest challenge Emmy has faced in her life?"

The question knocks the wind out of me a little bit, and I feel Grayson's eyes on me. I meet them and answer his silent question with a soft smile. He immediately starts writing, and I jot down my own response quickly.

"Okay, let's reveal those answers."

Grayson flips around his board. "Emmy's biggest challenge has been dealing with the loss of her father." His words are quiet, with any hint of competitive spirit dampened.

Crystal's expression softens. "Emmy?"

I flip around my own board, where I've written the exact same thing. I don't say anything, because if I open my mouth there's a decent chance I'll start crying and that's the last thing I want on some dumb promo video. But I keep an it's-no-big-deal smile plastered on my face, and when Grayson reaches over to squeeze my hand, I squeeze right back.

We wipe our boards clean.

"Same question. What has been Grayson's biggest challenge so far?"

Grayson immediately starts writing, and I study his profile, trying to discern what it is he might be scribbling. Not that I don't know about challenges he's faced—his relationship with his dad, for one—but more so not knowing what he would want me to reveal. I take a chance, jotting something down quickly, just in the nick of time.

"Reveal your board, Emmy," Crystal gently instructs.

"Grayson's biggest challenge is overcoming the perception that he's just a dumb jock." That's all I've written on my board, but I push on with an unprompted explanation. "I think people in this industry often see him as just a hunky action hero who's good at stopping the bad guys while shirtless, but in reality, he is capable of so much more than that." I chance a glance to my right, and something is shining out of those gorgeous baby blue eyes that I don't want to think about or name.

"You think I'm hunky?" Grayson deflects the tension with his usual cocky swagger, flipping around his board to reveal his matching answer.

Crystal whistles. "You guys are too good at this. One more question, and we'll see if we can break this tie! If the movie industry were not an option, what would your costar being doing instead?"

I inhale sharply. I immediately know Grayson's answer—

his honest answer, anyway. The day on the skating rink and his dad's prescribed life plan for him left no doubt about that. I also know there's no way he could possibly know mine. I could win it, right here, and take home the very enticing prize of whatever I want from Grayson. My mind can come up with a lot of possibilities for cashing in on that win.

But as much as I want to win, I don't know if I want to do it at that cost. I doubt Grayson wants that wound—a reminder that he could have had a different life—reopened on camera. So I write down something totally off the cuff, knowing it doesn't matter because he'll never guess mine.

"Okay, time to reveal your final answers."

I meet Grayson's gaze over the top of our whiteboards and notice just a touch of anxiety swimming in his eyes. I flash him a reassuring smile before turning around my board. "If Grayson wasn't acting, he would most definitely be an underwear model. Gotta put those abs to good use, you know?"

Grayson lets out a small sigh of relief that only I notice. "Ha! That's a good guess, but if I weren't acting, I would probably be a personal trainer." He flips around his own board. "If Emmy weren't acting and writing, she would be a teacher."

My mouth drops open in total and utter shock. "How did you know that? We've literally never spoken about that."

He shrugs and gives me a wink. "Maybe I know you better than you think, Harper."

Crystal's eyes dart back and forth between us. "Well, this has certainly been an enlightening afternoon. Thank you both so much for playing, and Grayson, congrats on your win!" She stops the recording and turns to both of us with a smile. "You guys are going to make my job almost too easy. I'll be in touch with more soon!" Crystal packs up her stuff and heads out.

Grayson tries to duck out of the little makeshift recording studio, but I stop him. "Okay. 'Fess up. How did you know that, really? We haven't talked about how I thought I was going to be a teacher."

He shoves his hands in his pockets. "You mentioned it once. Back when we were working on *My Love on Top*. I guess it just stuck in my head."

I check to be sure there's no one around us before stepping into him. "I can't believe you would remember something so insignificant after all these years."

He tucks a strand of hair behind my ear. "Nothing about you is insignificant, Emmy." His fingers curl around my waist, and he pulls me in even closer. "I can't wait to collect my prize." He brushes his lips over mine in the softest of kisses before grinning impishly and ducking out of the room.

Leaving me with an uncomfortable anticipation. Because I can't wait either.

THE KNOCK ON THE DOOR COMES DURING ONE OF the blessed thirty-second reprieves my bitch of a uterus has decided to reward me with. It's two days after the blasted promo video, and I'm holed up in my room.

"It's open." I manage to choke out the words just in time. Another cramp is coming and I screw my eyes shut, my arms clutching my lower abdomen as the door to my room opens and then closes. "Please tell me you have pads and painkillers and a heating pad, Liz."

"Emmy? Are you okay?"

My eyes fly open when someone who is most definitely not Liz answers.

Grayson strides across the room, closing the distance between the door and the bed in a few large steps. He kneels next to the bed, bringing him right to my eye level. His hand reaches out, smoothing a lock of hair from my face.

The worry is kind and genuine, and when I think back to how I treated him when he was in a similarly vulnerable place, it almost makes me feel worse.

And then another cramp hits, and nope, this is definitely worse.

"What's going on? I got a text from Liz that shooting was canceled because you weren't feeling well. I thought you might have a cold or something, but this looks serious. Do we need to go to urgent care? Or the ER?"

If I wasn't folded over in pain, I'd probably find it adorable how frantic he sounds. I use one of my thirty-second relief periods to calm him down. "I'm fine. It's just cramps."

"Just cramps? Are you sure?"

I breathe through another one. "Liz is bringing me painkillers and a heating pad. And then I'll be okay." At least, she better be bringing them. It's been at least twenty minutes since I texted her, and she knows time is of the essence when it comes to knocking out my cramps. I internally kick myself for being unprepared, but of course the one time it really matters, my period shows up two weeks early.

Grayson plants a quick peck on my forehead. "I'll be right back."

I give him a sarcastic thumbs-up, but I don't think he sees it, because he's already headed out the door, not bothering to close it behind him.

He returns a minute later, a small plastic bottle and a fabric-covered heating pad in his hands. "I grabbed these from my room. I can't help with the pads, I'm afraid, but I've got the rest covered. My knees are shit after all that hockey, so I always have these with me on location." He pops open the bottle. "How many do you want?"

"Four." I shift myself into a slightly upright position and hold out my hand.

"Four? Ems, the recommended dose is two."

"Yeah, and when one of your organs decides to rip itself apart and expel itself from your body, then you can take two."

He hands me four pills and a glass of water from my nightstand. While I swallow the capsules, he reaches behind the table to plug in the heating pad and hands it to me after I set down the water. I roll over so I'm flat on my back, pressing the welcome warmth to my lower stomach.

"Grayson West, you are my new favorite person." I close my eyes and sigh with the smidge of relief the heat brings me.

"Is there anything else you need? Do you need me to run to the store and get pads?"

I peek at him out of the corner of one eye. "Are you serious?"

He kneels down next to me again and takes one of my hands in his. "Yes?"

I grip his fingers as another gut-busting cramp rips through me.

"Jesus, Emmy. This seems serious."

"Happens literally every four to six weeks, my dude."

He rises, but I don't let go of his hand. "Let me run to the store for you. I can be back in a half hour."

"I appreciate the offer, really, but you don't have to. The painkillers were the most pressing need. The rest can wait." Somehow, the whole thought makes it through before another cramp causes me to tighten my death grip on his hand.

"Okay." He leans over, pressing another kiss to my forehead. "I'll leave you alone then. Let me know if you need anything else, though."

"Wait," I say before he even has the chance to turn away. "The painkillers will kick in in thirty minutes and then I'll probably fall asleep. Will you stay? Until then?"

He doesn't hesitate for a single second. "Of course."

Grayson kicks off his shoes and circles around to the other side of the bed, climbing in next to me. I turn so I'm facing him, keeping the heating pad pressed to my skin and away from his. He lifts his arm with a question in his eyes. It's the same motion he made that night after ice-skating, after he bared his soul and I freaked the fuck out. But this time, I scoot myself into his embrace, letting my head fall to his chest. One hand immediately works its way into my hair, the other rubbing slow circles on my back.

I'm gripped with a few more cramps, but it doesn't take long for the medication to kick in. When the relief overtakes me, my worn-out body drifts into a peaceful sleep.

———

AS SEEMS TO BE THE CASE LATELY, I WAKE UP REACH-
ing my hand across the bed. Only this time, it connects
with something hard and warm.

A crack of one eyelid lets me know it's biceps, luckily
(or sadly) not the other hard and warm part of Grayson
West.

Both eyes slowly blink open, taking in the full picture
next to me. Grayson is wearing gray sweatpants and a
hooded sweatshirt. He's not tucked under the covers with
me, but he's close enough for the heat radiating off him to
warm me from the outside in. Oh, and he's reading one of
the romance books I brought with me. And he's wearing
glasses. I might have just spontaneously orgasmed.

"You stayed." My voice croaks, groggy with sleep and
the remnants of the painkillers.

He sticks his thumb in the pages to mark his spot, looking down at me with a hint of a smile. "I stayed."

I push myself up on the pillow. And may or may not
move closer to him while doing so. "I didn't expect you to
stay after I fell asleep."

He sticks a bookmark in the pages and closes the book.
"I can go if you'd like."

My hand jets out, gripping his forearm. "No. I didn't
mean that. I'm glad you stayed. I just didn't expect you to
after . . ."

"After you left me alone after I revealed all of my most
vulnerable secrets?" His tone is light and teasing, but the
shadows in his eyes give away the depth of hurt behind
them.

I gulp down a dry swallow. "Yeah, that." I reach over

and take his hand in mine. "I'm really sorry, Grayson. That was a shitty thing for me to do that night."

"It was." He picks up our joined hands, brushing his lips across my knuckles. "I like you, Emmy."

I sit up even straighter. "You do?"

He meets my gaze, a small smile tugging on his lips. "Is that so hard to believe?"

"I mean, yes?" I poke him in the ribs when he sends me a glare. "Given everything in the past. And given how much of an asshole I was the other day."

"Everyone's allowed to be an asshole sometimes."

I tuck myself into his side, forcing his arm around me and burying my face in the soft cotton of his sweatshirt, mostly so I don't have to look at him. "I got scared."

I wait for him to press me further, but he doesn't. And his silence makes me want to fill it.

"It was supposed to be just sex." The words are barely a whisper, but I can tell by the way he freezes, his whole body stiffening, that he heard me just fine. "There weren't supposed to be feelings, Grayson."

He presses his cheek to the top of my head. "I know."

I lace my fingers through his, our joined hands resting on his stomach. "And there might be some feelings."

"Might?"

I can practically feel his smirk.

I pinch his hip and he wiggles out of the way, only to pull me in closer. "I like you, too, Grayson."

He takes my chin in his hand, tilting up my head so we're face to face. "Now, that wasn't so hard, was it?"

Before I can offer him a sarcastic retort, his lips are on

mine. The kiss is soft and sweet and melts any remaining solid parts of my heart to total goo.

I pull away when the kiss deepens, gesturing to my lower half. "As much as I am enjoying this, I think I'm closed for business for the next couple of days."

He moves his hand to my cheek and then to the nape of my neck. "Am I not allowed to just kiss you?"

"You can kiss me anytime you want," I say, before I realize the blanket permission I've just awarded him.

"I'm going to hold you to that." He plants a closed-mouth peck on my upturned lips before settling me back in the crook of his arms. "How are you feeling?"

"Much better. It's usually mild after the first couple of hours and then I'm just uncomfortable rather than writhing in pain." I slip my hand under the hem of his sweatshirt so I can trace light circles on the bare skin of his stomach.

He mirrors the pattern on my back. "I'm glad you're feeling better, but it sucks you have to go through that every month."

"Indeed."

We sit in the silence for a few minutes. And it's lovely, and comfortable, and safe. And perhaps I'm still under the haze left behind by the painkillers and seeing Grayson reading one of my romance novels, but it feels good, and right, and not nearly as scary as I made it out to be in my head.

Grayson heads out later in the evening to grab some dinner, bringing back pizza that we eat at the small table in the corner of my room. After a shower, I change into fresh pajamas and climb back into bed. Even though I've barely been out of bed today, my body still feels wrecked and exhausted.

Grayson hesitates for a second after cleaning up the trash from our dinner. "I should go shower. We've got an early call time tomorrow."

"Okay." I wait for him to reach the door. "You can come back, you know. When you're done. If you want to, I mean. You obviously don't have to, because no sex is happening here, and I wouldn't expect you to come back if you're not into that, but you did win a night with no leaving."

He crosses the room in a few short strides, kissing me before I can blab any further. "I'll be back in fifteen minutes. And this doesn't count as my prize. That will have to wait until you're ready for *activities*." He raises his eyebrows, wiggling them around like a total dork. A totally adorable, sexy-as-fuck dork.

I fist my hand in his sweatshirt, bringing his lips back to mine for another kiss. "Good."

Screen Scandals

I'm afraid I have some devastating news to deliver to you today, dear readers. As much as we have enjoyed ogling him over the years, dreaming about the day when he might come along and sweep us up into those huge, beefy biceps and carry us off into the sunset, it appears the one and only perpetually single Grayson West might be officially off the market.

As you may remember, Grayson was cast last minute in the upcoming rom-com *No Reservations*, penned by and starring our eternal fave Emmy Harper. And although word on the street led us to believe there might have been some long-standing animosity between the two, these photos tell quite a different story. Yes, we realize it is highly likely these photos were captured during filming, and yes, we realize the sizzling chemistry might be due solely to fantastic acting.

But let's be real. The heat between these two is literally jumping off the page. So although we will acknowledge there could be nothing here but a blockbuster movie in the making, we're placing our bets that these two are more than just costars.

Need some more evidence? Check out this promo video (below) released by the *No Reservations* PR team recently. If these two aren't hooking up in between takes, I'll delete my Instagram account. Look at that eye contact and that hand squeeze! My heart literally clenched.

If Emmy and Grayson do indeed turn out to be Hollywood's next A-list couple, well, we would like to be first in line to congratulate both of them on their impeccable taste. We already stan them as individuals and will be anxiously awaiting their official relationship confirmation. Now, what do we call them? Emson? Graymy? Let us know!

CHAPTER

SIXTEEN

FROM THE MOMENT I WALK INTO HAIR AND MAKEUP two days after the cramps from hell, I practically can feel Sam's restless energy. He's walking around the room, bouncing on the balls of his feet like a little kid about to perform in their first dance recital. When he bends his knees to bring himself to my eye level, his lips are pursed like he's holding in the world's greatest secret.

"Dude, please, just spit it out." The words come out muffled because Sam is currently applying liner to my parted lips. But I can't handle the tension any longer.

He practically throws down his tools and whips his phone from his pocket.

"Thank you for putting him out of his misery." Amanda fluffs my hair, smoothing in some anti-frizz cream. "I made him promise he wouldn't bring it up if you didn't."

"Bring what up?" I reach for Sam's phone. "Ho-ly shit."

"I know," Sam squeals, clapping his hands together in pure, unfiltered joy. "Look how good you guys look! Mostly thanks to me, but also thanks to your own natural beauty, of course."

Sam's phone is open to a celebrity gossip blog, and splashed all across the home page is a series of photos from the ice rink. They're taken from far enough away that I know they weren't shot by someone on set, but thanks to the wonders of technology, zooming in shows all the close-up details. The two of us laughing. Grayson holding me up and preventing me from falling.

Grayson and me lip-locked like we might never again come up for air.

"I had a feeling about the two of you, in here acting all snippy and *The Hating Game*." Sam reaches for the lipstick and goes back to attending to my face.

Which works out well because I am now speechless and my mouth is hanging wide open.

"Blot," he instructs, handing me a tissue and taking back his phone.

I do as he says.

Amanda gives my shoulders a slight squeeze. "Is there actually something going on with you two? If not, it's no big deal. Pieces like this come out all the time, especially when two hot people are filming anything remotely romantic."

I meet her eyes in the mirror and give her a grateful smile. "I don't know what's going on with us, honestly. But I definitely wasn't planning on having whatever it is splashed across the internet for the world to see."

Sam frowns, swiping at a smudge near my eye. "I'm sorry, love. I just assumed with all the chemistry and the way things have been going with filming that something good must have happened between you two."

"It did. I just don't really know what it is yet, you

know?" I want to reach for Sam's phone again, to read through every word accompanying the multiple photos from the day that changed everything. But I know myself well enough to realize that no good can come from me obsessing about some pictures and shoddy reporting posted on a blog. Especially not when we have extra scenes to shoot today to make up for my sick day.

As soon as I get the all-clear from Sam and Amanda, I push out of the trailer and into the cold morning air. I immediately take in a giant breath, hoping it will help clear some of the fog from my brain. My chest feels like a swarm of bees have taken up residence there. I don't love having my personal business splashed around and speculated about, that's for sure. It's always been a part of my life, but one I've never gotten used to. I also don't know how I feel about the masses speculating about Grayson and me being in some kind of relationship. Because for once they aren't totally off-base: we are in *something*. Even if we don't know exactly what that means just yet. Even if the thought is somewhat terrifying.

I see him for the first time in wardrobe, when I'm on the way out and he's coming in. He stops me just outside the doorway, his hands automatically finding a place on my hips.

"Good morning." He places a kiss on the top of my head because my face is already perfectly made up and he knows better than to mess with Sam's work.

"Have you seen the blog post?" I don't mean for it to come out accusatory, but given the sharp look of surprise in his eyes, it definitely doesn't come out as a casual question.

His brow furrows. "I try to avoid that stuff as much as possible. Why?"

I shrug and tuck my hands into the front pocket of his hoodie. "Someone took photos of us during our ice-skating shoot. At least half the internet assumes we're a couple."

"Is that it? That happens to me at least once every time I'm shooting with a new costar. Kevin will be thrilled; he loves this shit." He chuckles, and rather than making me smile like it normally does, it stings. As if he's somehow likening our whatever-this-is-ship to ones he's shared with countless other costars.

I pull my hands from his pocket and shove them into my own. "Yeah. Totally. It's no big deal." I turn to walk toward set, but he loops his hand around my arm and gently tugs me back.

"Does it bother you, having people speculate?"

I shuffle my feet, staring at the ground so I don't have to look at him. "No. At least, I don't think so. I know it comes with the territory."

He takes my chin in his hand, tilting my gaze up to meet his, a smirk tugging on his lips. "Does it bother you because you want it to be true?"

I roll my eyes and scoff at the same time, which is really an impressive feat, if I do say so myself. "You wish, West."

He crowds closer into my space, his arm wrapping around the small of my back, bringing our hips together. "Do you want to be my girlfriend, Emmy?"

Sighing loudly, I turn my head away from him as he nuzzles into my neck. "I'm not dignifying that with an answer."

"That means yes," he murmurs into my skin.

The door to the wardrobe trailer bursts open, and we jump apart like we aren't two consenting adults who are totally allowed to have the hots for each other.

"I'll see you on set," I mutter underneath my breath, turning and walking away as fast as my frozen legs will carry me.

"We're not done with this conversation," he calls from behind me, loud enough for the entire cast and crew and town of Pine Springs to hear.

"You are the actual worst," I shout back over my shoulder.

"You know you love me!"

And I obviously slip on some unseen patch of ice because that's the only explanation for how much I stumble when I hear those words. My almost face-plant is definitely *not* because every cell in my body chooses this moment to come to a particular realization.

Oh fuck.

I think I love him.

I BOLT FROM THE SET AS SOON AS DEIDRE SIGNALS it's time for lunch. I hole up in one of the trailers, closing and locking the door behind me. I ignore the suggestive texts from Grayson and the inquisitive ones from Liz.

And then I do the one thing I should've done days ago.

I pick up the phone and call my mom. She answers after the first ring, like she was staring at the screen, just waiting for my call. As soon as it connects, she switches it over to FaceTime and I suddenly regret my decision. Once Diane Brenner has you on FaceTime, there's no turning back.

"I like him." I blurt out the words the second our faces pop up on the screen. "I think I actually really like him." Relief courses through me at the admission.

"You *think*?" Her smile is all too knowing.

"I know. I know I like him." I cover my eyes, like that will accomplish anything.

"You *like* him?"

"Please don't make me say that part out loud again."

She chuckles, but there's nothing unkind in it. "Look at me, Emilia."

I peek through a small window between my fingers.

"Why is it so terrible to admit that you lo—that you have feelings for someone?"

"Because I used to hate him?"

She gives that response all the credence it deserves, answering it with an exaggerated eye roll.

"Because the world is already blasting our personal business out into the ether of the internet?"

She scoffs, which is fair. I've basically spent my whole life in the tabloids. I should be used to it by now. But somehow this feels way more personal.

I drop my hand from my face, tunneling it into my hair instead.

"Does Grayson West have some sort of shady background or terrible character traits that I don't know about?" she asks.

"To be fair, you don't really know him, Mom." I've barely mentioned Grayson in our weekly conversations, not wanting to fill in my mom on our costars-with-benefits arrangement, for understandable reasons.

She rolls her eyes again. "I've seen all his movies, and

ever since Liz clued me in that there's something going on between the two of you, I started studying him. He seems to be a charming and talented and compassionate young man."

"I'm going to kill her." Although at least my mom's research has led her to the right conclusions. Grayson is all of those things, and so much more.

"As usual, you've avoided the real question, Emmy. Is there something about Grayson that would lead you to believe you shouldn't have feelings for him?" She peers down her nose at me, and even with hundreds of miles separating us, I feel that look deep in my soul.

I let out a begrudging sigh. "No. Not even close. He's basically a perfect human specimen."

"And I'm assuming the sex is good?"

"Mom, seriously?" I bury my head in my hands, not that she'll let me hide from this conversation.

"A healthy sexual relationship is very important, Emmy. I just wanted to be sure the two of you are compatible in the bedroom."

"Oh my god, stop."

"I'll take that as a yes."

"Great."

There's a long pause, long enough for me to cautiously peek back at my phone.

"Why are you so freaked out, sweetheart?" Her soft words cut right to the heart of the problem.

"We were on some of the blogs today."

"And?"

"I don't know. It was hard enough when this was just between the two of us, but now that it's out there . . ."

Her forehead furrows, and I actually see wrinkles because she is staunchly against Botox. "Are you ashamed of him, Emilia?"

"No! Absolutely not." I sigh in frustration. "I guess I just don't like the idea of other people judging my relationship."

"Honey, whether you were dating Grayson West or some person with a regular job, there still would be people judging your relationship. It's part of the deal. You've known that."

"How did you and Dad deal with all of this?"

"You get used to it. And when you've been together for twenty years, people start to lose interest."

"Great," I mumble. "Only nineteen years and eleven months to go."

"The important thing is that the two of you keep something for yourselves. That you talk to each other when things feel shitty. And that you remember that, when it really comes down to it, it's about the two of you and no one else's opinion really matters."

I wipe my eyes on my sleeve, not fully sure when I started crying, and not wanting to recognize that my tears don't have much to do with a silly article posted on a blog. "So you're saying I should give things a shot with Grayson?"

She shrugs and smiles. "I can't make that decision for you, but what I am saying is that you shouldn't *not* give things a shot because you're scared. That's a cop-out."

"Gee, thanks, Mom."

"If your mother can't be honest with you, then who can?" Her hand floats up, like she can reach through the screen and wipe my tears. "Don't deny yourself something beautiful because you're already thinking about what happens if it goes wrong."

I nod, taking in the words I knew she was going to say, knowing that I needed to hear them said. "Thanks, Mom."

"That's what I'm here for, sweetheart. Now go wash your face and maybe slap on an eye mask for a few minutes before you go get your man. No one should declare love with snot dripping out their nose."

"You are the worst."

"I love you, too." She blows me a kiss and disconnects the call before I can return the sentiment.

Glancing over at the mirror on the back of the trailer door, I groan. Sam is going to have to do some serious work to salvage this face, and I can't imagine he'll be happy about it.

I text Liz, asking her to send him my way. Might as well get it over with.

When there's a light tap on the door, I peek out and, seeing Sam is on his own, I let him in, locking the door behind him.

"What's with all the secrecy?" He sets his kit down on the small table, and to his credit, only sighs a little when he takes in the damage to my eye makeup.

"Just having a day." I sit down and close my eyes, determined to be a good little patient.

"I didn't mean to upset you earlier."

I open my eyes to find Sam's face filled with compassion. I reach out and squeeze his hand. "You didn't. Promise. I just have some things I need to figure out."

Sam gestures for me to close my eyes again and gets to

work clearing up the smudgy mess. "He's a good man, you know."

"I know."

"Amanda and I have been rooting for the two of you to hook up from the beginning."

I groan. "Please tell me you did not place bets on my sex life."

"Oh, we totally placed bets on your sex life." He dabs on eyeliner. "Open up for me, babe."

We sit in silence for a minute while Sam applies a new layer of mascara to my eyelashes.

The tension must still be evident, because when Sam steps back and gives me a nod of approval, he doesn't immediately turn to pack up his things. "Is it really so terrible if the world thinks the two of you are dating, sweetie?"

I think about the question before offering my response. "I guess I should've expected it. The public and the paparazzi have been a part of my life since the day I was born. I'm used to people speculating about me, watching my every move."

"That sounds like a lot of pressure."

"It was. It is." I shrug, trying to brush it all off. "I know everyone is paying close attention to this movie anyway, what with it being my first one post-Oscar and my first time really acting. Maybe it's just a bad idea to give them all one more thing I could fail at, you know?"

"Oh, honey." Sam pulls me up from my chair and wraps me in a huge hug. "You are the opposite of a failure. And if I may pull out some Hallmark-card wisdom, the only way you can fail at love is by not letting it into your life."

I gently remove myself from his embrace so I don't start crying again. "You should get that stitched on a pillow."

He winks at me. "I just might."

"Thank you, Sam. For the touch-up and the advice. You're a miracle worker."

"I have been told that before." He blows me a kiss and heads back out to set, leaving me alone with my thoughts.

I still don't know much of anything, but I do think Sam and my mom are right. Maybe it's time to let some love into my life.

THE CONVERSATION WITH MY MOM RUNS ON A CON-
stant loop in my mind for the rest of the day, and the moment Liz calls cut on our final scene, I turn on my heel and
run. Well, I turn on my heel and walk as fast as I can
without slipping on the frozen ground and killing and/or
humiliating myself.

So unsurprisingly, Grayson is able to catch up to me
with just a few of his extra-long strides.

"Let's go get dinner in town tonight."

"You want to go get dinner in public on the same day a
blog posted an article about us possibly being in a relationship?" Like I even give a shit about the stupid blog post at
this point. I'm really just irritated with it for making me
think about things I was perfectly fine not thinking about.

"We are in a relationship." The words sound so calm,
so confident coming from his perfect lips, half of me en-
vies his surety.

The other half is annoyed he assumes such a thing
without asking me first.

I speed up my pace, attempting to put some distance between us. "Are we?"

He hooks a finger through one of the belt loops on my jeans, tugging me to a stop and ultimately catching me when I slip due to the sudden motion. He leans down to kiss me, but I pull away. Not because I don't want to kiss him, but because we are still on set and surrounded by people and he still hasn't answered my question.

"I seem to recall you mentioning I could kiss you whenever I want."

"Grayson . . ." I attempt to remove myself from his hold, but the action only sends me sliding on the ice again.

And of course, he is there to catch me. Of course he is there to steady me, even when pure, unfiltered hurt shines out of his gaze, knocking me back a step.

Suddenly, everything else around us—the trailers, the crew, the cameras, the lights—all of it fades to a silent black hole, and there is only Grayson and me, and I hate that I made him feel that way.

"Do you not want to be seen in public with me, Ems? Do you not want people to know about us?" His voice is so quiet, so rough, I have to lean in closer to hear him.

"No. Grayson, no. God no." I cup his cheek in my hand, relishing the scratch of his beard against my palm. "Do you really think I'm ashamed of you?"

"Maybe." He shrugs and pulls his eyes away from mine, like he can't stand to look at me. "And I would get it, if you were. You're smart and talented, an accomplished writer who has won all these awards, and I'm what?"

"The Sexiest Man Alive?" I mean for it to come out as a

joke, but I can immediately tell by the way his shoulders tighten that it's the exact wrong thing to say.

"I am that, yes." He hunches over like a weight is pressing him down.

I step closer into his space, taking his hand in mine and lacing our fingers together. "You are that. And you are much, much more than that. Grayson, I thought I'd made it clear the other night just how impressed I am by you. By all of you, not just this absurdly delicious physique you've got going on."

That earns me a hint of a smile.

"You did. And I know you meant it. I guess it's just different when other people start weighing in on your relationship. And I'd understand if that scared you away." His fingers tighten around mine.

I turn his cheek so he's forced to look me in the eye. "I wasn't totally joking when I asked if we're in a relationship, you know. It's not like we've ever really talked about it, other than when we agreed to being costars with benefits."

He turns his head, kissing the palm of my hand. "Safe to say that restriction is out the window."

"Most definitely." I rise onto my tiptoes and plant a soft kiss on his mouth, not caring who is around to see it at this point. "Maybe we should go get dinner in town tonight and figure it all out?"

"I think that could be arranged." He slides a hand into my hair, bringing me in for a deeper kiss.

"Is everyone staring at us?" I mumble against his lips.

"Does it matter?" His grip on me tightens, and I press my hips to his.

"Well, I am less likely to feel you up if we have an audience."

He breaks the kiss. "Then let's get the fuck out of here, yeah?"

I purse my lips and attempt to hold in the laughter, and it works for about five seconds.

He furrows his brow. "What?"

I slip my phone from the back pocket of my jeans, where I'd stuck it as soon as cameras were down, and snap a photo of his face. Emailing the evidence to myself first, I then flip the screen around so he can see for himself.

His nose wrinkles as he takes in his face, smeared with the remnants of my makeup. Because kissing wasn't in the script for today, Sam didn't bother to use the non-smudge stuff. "Oof. Crimson is not my color."

I laugh, tucking my arm into his and dragging him toward the makeup trailer. "I'm sure Sam has plenty of ways to get all of that off your gorgeous face."

He slips his hand into the back pocket of my jeans. "And then we'll get out of here and commence with the feeling up?"

"I thought you wanted to take me out to a nice, romantic dinner where we talk all about our feelings and hopes and dreams for the future?" I lean into him, unable to keep myself from needing as much physical contact as possible.

He gives my ass a squeeze. "I wouldn't say no to a little handy first."

"Oh my god." I swat at him and attempt once again to work myself out of his grip, but he doesn't let me, instead dipping me down and gifting me with another swoon-worthy kiss.

"You know I always return the favor," he says when he returns me to my original upright position.

"You're incorrigible."

"It's cute that you think I know what that means." He flashes me a wicked grin as we push through the makeup trailer door.

"I know you know what that means because I know I'm not the first person who's called you that." I shove him down into the makeup chair, and because Sam isn't around, I find the makeup remover wipes and softly clean off the remains of my deep red lipstick from his face.

With him in the chair and me standing between his legs, we're finally the same height. I can't deny how good it feels to be here with him, having acknowledged not just our crackling chemistry, but that there might be—that there definitely is—something more here. When I finish with Grayson, he pulls a cloth from the pack and ever so softly wipes at the remaining color painted on my lips. He's so exceedingly gentle, it takes minutes longer than it should, but I'm frozen, so absolutely transfixed by the care with which he cleans my skin. I'd stand here for the rest of the night if need be.

"All clear," he finally whispers, tossing the scarlet-stained cloth in the trash before taking my face in his hands.

When our lips meet, they're both a bit cold from the outdoors and the makeup remover, but it doesn't take long for the heat to swallow me whole. His lips move over mine as gently as his hands did, and I sink into him and his kiss.

"Emmy," he murmurs, parting us, leaving just a sliver of space between our faces.

It's enough for me to read the look in his eyes, to know

what he's going to say before he says it. And it hits me that I know him now. Not just his body, his lips, or the ridges of his perfect abs. I know his mind, and I know his heart.

And even though I thought the words to myself just hours earlier, I don't think I'm quite ready to hear them.

So I press my lips to his again, urgently and desperately. "Let's go home, yeah?"

There's a flash of disappointment in the bright blue of his eyes, but it doesn't last long. He covers it with a grin, hopping up from the makeup chair and lacing our hands together as we head out of the trailer and back to the inn.

WE MEET IN THE LOBBY A COUPLE OF HOURS LATER, having separated and gone to our individual rooms for a bit. I told Grayson I needed a shower, which wasn't exactly a lie, but it certainly wasn't the whole truth. I did need to wash the hours of being on set from my skin, but I also needed to stand under the stream of hot water and try to make sense of what's been going on in my head. And in my heart.

Because I'm not totally sure when my feelings for Grayson fucking West changed. That *fucking* used to mean one thing, and now means something totally different. But even with all the fucking aside, something is different now. We're different.

Was it the way we finally clicked and found our stride together in our scenes?

Was it how he opened up to me and allowed me to see his vulnerable side?

Was it when he took care of me when I felt like shit and looked even worse?

Or is it the way he kisses me, the way he cups my cheek

in his hand like I'm something to be treasured. The way he puts my pleasure first, always. The way he makes me laugh and the way he looks at me like I'm the most beautiful woman he's ever seen.

It's a lot. And I don't know if I'm ready for it. I also don't know what happens when we venture outside our perfect, happy showmance bubble. What will it be like when we go back to LA and he goes on location, or I'm on a writing deadline, or one of us has to film a sex scene with someone else? What happens when the press hounds us or the fans talk shit about us? What happens if *No Reservations* tanks or if the critics say we have no chemistry?

Hmmm. At least I'm confident that we don't have to worry about that last one.

But even still, a whole host of unknowns lies before us, and it was only a few weeks ago that we couldn't stand the sight of each other. Is it possible to go from enemies to lovers in a matter of days? The romance screenplay writer in me says absolutely yes. The realist might need a bit more convincing. Because now if we fail, if the two of us don't work out, the whole world will be watching.

None of these overwhelming thoughts keep me from spending longer on my appearance than I normally would. Despite Grayson having had his mouth and hands on practically every part of my body, this is technically our first date, and I want to look good.

It's also negative freezing outside, which greatly limits my ability to show off my best assets. Still, by the time I come down the stairs dressed in tight jeans and an over-sized cream sweater, a red wool coat draped over my arm, and long curls swinging down my back, I feel pretty. My stomach is hosting its own performance of the Irish-jig scene from *Titanic*, but at least I feel pretty.

And so it's kind of a low-key shame when I find Grayson waiting for me at the front door, out-prettying me in every way. He's also dressed in jeans and a sweater, only his chunky blue one is the exact color of his eyes. He's already donned his gray coat, and he basically looks like he stepped off the cover of *GQ*.

My breath flutters in my chest as he bends down to drop a chaste kiss on my cheek and helps me into my coat. "You look gorgeous, Ems."

"Yeah. Same." You'd think a woman who makes her living writing love scenes would be able to form some coherent responses to the most basic of first-date greetings, but in this case, you would be horribly wrong.

It doesn't stop the slow grin from spreading across his face. He holds open the front door for me, and we exit out onto the stairs, the railings lining the sweeping porch still covered in a smattering of snow despite the fact that we're heading into April.

"You wanna walk or drive?" Grayson offers me his arm as we head down the snow-covered steps.

I take it gratefully and shiver as the cold seeps in even through my coat and sweater. "Drive, please. I was not made for snow."

He bumps his hip with mine. "Oh come on, it's practically balmy."

"You people from the middle are weird."

He unlocks his midsize SUV, opening my door for me like a real date. "You're the born-and-bred Angeleno who doesn't like avocados."

I scoff in mock indignation, but before I can respond, he's shut the door and is crossing to the driver's side of the car. He climbs in, and as we buckle up, I hold my hands up to the heater while it kicks in. "Where are we going?"

"There's not much fine dining in Pine Springs, but Linda told me about a pub downtown that should have some good food."

"Sounds like a plan."

We arrive just a few minutes later because "downtown" is really just an expression here more than an actual destination. We find parking right away, and Grayson hops out quickly enough to race around and open my door for me.

"I'm perfectly capable of opening my own doors, you know." A sentiment that doesn't stop me from leaning on him as I jump down into the slushy snow.

"Trust me, Emmy. I'm well aware of all the many things you are capable of."

"Are you making a sex joke on our first date?"

He slips his hand under my coat, clutching my ass and pulling me into him. His head dips down, lingering a fraction of an inch away from my lips. Our breaths mingle and he turns his head, skirting his mouth down my neck, sucking lightly on my slightly exposed collarbone.

And each of my frozen extremities melts into a gooey puddle.

He pulls away from me suddenly, leaving me even colder than I already was. "Ready for dinner?"

"Huh?" Apparently my brain also has frozen to the point of losing all function, not that I ever had much to begin with in the presence of Grayson West.

He chuckles and pulls me into his side, guiding me into

the pub, which is right in front of us because parking here is plentiful and convenient—a foreign phenomenon.

The warmth of the interior instantly envelops me, and I sigh at the comfort of it. The pub is decked out in old gray stone and wooden beams, and there's a huge fireplace roaring with flames. There's a long bar made of a dark polished wood, but Grayson leads me over to a booth near the fire, like the very smart man he is. We settle into the comfortably cracked burgundy leather and order a round of beers when our server stops by a minute later.

I wait for him to bring it up—the big relationship-sized elephant in the pub. But he doesn't and so I don't, and instead we have a delightfully pleasant conversation while we eat fish and chips and drink our beers. And it's nice. Not just because I'm dreading the awkward "Where do we stand?" conversation, but because I actually like talking with him.

After our plates are cleaned and cleared, and with just the final sips of beer remaining in our steins, Grayson levels me with a serious look. But he doesn't say what I expect, what I've been waiting for.

Instead, he leans forward, reaching for my hand across the table. "Will you tell me about your dad, Ems? I know the basics, of course, and what happened, but I don't know much about your relationship with him."

My heart stops in my chest for just a minute as I have that realization. The one that sneaks up on me every once in a while. The realization that he's gone.

He squeezes my hand. "You don't have to, of course, but I'd like to hear about him if you want to tell me."

I nod, taking in a long breath, steadying my nerves and

my voice before I open my mouth to speak. "He died four years ago. Heart attack. It was pretty sudden. One day he was completely healthy, and the next day he was gone. But you probably knew most of that."

Grayson keeps a tight hold on my hand but doesn't interrupt me.

"He was the greatest." The words choke out of me, not just because it's still hard to talk about my dad, but because I now know Grayson's struggles with his own dad. Yes, I lost mine much too soon, but while he was here, he was everything I needed him to be. "Supportive and caring and loving. Never missed a school play or a dance recital, even when showing up caused a lot of stares and awkward photos. Took me book shopping and taught me how to ride a bike. Everything I could've ever wanted him to be."

"He sounds like an amazing man." The emotions are layered in Grayson's voice and in the tight smile he gives me.

"He was. I was very lucky to have him in my life."

"How's your relationship with your mom?"

I roll my eyes but pair it with a smile. "She's irritating in the best possible way. Pushy and overinvolved, but hilarious and has the biggest heart." My smile fades just a tad. "I can't imagine what it was like for her, what it's still like for her. They really, truly loved each other. Soulmates, as cliché as it sounds." An ache appears, right at the center of my chest. Obviously, I know how hard it must have been for my mom to lose the love of her life—she and my dad were the kind of couple I write movies about, so perfectly suited for only each other. But not having experienced anything close to that myself, I could never really imagine the full extent of her pain.

Now, as I look across the table at this beautiful man, I think I might have an inkling of an idea.

And it's at that moment when the tears spring to my eyes.

Grayson hands me a napkin, still keeping a hold on my hand, his thumb tracing a soothing pattern over my knuckles. "Ready to go?"

I wipe my eyes and nod, grateful he seems to know exactly what I need in the moment. "Thank you for asking about him. And for listening."

"Of course. I want to know about everything, and everyone, that's important to you, Ems." Grayson clears his throat, and the mood shifts. "You wanna walk for a little while before we head back?"

I fake a smile, knowing that it won't be long before Grayson turns it real. "Only if there's somewhere to grab hot chocolate along the way." I scooch out of the booth and hold out my hand to him.

He takes it, sliding his own way out and tucking my hand into the crook of his elbow. "I promise we'll find you something warm and sweet."

"Are you expecting me to go for the obvious and say you're the only thing warm and sweet I need?"

He chuckles, pushing the door open wide enough for us to both exit. "I think I know you better than that by now, Ems."

I tuck myself closer into his side the moment we step outside and the cold air hits me. The café is only two doors down, and after a quick stop for some cocoa, we take our drinks and meander down the main street of Pine Springs.

I sip from my cup, letting the warmth seep into me. "It's kind of a bummer we missed the winter holiday festival. I bet it's super cute."

"The cutest." He grins down at me before swigging from his cup. "We could always come back during the holiday season."

The words hang there for just a minute, the perfect segue, dangling right there in front of us.

I break the silence first. "You think you'll still want to be banging me in a year?"

"Technically, it's only eight months."

I elbow him in the ribs.

He dodges my half-hearted blow but still doesn't answer my question.

We end up at the tiny park at the far end of downtown. I finish the last of my drink and toss my cup in a trash can. Grayson does the same before lacing our fingers together and pulling me into the tiny white gazebo at the entrance of the park.

I slip my hands underneath Grayson's jacket, between his coat and sweater, because I'm already cold again and also because I need to feel him. He wraps his arms around me, settling them at my lower back.

It doesn't take long to realize he's not going to let me out of this one. He rests his chin on the top of my head like he's content to stay in this silence for as long as it takes, and dammit, I'm too freaking cold for this emotional warfare.

"What if we suck together when we get home?" I finally blurt out, clearly not having thought through my phrasing at all, even the slightest bit.

His laughter rumbles through me. "That one's just too easy."

I put a little distance between us but not much because fuck the cold. "I'm trying to be serious here."

"I know." He dips down to plant a quick peck on my pouting lips. "But I'd hope you know by now I am going to rib you at every possible moment."

I slip one hand under his sweater and pinch his hip.

He squeals, and revenge tastes sweet. "Okay. Okay. Why would you think we would su— Why do you think we won't work when we get back to LA?"

I shrug my shoulders, hoping he gets it as the helpless gesture it is. "This isn't real life, West. What we've been doing for the past few weeks isn't real life. And when we get home and are smacked in the face with reality, well, maybe we'll find we really do despise each other after all." Just the thought cracks my heart.

"Hey." He takes my face in his hands, his gloves scratchy yet warm on my cheeks. "I never despised you, Ems. Never. I didn't even dislike you. I mostly thought we gave each other a hard time because it was fun."

I roll my eyes. "Of course. But that doesn't mean we're well suited for a relationship. A relationship comprised of more than just sex."

His eyes heat, and a grin tugs on his lips. "It is pretty good sex though, isn't it?"

I glare at him. "Not the point."

He moves his hands to my hips, pressing us together. "I

don't know what to tell you, Emmy. We don't know if we'll work in the real world until we try it out and see."

"Do you want us to work in the real world?"

"Do you?"

I shift my hips subtly into his. "I asked you first."

He leans down and kisses me softly, a gentle press of his lips that's over far too soon. "I want us to work in the real world."

My hands travel around his back, coming to rest on his chest. "I do, too."

"Yeah?" A slow smile spreads across his lips.

"Yeah." I press my palm flat over his heart, relishing the accelerated beat pounding against my hand. "But that doesn't mean I'm not scared, Grayson. Everyone will be watching us, just waiting for us to combust."

"Fuck them, Ems. The only people who matter in this are you and me." He covers my hand with his. "You don't have to be scared, but I understand why you are."

"Can you be patient with me?"

"Always."

I push up on my tiptoes, sliding my arms around his neck and bringing his lips to mine.

This kiss starts soft and gentle, but it doesn't take long before my mouth is opening under his, both of our arms tightening until we're pressed together, every inch of us melding into one. We don't part until we have to; sadly, needing to breathe is still a thing.

Grayson's pupils are wide and dark, his lips pink, and his eyes bright. "I think I'm falling in love with you, Emmy Harper."

"Yeah?" I let the grin take over my face.

"Yeah." A flash of something not wholly confident passes through his eyes. He tries to cover it with a smile, but it's there, and I see it.

I tangle my fingers in his hair. "I'm falling in love with you, too, Grayson West."

The light that fills his eyes is so blinding, I have to pull him in for another kiss. It deepens, and I am desperate for him, aching to strip the remaining barriers between us.

"Think we can get away with doing it in the middle of this park?" he mumbles into my neck, his teeth grazing my skin, making me gasp.

I clutch him tighter. "Pretty sure not even you could make me desperate enough to have sex in the snow."

He laughs, separating our limbs just enough so he can pull me out of the gazebo. We sprint to the car, as fast as the snow-covered ground will allow. Grayson peels out of the parking spot, and we're back at the inn within minutes.

We shout a harried hello in Linda's general direction at the front desk before racing up the stairs and barreling through the door of my room.

"I think we just erased any and all doubt about our relationship status." I head directly toward the fireplace because despite all the physical exertion, I'm still chilled to the bone. Luckily, Linda has been in to stoke the flames, and the heat seeps through me almost instantly.

Grayson wraps me in his embrace from behind, pulling my back against his chest. He sweeps my hair to one side, his lips trailing down the exposed skin of my neck. Warm hands settle on my shoulders, removing my coat and tossing it on one of the armchairs.

I lean into him with a sigh, relaxing into the strength and warmth of his arms. "I don't normally sleep with guys on the first date, you know."

"Well, I don't normally declare love on the first date, so I think we're even." His hands travel down to my hips before slipping under my sweater.

"So you actually meant it? It wasn't all just a ploy to get me into bed?"

"I'm not dignifying that with a response." He shifts his hips, brushing against the curve of my ass, letting me feel how hard he already is. "And I've never really had a problem getting you into bed, Harper."

"It is one of your many talents, West." I guide his hands up to my breasts before I unlace our fingers so I can remove my sweater.

Grayson wastes no time divesting me of my bra, his fingers brushing over my already peaked nipples, the hint of contact enough to make me lose my breath. His mouth finds my neck again, lips tracing the faintest path, leaving behind an explosion of goosebumps in their wake. When his fingers stop their incessant teasing and turn to rolling and pinching my nipples, I turn my head, my mouth searching for his.

I find it, my tongue sweeping into his mouth with languorous, delving strokes. He spins me around, his hands covering my bare back and pressing me into his chest. His still very clothed chest.

I break the kiss for a half second so I can yank his sweater over his head. And then it's right back to a kiss that knocks my entire world off its axis. Our hands and lips and tongues explore each other in a way that's both desperate and lazy. Like we have all the time in the world but also could never find a way to take our fill. My heart pounds, and when our chests collide, the same beat echoes through his.

Grayson takes my face in his hands, parting us the tiniest sliver so we can both catch our breath. My hands come to a rest on his chest, his smattering of hair tickling my palms.

Our eyes meet, and I absolutely shatter. For the second time in my life, Grayson West has destroyed me, only this time couldn't be more different from the first. It's like he came in and broke me only so he could build me back, better and stronger than I've ever been before. Because the look in his eyes makes me feel beautiful and powerful and like I can conquer the fucking world.

"I love you," I tell him.

"I love you, too."

My hands move to the button of his jeans, unfastening and unzipping and shoving them down to his knees with his boxers in tow. He kicks them off to the side, somehow managing at the same time to release my own button and zipper. He peels my jeans from my legs, my hands finding stability on his broad shoulders while he helps me step out of them.

His lips trail up my legs, and he places a soft kiss below my belly button. He hooks his thumbs in the waistband of my panties, dragging them down slowly until I can kick my feet free.

When he rises, we both stand back a bit, fully and finally bared to one another.

Grayson reaches out, tracing the tips of his fingers

across my collarbone, down along the swells of my breasts, over the plane of my stomach. Our mouths meet again, and still, we take our time. We know each other's bodies pretty well by now, but that doesn't stop the exploration, as if by exchanging these new words, setting a new path for our relationship, we're discovering each other again like it's the first time.

My fingers skirt over the bulges of muscle in his back, the individual ridges of his abs, the solid trunk of his thighs. I send them back up, brushing over the thick and hard length of him. He groans into my mouth, and I swallow it like it's champagne.

His arms wrap tightly around me as he lowers us both to the soft, fluffy rug directly in front of the fire. I have a hard time remembering what it felt like to be cold, because the heat of him, of us, is everywhere. The hard, hot length of his body covers me, and I don't think I'll ever be cold again.

His mouth trails down my neck once again, although this time he doesn't linger. He cups my breast in his hand, his tongue swirling around the bud of my nipple until it's peaked and aching. When I moan, he takes it in his mouth, sucking until my hips buck beneath him, before moving on to the next and delivering the same deliciously frustrating treatment.

My core is throbbing, begging for pressure, and my body shifts under his, searching for relief. His mouth finally moves farther south, kissing every inch of my exposed belly before he settles himself between my legs. He nips at the thin skin of my inner thighs as his fingers part me, skirting the edges, touching me everywhere except where I need to be touched.

"Grayson, please," I beg. "I need you."

He growls—legitimately growls—and his lips are so close to my core it sends a vibration through me.

When his tongue finally traces me, opens me, I cry out. I lace my fingers through his hair, and when our gazes meet, his pupils are so blown his eyes look black.

He teases me, the tip of his tongue licking up my seam, swirling my clit before he takes the bud in his mouth, sucking until I can't breathe. Two fingers slip inside me, and all at once I shatter, convulsing around him, my hips rocking against his mouth, his name caught in the back of my throat.

He removes his fingers, planting soft and light kisses on my now slightly sweaty skin while I try to piece myself back together.

"You're so fucking gorgeous," he mutters into my neck. "I almost came just watching you."

I take his face in my hands, bringing his lips to mine. "I'm glad you didn't." I give him a wicked smile, wrapping my hand around his cock.

"I need to fuck you, Emmy." He reaches for his jeans, searching for a condom.

I stop his hand. "I'm on birth control, and I get tested regularly. I haven't been with anyone else since we started sleeping together."

He swallows thickly, his hand coming to cup my cheek, his thumb running over my jaw. "I haven't either." He brushes his lips against mine in the faintest of kisses. "I don't want to pressure you."

I place both hands on his chest. "It was my idea. I trust you, Grayson."

His hand travels from my cheek down my sternum to my belly until it lands between my legs. He strokes me slowly, until I'm aching for him. I take him in my hand, guiding him to me.

"You're sure?"

I nod. "Are you?"

He answers by pushing into me with one hard thrust.

It knocks the wind out of both of us, and for a minute we just lay there, our limbs intertwined, Grayson buried deep inside me.

His movements start slow, his thrusts long and deep, filling me to a completeness I've never felt before. He grunts my name, burying his face in my neck and the tangles of my hair. He thrusts harder and faster, and I clutch at the muscles of his back as the tension starts to rise inside me.

My muscles clench around him, and he groans. "Fuck, Emmy."

His mouth finds mine as we tumble over the edge together, every part of us connected. We ride out the aftershocks, all trembling hearts and intertwined limbs and desperate kisses.

When we're finally settled and whole, Grayson stands, scooping me into his arms and carrying me the short distance to the bed. We tuck ourselves under the covers, his huge body curling around me.

And I fall asleep in Grayson West's arms.

I WAKE UP ON THE FINAL DAY OF SHOOTING TO THE sound of my alarm and within the warmth of Grayson's arms. He groans as my phone continues to beep. His call time is—once again—not for another two hours, so I silence the incessant ringing and slip out of bed.

Or I would slip out of bed if it weren't for the muscled and incredibly strong forearm locked around my waist. I pull gently at first, but he doesn't give even an inch. Rotating to face him, I give him my best I-hate-Grayson-fucking-West glare. "Excuse me. Some of us have to be at work at a normal hour this morning."

He flashes me a sleepy grin, eyes barely open. "I'm not ready to let you go yet."

"You will literally see me in two hours." I try to wiggle out of his embrace, but he only clenches me tighter.

"You're not sneaking out of this bed without kissing me first."

I wrinkle my nose. "Can I at least brush my teeth?"

His eyes flutter open. "No." And he presses his lips to mine.

I fight it for point one second before I give in and sink into his kiss, morning breath be damned.

Grayson presses his hips to mine, the hard length of him teasing me. "Sure you have to leave right now?"

I groan into his mouth. "Yes." Forcing myself to break the kiss, I finally slip out of bed and head to the bathroom for a quick shower and toothbrushing. Grayson is asleep when I emerge, so I don't bother him, slipping quietly out of the room and shutting the door silently behind me.

"Last day!" Sam trills when I push into the makeup room.

We're shooting at the inn today, which means I had a short commute and managed to make it to the chair on time. And it isn't until Sam says the words that they really start to sink in. Today is our last day of filming. It's been a long time since I felt like an actual member of production, so that feeling of loss when a project wraps is somewhat foreign. Normally, I get to send off my baby to production and I'm not really involved from that point on, but it's been a new—and rewarding—experience to help shepherd her into her final stages.

But my heart is heavy at the thought of packing up tomorrow and heading home. I'll miss Linda and the inn, and early mornings with Amanda and Sam. I'll miss working with my best friend, and the new friends I made among the cast and crew. I'll miss my huge bed and the roaring fires. And I'll miss this magical bubble I created with Grayson.

Definitely won't miss the snow, though.

And thankfully, I won't really have to miss Grayson either. We're both based out of LA, close enough in the city that even a rush-hour commute won't take more than a half hour.

Yet I know things will be different. And different doesn't mean bad, necessarily. Just different.

"Don't you start crying on me," Sam scolds, waving his hand in front of my eyes.

I didn't even notice the welling of tears, but I blink rapidly to keep them from falling. "Sorry. I don't know what came over me."

"Happens all the time on last days." Sam swipes mascara onto my eyelashes and then shoos me over into Amanda's chair. "I'd cry, too, if I knew I wasn't going to see me every day."

I laugh, settling in in front of Amanda. "I am going to miss you guys."

Amanda winks at me in the mirror. "We'll miss you, too."

She's finishing up my so-casual-they-took-an-hour-to-style loose waves when the door opens and Grayson walks in. Our eyes meet in the mirror, and when he smiles, my heart grows three sizes.

Amanda gives me a final spritz of hairspray and sends me back to Sam for final touches.

"Did you do her lips yet?" Grayson asks, striding over to my chair.

"Does it look like I did her lips yet?" Sam gives me an incredulous look, offended that Grayson can't seem to tell the difference.

I purse said lips to hold in my laughter. "No, he hasn't."

"Good." Grayson leans down, planting a long, lingering kiss on my naked mouth. "Now that we've both brushed our teeth," he whispers, before hopping into Amanda's chair.

My cheeks flame, and I really hope no one else heard that. When I finally bring myself to look at Sam, his gleeful smirk makes it clear he most definitely did.

"Shut up," I mumble to him under my breath.

"I didn't say anything." He lines my lips and fills them in with a berry-colored stain.

I wait until he's done so the words come out clearly. "I know what you're thinking."

"I'm just glad to see you happy! It's about fucking time you two made it official." He shoots me a devilish grin.

"There are so many places I could go with that." Grayson reaches over to poke me.

I intercept him before he can make contact, hooking our index fingers together. "It's too early for sex puns."

"It's never too early for sex puns," Grayson and Sam say at the exact same time.

There's a knock on the door, and Deidre pokes her head in. "Are these two almost done?"

Sam swipes a slick of gloss on my lips. "Emmy is all set."

Amanda gives Grayson's hair a final tousle. "So is this one."

"Good. Go get changed, you two. We've got a tight schedule today because we have a reshoot in addition to our final scene."

I groan, knowing I have no one to blame but myself and the hot piece of ass next to me for the extended day. Because some of our essential scenes were shot during the early days of filming, when our acting was cringeworthy, we've had to reshoot a bunch of stuff in the intervening weeks to catch up.

The two of us head to the wardrobe room and don't even bother moving into private spaces to change, stripping down in the middle of the room and stepping into our assigned clothes.

Grayson catches me checking him out and gives me a cocky grin and a biceps flex.

I roll my eyes, but it doesn't cover the hint of drool that escapes my mouth.

We stroll onto set hand in hand, and Liz gives us a low whistle and a slow clap. "My, my, how the turn tables."

She's awarded with her own eye roll. "Yeah, yeah."

Liz turns to Grayson. "I'd love to give you the whole hurt-my-best-friend-and-I'll-kill-you routine, but we don't have time for that, so let's get to it, shall we?"

Deidre comes over to give us the run-down for today. I make it a point to have fun, to enjoy these final moments, and I lose myself in the story and the character. Grayson and I are a well-oiled machine at this point, our give-and-take a perfect balance. I know this final day is going to end before I want it to, and when Liz calls cut for the last time, announcing it's a wrap to cheers and applause, Grayson gathers me in a sweeping hug.

I bury my face in his neck, breathing in the pine and charcoal embedded in his skin.

"This is only the beginning, Harper," he murmurs, his mouth tracing the shell of my ear.

I separate us enough so I can look him in the eye. "Do you have any pressing engagements coming up this week?"

He raises his eyebrows. "I don't think so."

"I'm pretty sure Linda would be happy to extend the lease on my room for a few more days." I loop my arms loosely around his neck. "Wanna stay here for another week?"

He grins, and his eyes light up like the red carpet on Oscar night. "Hell yes, I want to stay."

And so we do.

Screen Scandals

Be still our very hearts, dear friends, because we are beyond excited to confirm our earlier suspicions: Grayson West and Emmy Harper are *officially* a couple. Okay, not officially in the way where they've confirmed it to the press or anything, but based on the photo evidence we've been collecting from their time on set shooting *No Reservations* (see that oh-so-romantic gazebo kiss) and the several sightings of the two of them together out and about in Los Angeles now that filming has wrapped, we feel pretty confident that we can declare #Emson the new Hollywood It Couple. Although it might not seem like these two have a lot in common—she's known for her witty and brilliant writing and has been dubbed the next Nora Ephron, while he's . . . got really nice abs . . . not to mention neither has a particularly stellar dating record—you can tell by the way they look at each other that these two have a love that will last (hopefully at least until the premiere of *No Reservations*, which, sadly, won't be until early next year). We'll keep an eye on these two hotties. Let us know if you spot them out in the wild!

CHAPTER

NINETEEN

LIZ SENDS ME A LINK TO THE LATEST REPORTING ON "Hollywood's Newest It Couple," along with a string of laughing-face emojis. I respond with a GIF of a kick line of middle fingers.

ME: You're welcome for all the free publicity.

LIZ: You say that like it doesn't also benefit you.

ME: Yeah, well, I'm the one whose personal life is now being stalked by low-budget paparazzi.

LIZ: What did you think would happen when you started dating Grayson West?

ME: People would respect our privacy and let us live our lives in peace?

LIZ: ...

ME: Yeah, yeah.

LIZ: How are things going now that you're back at home and not wrapped in a showmance fantasy bubble?

ME: Honestly?

LIZ: Yes?

ME: ...

ME: It's been pretty fucking perfect.

WE FALL INTO OUR ROUTINE EASILY, LIKE WE'RE BACK on set and all the moves have been planned out for us. Except instead of a script, it's just us. We fit together, and it's scary how seamless and easy it is. None of my past relationships could ever be described that way, and yet Grayson, a man I once thought of as the bane of my actual existence, slips into my life like he should have been there from the beginning.

We split our time between my condo in Los Feliz and his house in the Hollywood Hills. When I mention it would be nice to have a drawer at his place, he clears out an entire dresser. When he tells me he'll meet me at mine after an audition, I hand him my spare set of keys without a second thought.

If I were reading our story in a romance novel or a romcom screenplay, I'd be waiting for the other shoe to drop. Surely our black moment is just around the corner. One of us will be hit with some unexpected tragedy that will pull us apart and leave us broken and miserable, only so we can find our way back to each other in the end and have our well-earned happily ever after.

But this isn't a movie, and it's not a love story. We're simply living our lives, and so for the first time in a long time, I don't look for the problems. I sink down into the ease and the comfort and the unshakeable knowing I have that this is it. He is it.

When we wake up together in my bed three months after filming has wrapped, the sunlight peeking around the edges of my white curtains, tinting his bare shoulders a shade of honey gold, I almost tell him. I almost let it slip that he's the one. It's not like I'm hesitating to say it out loud because I doubt the sentiment, or even because I think he might not feel the same—I'm pretty sure he does. But I know what hearing those words can do if you're not ready to hear them.

And so I hold them in, showing him instead. Letting my lips trace over all the beautiful parts of him. The hard ridges hiding his soft soul. Our kisses are sleepy and fuzzy-edged, and yet when he pushes into me, we could not be more present in the moment. Our eyes meet when we tumble at the same time, and I know I don't need to tell him he's my person. He already knows.

After we've showered and made coffee and breakfast, settling in across from each other at my tiny dining room table like the disgustingly domestic couple we've become, Grayson clears his throat in the way I now know means he has something important to tell me. For a half second, a dart of fear shoots through my lungs, but I catch his eye and his smile is sheepish and I know whatever it is isn't going to hurt me.

"I have a premiere coming up in two weeks." He chomps down on a bite of toast to buy himself some time, as if he just announced a major revelation, not something that's been on the calendar for weeks.

"Yeah, for *Hostile Hostages 4*, right?" We've only talked

briefly about the movie, but the poster has been popping up on my Instagram feed for a couple of weeks now, as if the algorithm somehow knows I'm never opposed to seeing my boyfriend in a tight tank top, all fake dirty and sweaty and basically looking hot AF.

He swallows his toast and takes a long swig of coffee. "That's the one." Fiddling with his napkin, he looks everywhere but at me. "So do you think you might want to come with me?"

I bite my lip to hold back a smile. "Grayson West, are you freaking out about asking me to come with you to your premiere?" And if so, is that not the cutest thing I've ever heard?

He shrugs and runs a hand through his still-damp hair. "You don't have to come if you don't want to, of course. The movie is probably not going to be great, and if we walk the red carpet, you know how that will be. Everyone's going to ask about us, and I understand if you don't want to make it a big thing. I get it if you don't want to go, but I also wanted to make sure you know that it might be cool if you did want to come."

I push out of my chair and walk the two steps to his, straddling his lap and taking his face in my hands. "Hey. First of all, I'm sure the movie will be great because you're great. Second of all, I think the cat is already out of the bag about us, given how many times I've been tagged in posts from heartbroken fans of yours. And third." I brush a kiss over his lips. "Of course I want to be there for you. If you want me there, I'm there."

"I want you there." His hands loop around my back, and he brings me in for another lip-lock. "I also don't want to put you in that position if you're not ready to willingly and intentionally put us out there for the whole world to see."

I do my very best to hide the hesitation that comes along with his warning. He's not wrong. The second the two of us step out on a red carpet together, it's going to be a paparazzi feeding frenzy. But I push that out of my mind and focus on him. "Do you want the world to see us?"

He shrugs, his thumbs finding the bare skin above the waistband of my pajama shorts. "It's not that so much. I know Kevin is excited for us to make our public debut, but I'd just really like to have you by my side."

"That's all you had to say." I kiss him again, deeper this time, tightening my arms around his neck and licking at the coffee taste lingering on his tongue. The warmth of his embrace and the feel of his mouth on mine wipe away any lingering doubts about making our relationship public.

He breaks the kiss first, leaning back a tad so he can look me in the eye. "People are really tagging you on social media?"

I roll my eyes. "Good god, yes. Apparently I have crushed the dreams of approximately seventy-five percent of the population."

He groans, his forehead falling to rest on my shoulder. "I'm sorry you have to deal with that."

I kiss the top of his head. "I'm pretty sure you're worth it."

His lips skirt along my collarbone. "Only pretty sure? Anything I can do to change that to definitely sure?"

"Oh, I'm sure you'll think of something."

And with that, he hoists me up and carries me straight back to bed.

CHAPTER

TWENTY

SAM SWIPES A FINAL SWISH OF EYELINER OVER MY LIDS before stepping back to look over his creation. "Absolutely gorgeous, if I do say so myself."

I bat my very long and very false eyelashes at him. "Thank you so much for coming over to help me out, Sam. I could not have done any of this without you." I mean the makeup and hair, of course, but I've also used this time to catch up with Sam as a nice distraction from what's to come later this evening.

"I wouldn't trust your beautiful face in any hands other than my own."

"You're the best." I hop out of his folding chair and head directly to Grayson's closet, where my dress is hanging in a garment bag. "Can you stick around for one second and do up my zipper?" I call, carefully removing the dress from its wrapping.

"I'd much rather undo your zipper." Grayson's deep voice rumbles as his mouth finds my neck. He pulls me into him, lips skirting over my bare skin.

I squeal and push him away. "Do not mess up my hair, or Sam is going to kill you."

"And please do not have sex in that closet right now, or Sam will kill you!" Sam begins packing up his stuff, loudly, just in case we might forget he's still here.

Grayson spins me around, taking me in and groaning. "How am I supposed to not have closet sex when you're wearing that?"

My hands move to the buttons of one of his shirts, the only thing I currently have on. "I needed something that didn't have to slip over my head. I figured you wouldn't mind." I start pushing the buttons through their loops, one by one, taking my time because it's fun to torture him.

"I don't mind as long as you promise to put it back on the minute we get home tonight." He watches me shamelessly as I pop button after button.

Slipping the shirt off my shoulders, I reach for my dress, stepping into it carefully before Grayson has the chance to maul me. As far as red carpet dresses go, this one is pretty basic, but it fits like a glove and the deep emerald green brings out the hints of red in my hair. I spin around so Grayson can pull up the zipper.

His lips find the nape of my neck, naked because my hair has been swept up in a mass of unruly loose waves. His hands fall to my hips, turning me so I'm facing him, his eyes taking in every inch of me. "You look fucking gorgeous, Ems."

I don't know why the compliment makes me feel shy, but I can feel the heat rising in my cheeks. "Thanks." I straighten his already straight bowtie, indulging in my own head-to-toe perusal. "You look pretty fucking gorgeous yourself."

He dips his head, sucking gently on the junction of my neck and shoulder. "We don't really need to go to this premiere, do we?"

"You most definitely need to go to the premiere of your own movie, yes." I push him away, even though I wouldn't mind ripping off all these fancy clothes and spending the night curled up in bed.

"You're no fun." He pouts, sticking out his lower lip.

I lean in and kiss it. "That's not what you said last night."

"Okay, you two. I need to head out so please step out of there fully clothed and let me have a last look at you!"

I use Grayson to steady myself as I step into my shoes. He drops to one knee, buckling each shoe for me, and the sight of him kneeling before me takes my breath away.

"I could get used to you in this position." I mean for the words to come out as a joke, a clear sexual innuendo, but when he looks up at me, it's not flashes of where his hands and mouth and tongue could go from here that spring into my mind. It's a ring and a home and a future. And the picture-perfect image doesn't terrify me. Quite the opposite, actually.

"I'll keep that in mind," he says after one heartbeat too many. Long enough to let me know he had the same vision.

He rises and we exit the closet, hands locked together.

Sam gives us each a final once-over before handing me a tube of lip gloss. "Your liner and lipstick are kiss-proof and nude." He gives Grayson a pointed look. "But please, for the love of all that is holy, swipe on a coat of this before you get out of the limo."

I give him a mock salute. "Yes, sir."

He rolls his eyes but leans in to bestow an air kiss on each cheek. "Knock 'em dead out there. You both look fabulous, and even more importantly, you look fabulous together. This is going to be a first official appearance for the ages. People are going to eat you up!"

I blow him a kiss as he and his stuff make their way downstairs and out the front door. I turn back to Grayson. "You ready?"

He tugs a little on his tie. Any heat that was blazing in his eyes just minutes ago has been doused. "Yeah, let's go."

I wait until we're settled in the backseat of the limo before I reach over and take his hand. "Hey. What's going on? What happened?"

He doesn't meet my eyes, focusing his gaze on his feet, tapping an incessant rhythm on the limo's plush carpet. "Nothing. I'm good."

"Grayson. Seriously. We don't have to talk about it if you don't want to, but don't try to pull that 'nothing' crap with me." I nudge his ribs with my elbow. "I know you better than that now."

He drapes an arm over my shoulders, pulling me closer into him. "I just want to be sure you're ready for this."

I glance down at my designer gown and excruciatingly painful shoes. "I've been getting ready for the past four hours. Trust me, I'm ready."

"I don't mean physically, Emmy. I mean are you ready to step out on that carpet together and have people talk about you, and about us?"

"Hey." I take his cheek in my hand, forcing him to turn his head and look at me. "People are going to talk about us whether I walk this carpet with you or not. They've been talking about me my entire life. So let them talk. Who cares?" I repeat the advice my mother gave me with conviction because the one thing I've learned during the past couple of months of dating Grayson West is that people will talk no matter what, and in the long run, what they say means nothing.

"You might, when people start judging Hollywood's golden child for being with me." His brow furrows, and there's so much emotion in the deep pools of his eyes, I have to take a second to parse it all out.

"Anyone who thinks like that is an idiot and an asshole and doesn't matter to me anyway." I lean in and place a soft kiss on his lips. "I'm proud to be with you, Grayson. I feel so lucky to be with you, and I can't wait to step out on that stupid carpet and tell the whole world that you're mine."

His eyes soften, and he presses his lips to my hand. "I've never brought a date to a premiere before."

"Me neither. Well, except for my parents. They're usually my dates." The jolt of pain catches me unaware. It's not that I haven't been thinking about my dad—not a day goes by when I don't—it's just that lately the happiness in my life has overpowered the grief.

Grayson squeezes my hand. "You miss him."

"Every day."

His own sadness pulls down on the corners of his mouth.

"Have your parents ever come to one of these?" I ask quietly.

He shakes his head. "Nope. You're not just the first partner I've brought. You're the first person."

"It's an honor to keep being your first, Grayson West." I plant a kiss on his cheek and am happy to see the slight smile on his lips.

"I love you, Ems."

"I love you, too." I fist my hands in the lapels of his tux jacket. "Now kiss me good and proper before I have to put this junk all over my lips."

And he does, because of course he does. His lips are warm and searching and passionate, and I ache for him, so it's a good thing we pull up in front of the theater when we do. Otherwise, we'd be rolling up that partition window and going for it in the backseat.

We take a couple of seconds to right ourselves. I swipe on the lip gloss and smooth Grayson's hair. When we're all set, he knocks lightly on the window and the door magically opens from the outside. Screams and cheers immediately infiltrate the space, and we exchange a wary grin.

Grayson steps out of the limo in a graceful swoop, buttoning his jacket before reaching his hand back to help me out. I place my hand in his, climbing out much less gracefully but at least managing not to flash anyone in the process.

The reaction is so instantaneous, it almost knocks me back a step. The crowd went wild for Grayson, but they completely lose it when we join hands and take our first step onto the plush crimson carpet together.

"Holy shit," I mutter under my breath.

"Told you."

This is far from my first premiere—I couldn't even count how many I've been to for my parents' films, and then, eventually, my own—but this is the first time I've felt like the people crowded behind the metal partitions actually care about seeing me personally. Obviously, most are there just for Grayson, but I'm definitely hearing my own name shouted at me repeatedly as we begin the long short walk. It hits me again just how public this is. How public our relationship will be. How public our failure would be. I struggle to remember the words of advice I delivered to Grayson only moments ago.

The first stretch of the carpet is lined with fans, and I let Grayson take the lead, trailing behind him as he signs autographs and poses for selfies. Multiple people ask for a selfie with both of us, so I join in when requested, but I have no problem hanging back and letting him be the center of attention. This is his night, and honestly, the whole thing is a little overwhelming.

When we reach the step and repeat backdrop, Grayson poses for a few photos on his own, but it becomes clear quite quickly that the photographers are more interested in pictures of the two of us together. When he holds out his arm for me, I tuck myself into his side, remembering to keep one foot slightly in front of the other, hand on my hip.

"Do you hate me yet?" His lips barely move, but the words come out perfectly clear.

"Are you kidding me? Do you even know how good you look in that tux?" I keep a smile plastered on my face so big it starts to hurt after a couple of minutes.

His hand travels up to the nape of my neck. "I'm already counting down the minutes until we can go home."

I lean into his touch. "Does it make me a total and complete sap if I admit I love hearing you refer to it as our home, even if it's not actually our home?"

He tilts his head down, eyes meeting mine. "Well, what if it was?"

My fake smile falls, a real one taking its place. The crowds and the cameras and the screaming and the flashes fade away. "Are you asking me to move in with you?"

"I think I am. Or I can move in with you, whichever you prefer." A hint of a grin pulls on his lips.

"Did you always plan on springing that on me in the middle of our first red carpet walk?" I slip my hand underneath his tux jacket, pinching his hip in his one ticklish spot.

He jumps, chuckling. "No, but I'm seizing the moment." He tucks a stray curl behind my ear. "So what do you think?"

"I think yes."

"Yeah?"

"Fuck yeah." I grin up at him, and thanks to the height of my stupid shoes, he barely has to lean down to kiss me.

Which is of course the moment a thousand flashbulbs explode. Our lips don't even get the chance to touch before we're both pulling back with a sigh.

Grayson groans and tugs on my hand, pulling me away from the photo zone, farther down the red carpet. "Let's finish this bullshit and go find an empty closet somewhere."

"I know just the one, actually."

He shoots me a look. "Should I be worried that you know the best closet here for a hookup?"

I shrug and flip him a wink. "I've been to a lot of premieres at this venue, and sometimes I just need a minute of quiet time, you know?"

He squeezes my hand. "I know."

We come to a stop at the first reporter lining the carpet, and I paste my fake smile back on. I position myself slightly behind Grayson, but he tugs on my hand, making sure I'm standing right at his side.

The reporter asks him some standard questions about the movie and how he feels about his role and the franchise—all the usual queries he'll have to answer a hundred times. I tune them out for the most part, still reveling in the fact that he asked me to move in with him. I bite my lip to keep my giddy grin from spreading, mindful that it could look creepy to an errant camera. Every so often Grayson breaks eye contact with the reporter, meeting my gaze and flashing me a secret smile. He keeps a hold of my hand the entire time, his thumb rubbing my knuckles.

We move down the line, Grayson answering questions and me staring up at him all goofy and lovelorn. We're almost to the end of the line when one of the reporters snags my attention as Grayson is moving on to the next. I squeeze his hand and let him go ahead without me.

The reporter is a young white woman, probably in her early twenties, and she greets me with a mix of earnestness and professionalism. "Thank you so much for stopping, Ms. Harper. I have to say, I'm a big fan of your work."

I smile back. "Thank you so much. That's always nice to hear."

"Can we take tonight as officially official confirmation that you and Grayson West are officially a couple?"

"That's a lot of 'officials,' but yes, I suppose you can." I clutch my tiny purse so I have something to do with my hands. It's not like this is my first red carpet walk, or even my first interview, so I don't know why the nerves are fluttering, but something about tonight just feels different, more impactful somehow.

"Can I ask what it is about Mr. West that initially drew you to him?" She's bouncing a little on her toes, signaling she might be just as nervous as I am, which actually makes me feel a little better.

I shoot the man in question, just a few feet away from me, an appraising look. "Well, if I'm being honest, the initial attraction was mostly due to all of that." I gesture over to him, taking another second to admire just how delicious he looks in his tux. "But once I got to know him, he blew me away. Grayson is the total package. He's smart and witty and so kind and caring. An amazingly talented actor—I can't wait for everyone to see how well he tackles this new genre in *No Reservations*. It would be stupid to deny a physical attraction, because he's obviously a perfect specimen, but it was his heart and his mind that really made me fall for him."

Her eyebrows raise slightly. "So you two are serious then?"

He catches me watching him, moving a few steps in my direction as if attracted by a magnet. A smile automatically spreads across my face. "Yeah, it's serious." I reach out my arm, my hand landing on his shoulder, needing that contact with him.

He's in the middle of another conversation with a different reporter, but it doesn't stop him from sliding closer to me. His head turns, and he plants a kiss on the crease of my elbow. The move sends a shiver down my spine, and I can tell by the wicked glint in his eye that he felt my reaction. His arm snakes around my waist, pulling me toward him, anchoring me to his side, my arm still draped around his neck.

He begs off the final questions from the rest of the reporters, and we make our way inside the theater.

"Where is that closet you mentioned?" His fingers dig into my waist, his mouth tracing the length of my neck.

I nod my head toward a supply closet tucked away in the corner near the entrance.

But before we can make a break for it, an assistant ushers us to our seats. We're the last to sit down, and the lights fall a minute later.

"Next time," he mutters, his hand skirting up the silky material of my dress, landing on my thigh.

I intertwine my fingers with his. "Can't wait."

THE AFTER-PARTY IS HELD AT A PRODUCER'S HOUSE, a big square-and-glass modern monstrosity perched high in the hills. The view from the backyard is stunning, the full lights of Los Angeles laid out before us, but the house itself is a block of cold concrete.

As we step into the front hallway, Grayson leans down to murmur in my ear. "A half hour tops and then we're out of here and on our way home."

I check to be sure no one is directly in our sightline before I pull him into a deep kiss. "And what will we do when we get home?"

His hand skirts down the back of my dress. "First this dress comes off."

Wrapping my arms around his neck, I press my lips to his pulse point. "And then?"

"And then I make you come as many times as you want in our bed. Because it's ours now, yours and mine." His mouth captures mine, and he presses against me until my back hits a wall.

I pull myself from him at the contact. "How important is that half hour?"

"Let's make it fifteen minutes."

"Done." I push him away from me before taking his hand and guiding him into the throes of the party.

We're separated within seconds as the mobs of people surround him, congratulating and ass-kissing and fawning. I find myself a glass of champagne and step outside to enjoy the view, making note of the time and fully planning on holding him to the fifteen-minute rule, although something tells me it's going to be difficult to rescue him from the crowds in anything less than an hour.

Finding an empty cocktail table, I set down my glass and pull my phone from my clutch. A notification lights up my screen.

LIZ: Have you seen this gif? Holy shit, girl, you're a gif!

I swipe open my messages to find out what the hell she's talking about. And there we are. Someone captured the moment Grayson leaned down to kiss the crease of my elbow and the salacious look we exchanged after. If I wasn't already the subject, I'd be working out ways to include the moment in my next screenplay because we look hot—and in love.

LIZ: You guys are killing it in the free publicity game! 😬

ME: You're welcome.

ME: And you owe me a drink.

I tuck my phone back in my purse, noting that more than fifteen minutes have elapsed since I lost Grayson to the fray. Deciding I'll do a quick sweep of the backyard before I go to find him, I stroll over to the farthest corner, taking in the 180-degree views of the city.

I stop when I hear my name, coming from one of the dark pockets of the yard, one of the few places where there seem to be no guests or servers mingling. Creeping a few steps closer, I find a spot where I can eavesdrop without being seen, which maybe isn't the nicest thing I've ever done, but hey, they're talking about me so I don't feel too bad about it.

"This is what we wanted, G. You told me you wanted opportunities to audition for more serious roles, I told you that you needed to work with Harper, and now you've got an audition next week for one of the buzziest awards contenders out there."

"Yeah, I know. And I'm thankful, truly." The deep rumble of Grayson's voice is unmistakable.

My brows furrow as I subconsciously move closer to their conversation, something about Grayson's tone stirring some seriously icky feelings deep in my belly. It's clear he's talking with his manager, Kevin, but the words sound all wrong. Grayson hasn't mentioned any big auditions to me. Why would he keep something that exciting a secret?

"So what's the big deal? Keep dating Emmy for a few more weeks at least, just until you've landed the role, and then you can do whatever you want. Your relationship with her has had nothing but a positive impact on your reputation. People are looking at you differently, taking you more seriously."

"That's not the problem, Kevin." Grayson sounds weary and tired, like the conversation is annoying him.

"In one of her interviews tonight, she called you a 'talented actor.' Do you have any idea how many doors a comment like that from someone of her pedigree can open?"

I hold completely still, not totally sure what exactly I'm hearing, only knowing that I don't like it. The ick feeling has morphed into a full-blown tornado of bad energy.

"You seriously can't handle faking feelings for this girl for another month or two? Is she that bad?" Kevin spits out the words with such venom, I physically recoil.

Did he just say "faking feelings"? What does that even mean? The phrase turns over and over in my brain as I take another step closer to their conversation, needing to hear something, anything, to negate those two cursed words.

But the silence from Grayson is deafening.

Kevin sighs, audibly. "When I told you we needed to milk this situation with Harper—play up this whole relationship angle—you said you could take whatever she was going to throw at you, that you could hang with her for as long as we needed, until we saw some results. Don't tell me you're going to quit now when we're so close to everything working out."

"I've told you a million times, it's not that." Grayson's voice is low and resigned. "I haven't had a problem faking my feelings for Emmy . . ."

And that's when I bolt, pretty sure I'm going to actually throw up my stomach full of champagne bubbles.

Faking my feelings, faking my feelings, faking my feelings.

Not only did he not dispel the very idea that anything between us could ever be fake, he basically admitted it's true. His feelings for me are fake? What the actual fuck?

The overheard conversation runs through my mind on repeat as I push through the crowds of people and out the front door, phone already open, Lyft already called. I rush down the long driveway, past the valet stand, out to the sidewalk in front of the McMansion, as fast as my stupid shoes allow me.

Luckily, because we're in the middle of Hollywood, my ride is there in minutes. I climb into the backseat, slamming the door behind me.

"Everything okay?" my driver asks.

"Yes." I keep my tone polite but short, so she knows I don't feel like talking.

As soon as the car is moving, I text Liz.

ME: Can you meet me at my place?

LIZ: What, like now?

ME: Please. It's an emergency.

LIZ: Yeah, of course. On my way.

My head falls back against the seat, Grayson's words still looping through my mind just like that blasted GIF of the two of us.

Faking. Feelings. This whole thing has been fucking fake?

I'm an idiot.

I can't believe I fell for it. And so easily.

Grayson and his manager planned this from the beginning. Taking the role in *No Reservations*. Cozying up to me. Pretending to be attracted to me. Sleeping with me. Making me believe he actually liked me. Loved me.

And none of it was real.

I seriously underestimated Grayson's acting abilities, because he had me fooled from day one.

The Lyft driver drops me off in front of my condo, and I find Liz waiting at my front door, a bottle of wine in one hand and a tub of Ben & Jerry's in the other.

"You work quickly."

"I wasn't sure what kind of emergency this was." She holds up the wine hand first and then the ice cream hand.

"Both." I slip my key into the front door—making a mental note to have my locks changed because Grayson still has a key—and push inside. Kicking off my shoes, I turn my back to Liz. "Can you unzip me?"

She does, before heading into the kitchen and opening a cupboard.

I hear the sounds of her pouring wine and grabbing spoons as I head to my bedroom to shuck my dress and slip into pajamas. I make a pit stop in the bathroom to scrub my face clean of my makeup and take down my hair.

Plopping onto the sofa, I accept a glass of wine and a spoon. First a large gulp, then a big bite. Okay, two big bites. And then another gulp.

"You want to tell me what the hell is going on?" Liz asks after a minute.

"Grayson fucking West is what's going on."

She swigs her wine. "Ah, we're back to full-naming him. What happened?"

"Well, earlier tonight he asked me to move in with him." I ignore her eyebrows as they shoot up practically to her hairline. "And then later I overheard him talking with his manager about how our whole relationship is fake and he only started dating me because he thought it would improve his reputation and he would have the chance to audition for roles that don't require a six-pack and a penchant for blowing shit up."

Liz sets her wine down on the coffee table as if she can't possibly drink and sort out my life at the same time. "I'm sorry. What?"

"Yeah. Basically."

"That doesn't even make any sense, Emmy. How does dating you lead to more serious roles for Grayson?"

I shrug, finishing off my wine. "No idea, but apparently it worked because apparently he has a big audition next week for some movie that's apparently going to be a major awards contender."

"And apparently this guy has robbed you of your vocabulary."

"Apparently."

Liz leans over and refills my wine glass because of course she brought the bottle into the living room because she is both wise and kind. "I didn't even know Grayson was interested in exploring those kinds of projects."

I know exactly why Grayson is interested in exploring those kinds of projects, but I don't tell Liz that. He's an asshole, and I hate him, but he still deserves to have his family drama kept private. I shovel another bite of ice cream in my mouth before I blurt out something I shouldn't.

"I can't believe I'm saying this, but I thought he really loved you, Em. He seemed so real and so genuine; I have a hard time believing that was all fake." Liz takes the ice cream carton from me, digging out a bite of her own. "Are you absolutely sure that's what you heard?"

"Yup. I guess he's a much better actor than any of us gave him credit for." I pause for a minute, letting every one of our interactions from the past couple of months run through my mind. "Thinking back, I guess I did overhear a weird phone call once, and he wasn't ever concerned about the two of us being caught in the press. In fact, the first time we were mentioned in the blogs, he wanted to go out to dinner that same night." The evidence is weak, even in my addled state of mind, but coupled with what I overheard tonight, it paints a pretty compelling picture. I pull a blanket down from the back of the couch, even though I'm not cold. "He made me believe what we had was real. I actually thought I fell in love with him."

"What did he say about it? Did he have a good explanation for why he said that?"

I shove a huge bite of ice cream in my mouth so my answer is muffled. "I didn't talk to him."

"You didn't talk to him?"

I shake my head. "I left as soon as I heard enough."

Liz reaches for her wine, taking a large gulp before facing me. "Emmy. How can you claim to love this man and not even give him a chance to explain?"

"What possible explanation could there be? I know

what I heard." I pull the blanket up over my shoulders, burrowing down to try to hide from her penetrating gaze.

"I'm not saying what he said was okay, or that you shouldn't be upset." She hesitates for a second before continuing. "I just want to be sure you're not pushing him away because it's easier that way."

I'm quiet for a minute as I try to ignore the implications of her words. "Nothing about this feels easy, Lizzie."

Liz reaches over and squeezes my arm. "I'm so sorry." She studies me for another long second but seems to realize it's not the time to push the subject further. "Will it make you feel better if I tell all my friends never to cast him in anything ever again?"

"Yes." I flash her a smile so she knows I'm mostly kidding.

"Is it stupid of me to ask you if you're okay?"

I snuggle farther down into the blanket. "I think you're obligated to ask me that at least once a day for the next two weeks, according to the best friend code, section 213."

"Are you okay, Em?"

"I'm numb." I swig another long gulp of wine and hold up my glass for a refill. "And I plan to stay that way at least for the rest of tonight."

Liz pours the remainder of the bottle into my glass. "I fully support that plan."

"Are you going to make me talk about my feelings tomorrow?"

"I learned a long time ago that I can't make you do anything, my friend."

"Are you going to call my mom if I don't talk about my feelings tomorrow?"

"Most definitely."

I sigh and pull the blanket up over my head. "Rude."

"Where's your phone?"

"Why?" I don't come out of my hiding spot, so my voice is muffled by the thick cotton.

"Section 752 of the best friend code requires me to be sure no drunk texting happens tonight."

"My clutch is on the hall table. I already turned off my phone." I poke my head out of my blanket and point to the table, which is only a few feet away and clearly visible.

Grayson might be a lying dick, but I don't think he's not going to notice I ditched him and the party. I'm sure he'll be calling and trying to find me soon, if he hasn't already.

Liz gets up and walks the short distance to the entry-way, pulling my phone from my purse and tucking it into her pocket. She slides out her own phone and studies the screen for a second. "Grayson just texted me to see if I know where you are. What do you want me to say?"

I groan and bury my head in my hands. "Tell him I'm home safe, but I don't want to talk to him. And he shouldn't even think about coming over here, or I will punch him in the nuts."

"Going to leave off that last part, but yes to the rest of it." She taps at her phone before returning it to her pocket. "More wine?"

"Is that an actual question?"

A cork pops in the kitchen, and I burrow myself back into the comfort of the blanket.

CHAPTER

TWENTY-ONE

WAKING UP THE MORNING AFTER THE PREMIERE IS, well, not fun. The sunshine is bright, and the headache is fierce. Somewhere around the end of bottle of wine number two the tears started, and I don't remember them stopping. Which probably explains the dampness on my pillow and the snot crusted around my nose.

Super cute.

Liz is snoring next to me in bed when I throw off the covers and haul my ass up. I head straight for the kitchen, guzzling down two full glasses of water before even attempting to do anything else. A hot shower is up next. The steam helps my headache, but the time alone under the pulsing water doesn't do much for my aching chest.

Grayson's words keep echoing through my mind, and today, the numbness has abated and I feel every inch of the pain.

I trusted him.

I loved him.

And he was faking it the whole fucking time.

Liz is sitting at my dining room table when I finally

emerge from my makeshift steam room. She hands me a cup of coffee and a plate of toast like the best best friend she is.

I sink into a chair and gratefully sip from my mug.

"How are you feeling?" She pulls her knees up to her chest and studies me far too insightfully.

"Physically or mentally?"

"Both?"

"Shitty and shittier." I nibble on a bite of toast, making sure it isn't going to upset my fragile stomach.

She slides my phone across the table. "Now that you're sober, you can have this back."

I don't touch it, like it's a slug or a snake or something equally slimy and gross. "I don't know if I want it back."

She sips from her coffee, watching me over the rim of her mug. "Are you going to talk to him?"

Rubbing my temples, I avoid her gaze. "I don't want to."

"You should give him a chance to explain."

"I know what I heard, Liz."

"I know." She drops her feet to the ground and leans on the table. "But I also don't think I'm wrong about his feelings for you. Which were very, very real, despite whatever else happened. Maybe he went into your relationship with ulterior motives, but that doesn't necessarily mean that his feelings for you were fake."

I shrug and chomp down on another bite of toast. "I don't want to talk about it."

"Okay." She stands and heads into the kitchen, coming back with the pot of coffee. "Do you want to go do something today? I cleared my schedule."

I hold up my mug for a refill. "That was very nice—and

out of character—of you, but I think I just want to be alone."

"Are you sure?"

I nod. I know Liz means well, but I need some time to sit and process everything that happened the night before. I need to figure out how we went from making plans to shack up to breaking up in the course of a few hours. And I need to let myself wallow a bit. And probably eat some more ice cream.

Liz swigs the last of her coffee and gathers up her stuff. "I will be checking in on you throughout the day, so you're going to have to turn on your phone. And if you don't respond to my texts, I'm coming back." She smooths down my hair in a gesture that feels like my mom, and that's definitely a compliment. "If I come over here and see you've gone all Bella Swan sitting in that chair and staring out the window for months on end, I will call in reinforcements."

"Aye, aye, captain." I accept her hug, squeezing her tightly. "Thank you for coming over."

"Literally anytime." She blows me a kiss and heads out the door.

I push myself out of my chair and lock the door behind her. Not that that will keep him out.

I trudge back to the table, my cell phone staring up at me, glaring like I just stole the last parking spot at the mall on Black Friday. Picking it up gingerly, I hold it away from my body and make my way to the couch, burrowing back under my safety blanket before I power it on.

It takes a minute, but after I punch in my passcode, the text chimes start and don't stop.

GRAYSON: Hey, where'd you go?

GRAYSON: It's been way more than 15 minutes, let's go home.

GRAYSON: Okay, I looked everywhere in this house, where did you disappear to?

GRAYSON: Ems, you're starting to freak me out. Where are you?

GRAYSON: The valet guys said they think you left? Did you leave? Why did you leave?

GRAYSON: Ems, seriously, please just text me and let me know if you're okay.

There's a break in the messages, probably when he texted Liz and she told him I was home and safe. My heart feels like it's being punctured by a thousand tiny needles, but I keep reading his messages. They start up again early this morning.

GRAYSON: Emmy, please. I don't know what happened, but I just want to talk to you. Please call me.

GRAYSON: Whatever it is, I can fix it or explain or apologize. I just need you to talk to me.

GRAYSON: I love you, Ems.

GRAYSON: Please call me. Anytime. I'm here and I want to talk and figure this out, whatever it is.

My eyes squeeze shut, but that doesn't stop the tears from falling down my cheeks. I know they're just text messages, but he sounds so hurt. How is he still able to fake it so easily? Why is he even bothering?

You've got an audition next week for an awards-season contender . . .

Of course. The last thing he needs before going in for some serious audition is a tabloid breakup story. Not that I would ever plan to run to the tabloids. But word will get out sooner or later.

ME: I'll have Liz come by next week with anything you left at my place. Please pack up anything I left at yours and give it to her then.

GRAYSON: Jesus, Emmy. I've been worried sick over here and that's all you have to say? Pack up my stuff?

ME: I don't have anything else to say to you.

GRAYSON: You won't even tell me what I did wrong?

ME: You know exactly what you did wrong, Grayson.

ME: Don't contact me again.

GRAYSON: Emmy, we need to talk about this in person.

ME: No. And if you can't respect my wishes, I'll block your number.

GRAYSON: Why are you pushing me away right as we were about to take things to the next level?

ME: I'm not pushing you away.

GRAYSON: You are. You got scared, didn't you?

I scoff out loud, the sound echoing around my empty condo. This man, this lying liar who lies, thinks he can psychoanalyze me?

ME: I'm not scared. I just finally figured out who you really are.

GRAYSON: . . .

GRAYSON: So this is it? You're just writing me off for some reason you won't even share? Writing off this relationship we've built and my feelings for you? Seriously?

GRAYSON: One minute you love me and the next you're just done?

ME: Yup. Goodbye.

GRAYSON: I don't even know what to say.

GRAYSON: I'm here. If you change your mind. I love you.

I click off my phone before I'm tempted to tell him I love him, too. Because I still do, of course, even if his declaration is a lie.

Keeping the blanket wrapped around me, I shuffle into my bedroom, climb under the covers, and go back to sleep.

Screen Scandals

We have some devastating news to deliver to you today, friends, and although we hate to be the bearer of it, we must report the facts. It seems our favorite (and hottest) couple #Emson is already headed for Splitsville. Paparazzi captured photos of director and Emmy's best friend Liz Hudson delivering a cardboard box to Grayson West's house and leaving with a different, much bigger box. It seems Emmy recruited her BFF to do the final exchanging of the stuff. Neither West nor Harper has been seen out about town, individually or together, since they made a splash on the red carpet at the premiere of West's box office smash *Hostile Hostages 4* (aka the site of the GIF heard 'round the world). Although our initial impression was that the couple was a bit of a mismatch, no one could deny their obvious chemistry. We are super sad to learn of this split, but we gotta admit, we're now really looking forward to the *No Reservations* press tour, which is scheduled to take place in just a few weeks. Those should be some interesting interviews!

CHAPTER

TWENTY-TWO

THE KNOCK ON MY FRONT DOOR IS CHEERFUL AND unexpected and, therefore, I know before I reach said door that my mother stands on the other side. I still check, because I'm a woman who lives alone in a major city, but of course, all the peephole shows is my mom, dancing a little on my welcome mat to some unheard tune inside her head.

Luckily, she brought coffee.

I open the door with an exaggerated sigh. "We have these lovely things called cell phones nowadays, and they allow you to let a person know when you are going to be unexpectedly popping by for a visit."

She hands me a steaming cup from my favorite coffee shop and pushes past me. "Then it wouldn't be unexpected."

"Yes. That would be the point." I follow her into the living room, collapsing onto the opposite end of the sofa from where she already has made herself comfortable. "So, to what do I owe the pleasure?"

"Do I need a reason to come check on my only child?"

"It's been three weeks, Mom. I don't need the daily check-ins anymore." Fortunately, most of her daily check-ins have been by phone. Although she has been "in the neighborhood" a lot more these days.

"I know, and you've handled things remarkably well, all things considered. But in case you haven't checked your calendar . . ."

I take a long drink of coffee. "Yes, yes I know. And I really regret the day I introduced you to Liz. You two are a frightening pair when you're conspiring against me."

"She is a dear, isn't she?" She reaches over and pats my leg. "So are you ready?"

"Am I ready to sit in a hotel room with the man who broke my heart and answer questions about the romantic movie we filmed together and also probably be badgered to answer questions about our own relationship?"

"Should I take that as a no?" Her eyebrows raise, and she gives me a cheeky smile.

"You're incorrigible."

"Where do you think you got it from?"

I set my coffee down on the table so I can use both hands to massage my now-throbbing temples. "I don't really want to think about it, Mom."

"So you'd rather go in blind? Not mentally prepared for what it's going to be like to see him again?"

I don't need to mentally prepare, because I've thought about it every damn day since that stupid party. Some days the thought fills me with rage; some days, bitter sadness. And some days, the days I like to pretend are flukes, I miss him so badly that the thought of being trapped in a press room with him is the only thing I have to look forward to. But those days don't happen very often. Only three or four times a week or so.

Because as mad as I am, I do miss him. There's a hole in my chest and in my life, and it's most definitely Grayson West shaped. I miss his jokes and his teasing and the way he ran his fingers through my hair. I miss talking to him about my day and hearing his stories. I hate the fact that I wasn't there when he found out he's in the final round for that blasted awards-bait movie. I hate that he wasn't there when my new screenplay got the green light.

And a large part of me still hates him for making me love him.

My mom reaches over and squeezes my hand. "You miss him, don't you?"

For a second I think she's talking about my dad, because for so long he was the only man I ever had a chance to miss. "How do you get over the loss of someone, Mom? I mean, it's different with Dad, of course, but how did you get over missing him?"

She shrugs, her fingers tightening around mine. "I didn't. I miss him every hour of every day. I don't think that ache will ever really go away. It will be there with me until the end." She brushes a stray lock of hair out of my eyes. "But I loved your father for thirty years of my life, and he loved me, and it wouldn't honor that love if I let missing him keep me from living."

"I thought I might have found that kind of love with Grayson." The words come out hoarse. It's been a few days since I cried, and I don't want to let the tears fall, but they do. "I thought it was real and genuine and the kind of love

I write about, you know? The kind most people don't think exists. But I know it does, because I've seen it."

"Oh, honey." Her eyes well up with tears, too. "If you care for him that deeply, why won't you give him a chance to explain?"

I reach for a tissue, handing one to her before taking one for myself and blowing my nose. "How could he explain what he said? If he really loved me, there wouldn't be anything to explain away. That's not how true love works. You don't hurt the people you love."

She scoffs. "Emilia Harper, you have said a lot of ridiculous things in your lifetime, but that might top the list. Of course we hurt the people we love. We don't want to, and it should never be intentional, but it happens all the time."

"Did Dad ever hurt you?"

"We didn't talk for six months after our first film together came out."

"Wait, what?" That's news to me. My parents always painted the early days of their relationship as an idyllic showmance. "Why didn't you ever tell me that?"

"Because in the long run it didn't matter." She shrugs and calmly sips from her coffee like she hasn't just dropped a total bomb on me.

"What happened?" I ask quietly.

She studies me over the rim of her cup for a minute before sighing dramatically. "Our first movie together was *Running Springs*."

I roll my eyes. "Yes, I know that part. You were both nominated for Oscars. You won, and Dad didn't."

She preens for a second and then seems to remember the purpose of this conversation. "Yes, well, when the movie was first released, my reviews were shining, of course, but your dad didn't get as much of the praise. He said some petty things, I said some petty things right back, and we didn't speak for months."

"That doesn't sound like something Dad would do. He never seemed to be threatened by your success."

"He wasn't. He didn't mean any of what he said. We just sometimes get caught up in an emotional moment and make bad decisions. It doesn't mean we have to write someone off completely."

"So you gave him a second chance? After he acted like that?" I'm happy she did, of course, because I wouldn't be here otherwise, but I'm surprised she would, given her skill for grudge-holding.

"He was worth it," she says simply. "We both made some mistakes and handled things poorly; we learned from it and didn't let it happen again."

"Weren't you scared? That things would go wrong a second time?"

"I'm sure I was a little afraid of getting hurt again, but I loved him enough that it was worth it to try." Her head tilts to the side as she watches me, and I know she's piecing things together in a way that maybe only my therapist has before. "Did we ever give you the impression that it's not okay to make mistakes, Em?"

I turn away from her gaze, not sure I really want to be having this conversation right now. "No, you and Dad never made me feel like I had to be perfect."

"But?"

I pinch the bridge of my nose and avert my eyes from hers. "But growing up the way I did, with everyone always watching every move I made, a lot of times it felt like I didn't have the space to mess up. Like if I did, I wouldn't just be letting down you and Dad, but letting down the whole world."

She sighs. "The downside of being a nepo baby, I suppose." She nudges my shoulder with hers. "I'm sorry you felt that pressure, Emmy. Those were circumstances beyond your control, and I wish I would've been able to protect you from feeling that way."

"It wasn't your fault. It was out of your control, too." I lean into her shoulder. "And I should probably be finding ways to get over it."

"Well, we can work on that. You can't let fear hold you back, sweetie."

We sit in the silence for a minute, digesting and processing. Finally, I ask, "What was the biggest mistake you and Dad made? Back at the beginning?"

"Mostly it was not communicating." She gives me a pointed look.

I catch a stray tear with my finger, not even sure where it came from. I thought I was all cried out. "Is the moral of the story here that you think I should give Grayson another chance?"

"The moral of the story is that you should communicate with him. If for no other reason than you have to work together again for the next few weeks and it's going to be hella awkward if you don't."

"Nobody says hella anymore, Mom."

"I do what I want." She grins and pulls me in for a hug.

"What if I fuck it all up?" I murmur the words into the cotton of her shirt, half hoping she doesn't hear them.

"If you and Grayson are meant to be together, then you'll be together. And if you aren't, you won't."

"It's that simple?" I sit up, brushing back my hair, wanting nothing more than for it to truly be that simple.

"Love is only complicated when we make it complicated."

"That's very wise."

"It was in my fortune cookie last week."

"You're the worst."

She takes both of my hands in hers, and as her expression shifts into something serious, I sit up straighter. "Whatever happens between you and Grayson, don't let your fear of loss keep you from loving. I get it, Emmy. No one does more than I do. But don't cut ties because you think it's easier than forming an attachment."

"It definitely doesn't feel easier." The words come out in a whisper as I remember Liz telling me almost the exact same thing.

"If it hurts more to be without him, sweetie, you might want to think about giving him a chance."

The advice makes a lot of sense. Too much sense. I chug the rest of my coffee and stand, pulling her up with me. "It has been lovely chatting with you, as always, but I do have a pressing engagement to attend to."

"Does that pressing engagement involve watching hours of Bravo on repeat?"

"Maybe."

She sighs and heads toward the front door. "Call him, Emmy."

"Yeah, yeah."

She pauses in the doorway. "I love you."

"I love you, too."

"Don't be an idiot." The door closes behind her before I have a chance to respond.

"Rude."

I collapse back on the sofa, picking up my phone, going so far as to punch in my passcode and find Grayson's name in my contacts. But I don't press call. I'm not ready to hear his voice yet. I need to be well and fully over him before I can even think about talking to him. And because our press tour starts in three days, I guess I better get started on that whole getting-over-him situation.

Or I could binge the latest season of *Project Runway*.

Tough choice, but Christian Siriano always wins.

JUST LIKE A TYPICAL DAY ON SET, MY CALL TIME FOR the press junket is three hours before the damn thing is scheduled to actually start. Luckily, I was able to play my I'm-the-star card and insist on Sam and Amanda for my hair and makeup team. Neither of them knows the full story about the breakup—not many people do—but they both know enough that they are sensitive to the fact that today is going to suck. They fill the room with aimless chatter and gossip, and I'm able to spend at least the first portion of the morning nice and distracted.

After I'm all dolled up, a stylist hands me a comfortable yet cute outfit: jeans and a soft lavender sweater along with some dainty earrings and a gold necklace. A publicist pops by to usher me to the green room, briefing me along the way.

She stops just outside the door, checking around the hallway of the hotel to be sure we're alone before she leans in. "Everyone has been briefed to stay away from personal relationship questions, but of course, it's not unheard of for reporters to go rogue. Just remember to smile, and if you don't feel like answering a question, tell them you prefer to keep your private life private."

I nod, wiping my suddenly sweaty hands on the dark denim of my jeans. "Is he here yet?"

She gives me a sympathetic smile. "I haven't seen him, but he'll be stopping by here as well before we get you guys settled in the interview room."

"Thanks." I try to return her smile, but my lips feel numb and tight.

She opens the door to the green room for me, ushering me inside before closing it behind me.

It's a small meeting room with a long table in the middle covered with food and snacks. Coffee is set up on a sideboard underneath a window, and although I want something to do with my hands, I think even a dash of caffeine would send my already jittery nerves into overdrive. I pick up a bottle of water instead, popping the cap and taking a swig, hoping it will calm me down.

It doesn't. The only thing I can think to do is pace, so I start a lap around the table and am at the far end when the door opens.

I stop in my tracks, pivoting toward the door in absurdly slow motion.

It clicks shut behind him, and the tiny sound shakes me like it's a gunshot.

For a second there's only silence.

It's only been a few weeks, but I drink him in as if I've spent those weeks traversing the desert and he's a tall glass of water. He's still tall, still broad, still bearded, and still gorgeous. But his eyes, when I finally allow myself to meet them, are dull and faded, nothing like the bright lightning I fell in love with.

"Hi," I finally say, my hands twisting around my water bottle.

"Hey." He shoves his hands in his pockets, which does nothing to hide his clenched fists.

The silence returns, blanketing the room in a painful awkwardness.

"You look good." It's not a lie, exactly, because he's Grayson West and he always looks good, but it's definitely not the whole truth. He looks like he would rather be anywhere else than in this room with me. Which is fair, I guess.

"Thanks." He doesn't return the compliment. Also fair.

I suck in a deep breath because this might be the only minute of the day we're alone. If we're going to talk, this is the time to do it, and I want to clear the air at least so we can be professional. Really, I do. Even if the mere sight of him has stopped all brain function and I'm no longer able to produce words.

"Grayson, I . . ."

"Okay, guys, time to get set up." The door swings open, and the publicist gestures for us to follow her. "We've got a tight schedule, and we need to stay on it."

She takes us to a room down the hall where two director's chairs have been set up in front of the *No Reservations* poster. Fortunately, the team was able to grab enough still frames from the footage that we didn't have to pose for any photos. Looking at the images of us clearly happy and in love is a knife to the heart.

I hop into my chair after a cursory glance. Another chair sits opposite us, waiting to be filled by a carousel of reporters from every major entertainment outlet in the country, along with ample space for each of them to set up their video cameras.

The publicist is rattling off some probably highly important instructions, but I'm so tuned in to Grayson as he sinks into his own chair that I don't even hear her. There are a few inches between our armrests, but when both of our arms are actually settled, I can feel the heat of him. I pull my arm into my lap, clasping my hands together instead. He shifts in his seat, moving as far away from me as he can.

After opening the door for the first reporter, the publicist scoots into the hall to let the torture commence. I plaster a fake smile on my face as the questions begin.

"So, Grayson, what was it like shooting your first rom-com?"

He clears his throat. "It was great. Different, of course. But great."

The reporter nods and waits an awkward beat for him to expand. When he doesn't, she turns her attention to me. "Emmy, what was it like for you being in front of the camera for the first time in more than a decade?"

"It was—uh—it was really—really fun. A great experience."

"Great." The poor reporter looks between the two of us like she must be missing something. "How was it working together?"

"It was great," we both say at the same time.

When her time is up, she steps out of the room with a

sigh of relief and reporter number two comes in, only to repeat basically the exact same questions. We deliver the exact same stilted answers with the exact same fake smiles, and the cycle rolls on and on and on.

I don't even know how long we've been sitting in these chairs, but my body aches and my stomach is rumbling and I'm tired and cranky and sitting this close to Grayson is making me tense and, admittedly, horny.

"Last one for the day, guys," the publicist finally announces, holding the door open and ushering in our final torturer.

He gives us both a wide smile and his name, which I promptly forget. His first few questions are variations of what we've been asked all day, but after our standard answers, he turns his attention solely toward Grayson. "So congratulations are in order with the news of your potential casting in *Beautiful Water*."

Grayson tenses a little, enough that I can feel it. "Thank you. I'm honored to be in consideration to be part of such an amazing project."

"I think there were a lot of people who were surprised when you were announced as one of the final contenders, given the character is a recovering addict. Lots of facing the demons from one's past. The role will be quite emotional, I'm certain." The reporter smiles, as if that might distract from the bitchiness of his not-question.

I clasp my hands together tightly because I'm tempted to reach a hand out to Grayson's.

"I'm sure it will be," he responds without a hit of malice. "But I'm up for the challenge."

"Rumor has it you're also being considered for the next

Marvel movie. That seems like a project that would be more in your wheelhouse. Don't you think that would be a better fit?"

I roll my eyes, but no one seems to notice.

"I'm also honored to be mentioned in talks with Marvel, but I wouldn't have auditioned for the role in *Beautiful Water* if I didn't think I was well suited for it." Grayson's fingers tighten around the armrest.

"Well, sometimes we aren't really the best judge of ourselves. This will be quite a step up from *Hostile Hostages*, or even *No Reservations*."

I'm not sure who put this guy on the press list, but they'll be receiving an angry phone call from me later. Who the hell does he think he is? I peek at Grayson out of the corner of my eye, waiting for him to put this guy in his place. Instead, I watch him shrink before my eyes, curling in on himself like this reporter is making valid points instead of making a complete ass of himself.

This jackass poises his pen on top of his notepad like he's about to jot down an answer to his bullshit questions. "What makes you think you could play the part? Are you qualified for a role that requires such profound depth and emotion?"

"Are you kidding me with this shit?" The words burst out of me before I have the chance to stop and think about them. "First of all, you have no right to speak to anyone that way. Are you suddenly more qualified than the team of professional casting directors who decided to put Grayson up for this role? No. And second of all, if you have ever watched a Grayson West movie, you know how talented he is. It's so easy to deride and shame, but the truth of the matter is that action movies and rom-coms are hard fucking work. It takes real skill to portray these characters genuinely, and Grayson does it better than literally anyone else out there. Not only that, but he is extremely well-rounded as a performer, not to mention a supremely empathetic and kind person, which I'm sure is more than anyone has ever said about you."

I realize I'm halfway out of my seat only when Grayson's hand lands on my forearm, steadying me, guiding me back into my chair. I shoot him a grateful look, but his eyes are on his lap. I glare at the reporter. "Any further questions?"

"Uh, no, that's all." He hops out of his chair, grabs his camera, and scurries out of the room.

Air flows into my lungs the second he leaves, and I just barely keep myself from choking on it. "I'm sorry." I mutter the words as I practically fall out of my chair, rushing for the door.

"Emmy. Wait, please."

My hand freezes on the doorknob. The heat of him warms my back, and I know he's suddenly behind me. All I would have to do is take a step and his arms would be around me.

I take the step, but his arms stay by his side.

"Thank you."

Turning around slowly, I find myself mere inches away from him. He's there in my bubble, his pine-and-charcoal scent filling my nose, his warmth wrapping me up like a fuzzy blanket. My eyes travel slowly from his chest up to his face. He finally makes eye contact with me, and the force of it knocks my breath right out of my chest.

"I shouldn't have gone off on him like that. I'm sorry." I clench my fists to keep from reaching out for him.

"Don't be sorry. I appreciate you defending me." He runs a hand through his hair. It's longer now, like he hasn't had it cut since we've been apart. "I was just surprised to hear you say nice things about me."

Okay. I deserved that.

"I still care about you, Grayson. Those feelings didn't just magically disappear." I rock forward on my toes ever so slightly, needing to be closer to him.

"Normally when I care about someone, I don't completely cut them off without any kind of explanation." He takes a small step back, putting distance between us but making it easier for me to meet his gaze.

I take another deep breath, realizing that we *do* need to have this conversation. It should have happened days ago, but I was too chickenshit. It needs to happen now.

I release the breath I totally knew I was holding. "I heard you and Kevin, that night at the party."

His brow furrows. "Okay?"

I blink slowly, unsure of how that isn't enough of an explanation. "I overheard you and Kevin talking about how you were pretending to have feelings for me so you could get more opportunities for serious roles."

The confused look remains in his eyes for a second until it finally seems to click. His forehead smooths and his lips purse.

I wait for the guilt and the shame, but that's not what I find in the depths of those stupid blue eyes.

"You're telling me you heard me and Kevin talking?"

I nod.

"And you listened to the entire conversation?" His arms cross over his chest, his muscles bulging, not that I should be paying attention to his forearms at a time like this.

I swallow thickly. "I left when you said you'd had no problem faking feelings for me."

He nods, and it's knowing and a bit condescending and it feels like we're back at day one on set. "So you missed the rest of that sentence. The part where I said I had no problem faking any feelings for you because they were a hundred percent real and I was madly in love with you."

I try to work my throat again, but a huge lump seems to have lodged itself in tight.

"Did you miss that part?" Sarcasm drenches his words, doing a poor job of covering the hurt and anger underneath.

I don't respond because I don't know what to say. How could I have gotten it all so wrong?

Grayson steps toward me, but there's no warmth radiating from him now. "So you eavesdropped on my conversation, took my words out of context, and bolted before giving me a chance to explain. Then, you completely cut me off without the courtesy of even one fucking conversation? Did I get that all right?"

"Yes." I bury my face in my hands. "Fuck, Grayson. I didn't know."

"You didn't know because you didn't let me tell you. And you didn't let me tell you because you automatically assumed the worst of me." He retreats a few steps, opening the chasm between us. "Jesus, Emmy. How could you think that about me? How could you think I would do that to you?"

I pull myself up to my full height. "Well, Kevin didn't just get that idea from nowhere. That conversation had to be grounded in something. So was that your original plan? Pretend you like me so that any relationship between us could improve your image?"

His hand floats up like he wants to reach for me, but he clenches his fist and drops it at his side. "Kevin might have been hoping for something like that. Who the hell knows, and why does it even matter? I fell in love with you for the first time when I was seventeen years old, Ems. I was never faking anything."

"But you were happy to go along with it?"

He throws his arms out to the side. "Yeah, sure. I let my prick of a manager think I was playing along so he'd drop it! To me, I knew none of it mattered."

"You could have told me."

"I swear I was going to, when the time was right."

I've kept my emotions pretty in check, but the look of utter defeat in his eyes brings the water springing to mine. I purse my lips to hold back the sob. "I'm sorry. I should have given you a chance. I fucked up, Grayson. And I'm sorry." My voice breaks on the last word, and the tears spill over.

He sighs, but it takes him less than a second to sweep me up in his arms, tucking my head under his chin, letting my tears stain his shirt. My arms snake around his waist, and it feels so good to hold him again, his strength steadying me.

Sniffling, I pull away just enough to be able to look up at him. "Do you think you can give me a second chance?"

His thumbs swipe underneath my eyes, wiping away the last of my tears. He doesn't say anything but steps out of my embrace. "When you defended me to that reporter, Ems, I've never had someone stand up for me like that before. But the truth of the matter is, you didn't have faith in me. You didn't believe in me when it really counted."

I nod, wiping at my nose. "It won't happen again. I promise. I know who you are, Grayson."

"I don't think that's enough," he says quietly, the pain lacing through his words.

Words that punch me directly in the chest, knocking the wind out of me and kick-starting a fresh wave of tears.

He crosses toward me, and for a blissful five seconds, I think he's going to forgive me and sweep me off my feet.

Instead, he places a single kiss on the top of my head. "I'm sorry, Emmy."

"Yeah, me, too." But the words only reach an empty room. Grayson has already left, the door clicking shut behind him.

LIZ: Feeling any better today?

ME: I can't turn on my TV without seeing myself screaming at a reporter, defending the man I'm one hundred percent in love with, the same one who (rightfully) can't forgive me for being a heinous asshole.

LIZ: Should I bring over some wine?

ME: I don't know. I'm very comfortable sitting in this chair, staring aimlessly out the window while a camera circles me and Muse plays in the background.

LIZ: If you're making Twilight jokes then you must be feeling somewhat better.

ME: *shrug*

ME: I don't deserve to feel better.

LIZ: Knock that shit off, right now.

LIZ: You made a mistake, something people do literally every single day. Grayson has the right to respond to that mistake however he chooses, but you do not deserve to feel like shit for the rest of your life because of it.

ME: If I promise to stop beating up on myself, can I skip the premiere?

LIZ: No.

LIZ: But you should still stop beating up on yourself.

LIZ: You're a good person and I love you.

ME: Thank you, friend. Love you, too.

MOM: Is it weird that I keep watching your video on repeat?

ME: Oh my god, Mom, seriously?

ME: Yes, that's fucking weird.

ME: Why are you watching one of the worst moments of my life on repeat?

MOM: It's not this part that was bad. It was the conversation between you two that came after.

MOM: The video is fabulous. You defended your man's honor, and it's so sweet.

ME: He's not my man.

MOM: We'll see about that.

ME: Whatever it is you're planning, stop it immediately.

ME: Seriously.

ME: Stop it.

MOM: I'm not planning anything. Really, who has the time for that?

MOM: I just think the two of you will find your way back to each other. You're meant to be.

ME: I need a drink.

MOM: It's 10 a.m.

ME: Your point?

MOM: Eat something first at least.

MOM: And stay hydrated!

THE LIMO RIDE ON THE WAY TO THE PREMIERE IS SI-
lent. Liz sits on one side of me and my mom on the other,
like they're afraid I might jump out of this moving vehicle
just so I can avoid the events of the next few hours. Which
I definitely might do if given the chance.

When we pull up to the curb at the mouth of the red
carpet, Liz steps out first. I give her a minute to take a
quick sweep of the carpet and make sure Grayson's not
there. I only agreed to show up on the conditions that our
entrances were to be at separate times and there was to
be zero interaction between the two of us. Exactly what
everyone wants to see at the premiere of a romantic
comedy: two stars who can't be within ten feet of each
other.

It's only been a couple of weeks since the press junket,
and just a couple of days since the video of me defending
Grayson has started to fade into obscurity, and I'm just
not ready to see him.

Not talking to him after the premiere party hurt. I
missed him desperately. Not talking to him after finding

out the truth has been a million times worse. I could fill a bottomless mimosa glass with my regrets, but the one that looms the largest is how much I hurt him. He didn't deserve that.

And so, my very mature and totally plausible plan for the evening is to avoid him at all possible costs. Which I'm sure is going to work out great.

"You look beautiful, sweetie." My mom reaches over and pats my hand, giving me a forced smile.

"It's hard to do these without him." I'm not talking about Grayson, and based on the tinge of sadness in her eyes, she already knows that.

"I know, baby." She wipes a nonexistent smudge from my cheek. "But you can get through this. I know you can. It'll all work out."

"Your relentless positivity is irritating." I soften my harsh words with a small smile.

"My goal in life is to irritate you as much as possible."

I lean my shoulder into hers. "Thank you for being here with me."

"I wouldn't dream of missing it."

The car door opens, and Liz pops her head into the backseat. "We're all clear, but we should get a move on."

I slide over to the door and carefully step out of the limo, adjusting my long navy dress as Liz helps my mother. From the front, my dress is nothing special, aside from the luxurious silky material. It's high-necked and long-sleeved, even though the LA evening air barely holds a chill. But when I start walking, the high slit on the left side shows off both of my legs and the movement of the skirt. And when I turn around on the step and repeat, the crowd's appreciation is audible. My back is almost completely bare, the dress swooping down to just over my butt with one thin gold chain dangling down my spine.

Amanda swirled my hair into an updo, and Sam went simple with my makeup, letting the dress do the talking.

After posing for a million photos, I speed through the line of reporters, not answering a majority of the questions thrown at me and doing my best to get inside as soon as possible, before Grayson steps foot on the carpet behind me.

We make it to the front doors of the theater just as a raucous cheer alerts me to his arrival.

I tell myself not to look, but of course, I fucking look.

He's far enough away that hopefully he doesn't see me completely freeze in my tracks. He's wearing a standard tux, except his jacket is a dark navy velvet, almost the exact color of my dress. His smile, at least from a distance, seems genuine as he interacts with the fans lined up behind the metal barricades. Any hint of sadness I saw during the press junket seems to have completely faded away.

Which is a good thing. I don't want him to be sad.

Okay, maybe I want him to be a little bit sad, but I certainly can't begrudge him for moving on, even if the thought of him moving on does make me want to vomit all over the red carpet.

Liz links her arm through mine. "Ready to go in?"

I nod, letting her lead me away and into the theater. As we walk through, I throw a longing glance at my favorite supply closet of solace and solitude, but we're ushered to our seats before I can duck away. I force Liz and my mom to let me have the aisle seat because the chances of me making it through this without needing to step outside for some air are slim to none.

The seats around us fill with cast and crew as well as fans and critics. Jenna wraps me in a big hug before sitting in the seat right behind me. I should have done a better job staying in contact with her, but our relationship is just one of the many casualties of the big breakup. Everything that reminds me of Grayson is just too painful.

I feel him before I see him, the air in the room shifting as he walks down the aisle on the other side of the theater. Liz arranged for us to be seated in the same row but at opposite ends to ensure minimal potential interaction.

We're right back where we started, barely able to be in the same room with each other. Only this time the anger and hurt are real and not some leftover teen-angst drama.

The lights go down, and I clasp my hands tightly together in my lap. The beginning of the film is easy to watch. It's mostly me and Jenna, and we're good together on-screen. The audience laughs at all the right places, and for a half second, I let myself relax. I let myself actually enjoy this monumental moment. That's me up there on that screen. I'm not just a name in the credits; I'm there bringing my own character to life. I was terrified to step back in front of the camera, and I did it. That's something I should be proud of, all other drama aside. A smile tugs on my lips as I watch my conversation with my movie dad. Maybe tonight won't be such torture after all.

And then there he is. In all of his twenty feet of cinematic glory.

I dig my nails into the palm of my hand because hyperventilating at the sight of my ex in the middle of our joint movie premiere is probably not the best look. How the hell was I so naive all of five seconds ago to think I could do this, let alone enjoy it?

Liz reaches over and squeezes my hand, saving me from drawing blood. I keep a tight grip on her fingers and try to keep my shit together. And I do okay, for a while.

That is, until we watch Isobel and Josh share their first kiss in front of the fireplace and I know what's coming next. The raw footage Grayson and I watched in Liz's room all those months ago was enough to shift the entire course of our relationship.

I definitely can't fucking do it again.

"I need a minute," I mutter to Liz, dropping her hand and bolting for the door at the back of the theater.

People notice as I make my way up the aisle, but I couldn't care less. The door to the theater swings shut behind me, and ten seconds later I'm safely stowed away in my closet, my back pressed against the door. I flick on the light, illuminating the metal shelves towering around me.

I shuffle a few steps farther into the tiny room, one arm wrapping around my stomach and my other hand flying up to my mouth, as if that could keep in the sob.

It shudders through me, shaking my entire body until I'm doubled over and unable to catch my breath. The pain of seeing us, of knowing just how real those captured moments were, is more than I can physically bear.

I don't hear the door open behind me. I don't hear it shut. But I do hear him.

"Emmy."

I straighten, but I don't turn around. My chest heaves

as I try to catch my breath while hastily wiping what is surely a travesty under my eyes.

He doesn't say anything else but just waits for me to collect myself, the tension between us so thick it chokes my lungs.

After a minute, his hand skirts the bare skin of my lower back, and I can't hold back the gasp his touch elicits. His fingers wrap around my waist, and he pulls me into his chest.

"Do you have any idea how fucking miserable I've been without you?" The rumble of his words shudders down my spine.

I want to see him, to read the emotion I know is clear in those blue eyes, but I'm paralyzed, homed in on every place our bodies touch. My back pressed to his chest. His hand on my waist. His mouth tracing the shell of my ear.

"Yes," I answer honestly. I know exactly how miserable he's been because I've felt the same way.

"You destroyed me, Emmy, and yet all I do is think about you. Every time I pick up my goddamn phone, there you are, defending me like you actually see who I am and know me. And love me." His voice is thick, choked with what could be his own tears.

I close my eyes, as if that can keep the pain in his voice from knifing me in the chest. "I do see you, and I do know you. I love you, Grayson." I reach behind me, taking his free hand in mine and lacing our fingers together. "I love you, and I'm sorry, and I will say that a million more times if it means you can forgive me."

He spins me around so we're face to face. "I forgive you."

Tears I thought were under control stream down my cheeks. "Yeah?"

"Yeah." His hand snakes around my waist, pressing flat against the small of my back. "I should have told you about Kevin's intentions from the beginning, as soon as it became clear we were more than costars with benefits."

"I never should have jumped to conclusions about what I heard. You would never hurt me intentionally, and I know that." I place my hand on his chest, feeling the thud of his heartbeat beneath my palm. "I missed you."

His hand covers mine. "I missed you, too. Every second of every fucking day."

I tilt up my head, and thanks to my heels, my lips land just inches from his. He leans down, closing the gap to a sliver. The first brush of his lips over mine is like the drift of a snowflake, soft and light and gone before it truly lands.

He closes his eyes, his forehead coming to rest on mine. "Sometimes I feel like you're the only person in my life who's ever really believed in me, Ems. And then you didn't, and it killed me."

My heart constricts, burning in my chest. "Again, I'm so, so sorry—"

"I'm not telling you that because I want you to keep being sorry." He cups the nape of my neck in his large palm. "I said I forgive you, and I meant it." His thumb strokes the line of my jaw. "I'm telling you because that's something I need to work on. It's not up to you to make me feel worthy. I need to feel that for myself."

I press a soft kiss on his cheek. "I admire you for seeing that, and for wanting to do something about it." I take his cheek in my hand, delighting in the familiar tickle of his beard on my palm. "And I will tell you every day how worthy I think you are."

He turns his head, his lips finding the center of my palm. "God, I love you."

"I love you, too."

His mouth is on mine before I even finish the phrase. He kisses me like he wants to make up for our thousands of lost kisses in one single blow. I open to him and he takes me, his arms wrapping around me, pressing me into him. My fingers dig their way into his hair, and he groans into my mouth.

I don't even realize my feet have left the ground until my back is pressed up against the door, the full weight of Grayson anchoring me, holding me, supporting me. His lips travel down my neck, finding the sensitive spot along my collarbone. I slip a hand under his jacket, yanking the tail of his shirt from the back of his pants, needing to feel his skin underneath my palm. My fingers skirt around his waistband, tracing the ridges of his stomach and up over the hard planes of his chest.

His hips thrust, the hard length of him pressing into my belly, and this time the groan is mine.

"Grayson, I need you," I whimper, my hand traveling down to the front of his pants, cupping him through the fabric.

He grunts, his hands digging into my waist and pulling me closer. "You want our first time in all these weeks to be in a closet?"

I squeeze him gently. "I want our first time in all these weeks to be right fucking now."

He puts some space between us, his pupils so wide I can barely see the blue of his eyes. "Are you sure?"

I cover his hand, moving it down to the slit in my dress. "That's one thing about this dress; I'm not wearing any underwear."

His lips crash down on mine, his fingers wrapping around my leg, lifting it so his next thrust hits me right where I need him. I roll up my hips, desperate for pressure, for relief. He peels off his jacket, tossing it on some nearby shelf.

And then he falls to his knees in front of me. For a second he doesn't touch me, doesn't even breathe. Our eyes meet, and there is nothing but love in his gaze.

Then he licks his lips. "Hike up that skirt."

"What's the magic word?" I tease, breathlessly.

"Now."

I choke on a gasp and immediately obey, pulling my skirt to the side, baring myself to him.

The next look he gives me is greedy and salacious, and I almost come before he even touches me. He runs a hand up my bare leg, taking his sweet-ass time, considering how demanding he was just a second earlier.

But I don't rush him, because his skin on mine is electric. He places a soft kiss on the thin skin of my thigh, his movements slow and mesmerizing. I can't take my eyes off him. He positions my leg over his shoulder, his lips continuing to kiss a trail up to where I'm aching for him.

The first contact he makes is a soft kiss, reverent and promising. And then his tongue finds my center and I have to reach for something to hold onto, something to brace myself with. The cold metal of one of the shelves stings my hand, but I barely notice because all I can feel is Grayson. His mouth works me, tongue dipping and swirling, lips sucking and devouring. My hips roll, the movement completely beyond my control. When he slips two fingers inside me, I shatter. He groans as I tighten around his fingers, the vibrations of his mouth sending me further over the edge.

The orgasm rips through me and doesn't stop. Grayson rides the wave with me, his strokes and licks softening as I finally start to come down.

The minute he stands, my hands reach for his pants, unbuckling and unzipping until my fingers finally wrap around the hard, hot length of him. He thrusts into my hand with a groan, his hands planted on the door on either side of my head.

He lowers his mouth to my neck. "I don't have anything with me, Ems."

"I haven't been with anyone. But if you have and you would prefer to wait, I don't mind returning the favor." I capture his mouth with mine while I continue to stroke him.

He presses the full weight of his body into me, melding us together. "I haven't been with anyone else. How could I? You completely ruined me, Harper."

"I'm going to take that as a compliment."

His hands cup my ass as he hoists me up against the door. "Good."

I guide him to my entrance, my legs wrapped tightly around his waist. He pushes into me slowly, and I can't hold in the moan when he's finally fully seated.

"Fuck, Emmy. It's been so long, I don't think I'm going to last."

I thread my fingers through his hair, tugging gently so his gaze has to meet mine. "I'm not sure if you missed it, but I already had one mind-blowing orgasm. I think we're good."

He starts to move inside me, slowly, the swivel of his hips brushing my clit. "I want to feel you come on my cock, Emmy."

I suck in a breath, his words shooting right down to my core. "Keep talking like that, and I don't think it will be a problem."

His thrusts become faster and deeper as his voice goes guttural. "Touch yourself. Please, Emmy. I'm so close."

I don't hesitate, his commands and his thrusts and his grip on my thighs pushing me closer to the edge. I slip a hand in between our bodies, stroking myself until the pressure is building. "Don't stop," I manage to choke out, my breaths unsteady.

He buries his face in my neck, his lips and teeth digging into my skin. I tighten and tighten just as I hear his telltale grunts, the ones that mean he is about to explode. I clutch him to me, never more thankful for his action-hero strength than I am in this moment.

His mouth finds mine as we both careen over the cliff, together, a tangle of sweaty limbs and mussed hair and clenched muscles. His thrusts finally slow, and he cradles me in his arms, sinking to the ground and gathering me in his lap.

For a minute, all we can do is breathe.

Then I take his face in my hands and kiss him. "I love you."

He runs a soothing hand down my bare back. "I love you, too."

"Think anyone will notice if we dip out now and just go back to my place?"

"Mine's closer." He grins and smooths out the sleeves of my dress. "But you deserve this moment, Ems. You don't actually want to miss the entire premiere of your second starring role ever."

I sigh and kiss him on the cheek. "I hate it when you're right."

He pulls me close, his kiss deep and promising. "Besides, I plan on keeping you up all night, so we might as well relax and eat while we can."

I loop my arms around his neck. "I like the sound of that. But does that mean we need to go back in? There can't be much left."

He purses his lips, fighting back another grin. "Hate to break it to you, Ems, but I don't think you can go back. You look . . ."

My mouth drops open in mock outrage. "I look what?"

"You look like you just got fucked against a door."

I don't bother holding in my laugh. "Well. Shit. Do you have your phone?"

He shifts me to the side so he can reach for his jacket, pulling his phone from the inner pocket and handing it to me.

"Passcode?"

"031723."

I smirk as I punch in the numbers. "Wait, your passcode is the first day we hooked up?"

"Yup." He says it with a wide grin and zero shame.

I find Sam's number in his contacts and send him an SOS. "We should probably get up now."

Grayson grasps my waist and lifts me to my feet, hopping up next to me. I straighten my dress and he buttons his pants, and a minute later there's a knock on the door.

I open it just wide enough to pull Sam inside.

He looks between the two of us and sighs heavily. "You couldn't have waited until after the party?"

"Sorry." I flash him a sheepish smile.

"No, you're not."

"You're right, I'm not."

Sam gives us a weary look again, opening his emergency kit. "You're lucky I'm always prepared." He hands Grayson a makeup remover wipe. "Take that to your whole face."

Grayson winks at me, stepping to the side and wiping the remains of my makeup from his skin.

Sam gets to work on my face and five minutes later steps back and gives me a once-over. "Sadly, I don't think this hair can be salvaged, so have fun explaining that to Amanda. Turn around."

I do, groaning in relief as the mass of bobby pins are pulled from my hair.

Sam works his fingers through the curls before spinning me back around. "That will have to do."

"Is it obvious?"

"That you just got lucky in a supply closet? Yes." He

gives Grayson a nod of approval. "Fortunately, the just-fucked-and-madly-in-love look works for both of you."

My eyes meet Grayson's, and we share a wide grin.

Sam fake retches. "Gross." He heads for the door. "You should probably get your asses back in there. The movie's almost over."

We speed walk back to the theater, Sam making his way to his original seat while Grayson and I find two empty spots next to each other in the back row. We sink into the plush red chairs, and his hand automatically finds mine, our fingers lacing together.

We share another smile as Isobel and Josh reunite on-screen. My head falls to his shoulder, and his lips brush my forehead.

And we all live happily ever after.

EPILOGUE

I TAKE A CUP OF HOT CHOCOLATE, WRAPPING MY hands around the festive red cardboard and letting the heat seep into my chilled fingers. "Was it always this cold here?"

Grayson accepts his own cup before sticking a large wad of cash in the tip jar on the counter. "You just didn't notice because we spent most of our time naked in bed."

"Hmmm, and why are we not currently doing that?" I sip from my cup, walking slowly toward the front door of the café, wanting to delay entry into the frigid afternoon air for as long as possible.

He pushes open the door, guiding me outside. "Someone I know made a big stink about wanting to explore the Pine Springs holiday festival."

"I think I'd rather explore your holiday festival." I tuck myself into his side, burrowing into his warmth.

He chuckles. "Nice one."

We take our hot chocolates and stroll along Main Street. The timing worked out pretty perfectly. We both have a break for the holidays before starting our next projects. Mine is a new rom-com—one I didn't write but will be starring in. Grayson's is the latest Marvel movie, which he signed onto even after being offered the role in *Beautiful Water*. When I asked him why he would turn down a possible Oscar-winning role, he told me he would rather do something that makes other people happy, something that makes him happy. Just hearing him say those words made me happy.

The main road through Pine Springs has been closed to all vehicles, and each side is lined with booths, some selling their holiday wares, others fundraising, and others providing information about the happenings around town, both during the season and after. We peruse each booth, doling out lots of money and collecting ornaments and candy and jewelry and homemade scarves. By the time we reach the end of the street, Grayson's arms are laden with packages.

That doesn't stop him from nudging me in the ribs. "For old times' sake?" He cocks his head in the direction of the park a little farther down the road, separate from the festival but still within our line of sight.

"I'm still not going to have sex with you in the snow, West." But I link my arm through his as we meander down the sidewalk to the park.

We find ourselves back in the gazebo. Grayson sets down his load with a sigh of relief, and we both perch on one of the white wooden benches lining the inside. He holds out his arm, and I nestle in his embrace. His lips brush my forehead, and it's blissful.

"I think we should make this a yearly tradition." I reach over and lace my fingers through his.

"Oh yeah? You think you're still going to want me around, year after year?"

I scrunch my nose as if I have to think about it. "Possibly. Probably? I think the odds are in your favor."

"Good." He shifts away from me a bit, and I instantly miss his warmth. But then he's back, pressed up against my side, only now he's holding out his hand to me and there's a small red leather box resting on his palm. "Would've been a bummer if you weren't sure."

I sit up a little bit, my eyes darting between him and the box, back and forth. "It's not Christmas yet."

"It's not your Christmas present." He grins, nudging me to take the box.

I do, holding it gingerly like it's made of glass. "Grayson West, what the hell are you doing?"

He opens the box for me. "I think I'm asking you to marry me. Or I'm about to, anyway."

The ring is gorgeous—a solitaire cushion-cut diamond on a thin gold band. But it's not the shining rock that captures my attention. It's the excitement and love and the tiny bit of nerves I see in his eyes.

I bite my lip to hold back my grin. "All right then, get on with your asking."

Grayson laughs and sits up straight. He takes the ring from the box and holds it up. "Emmy Harper, you drive me absolutely mad. But you're my best friend and my partner and the only person I think I could tolerate being with for the rest of my life. Actually, the one thing I know for sure is that I couldn't tolerate a life without you. Will you marry me?"

I want to say something coy and snarky, but the word

yes flies out of my mouth before I even have the chance. I fling my arms around his neck, burying my face in his pine and charcoal–scented skin. He squeezes me, his lips finding the sensitive spot on my neck.

I pull out of the hug so I can kiss his stupid handsome face. When we finally separate, he takes my left hand in his, sliding the ring onto my finger. It's a perfect fit, and so is he.

"Grayson *fucking* West, I love you so much, and it's time to go back to the hotel literally as soon as possible," I say, in between stamping my lips on any inch of his bare skin I can find.

He jumps up and gathers our bags, and we race as fast as is safe back to the Pine Springs Inn. We leave our bags of festival trinkets in the car, and even though I'm tempted to spring upstairs to our room, I slow down as we enter the lobby, the bell tinkling over the door as we make our way inside.

There's a tree set up inside the doorway, and stockings are hung along the dark wood of the counter. The banister is wrapped in garland, and Linda is checking in guests while decked out in a bright green Christmas sweater. It doesn't look the same as when we were here filming, but somehow the holiday magic sprinkled around the room just makes it all the more special.

I squeeze Grayson's hand. "Right here is where I ran into your dumb rock-hard pecs and thought my whole life was over."

He takes my face in his hands and kisses me through his chuckle. "Funny. Right here is where you ran into me and I thought, 'I'm going to end up marrying that girl.'"

I swat his arm as we make our way up the stairs. "You did not think that."

"I definitely did."

"Then why were you such an asshole?"

"You were an asshole first." He shrugs and pushes open the door to our room, the same one I stayed in during filming, our little Pine Springs home.

I toss my coat on one of the armchairs, warming myself up in front of the blazing fire.

Grayson catches my eye, raising one eyebrow and directing my attention to right above my head. Where a sprig of mistletoe hangs, because of course it does. As if our life could be any more of its own rom-com.

"Did you hang that there?" I ask as he stalks across the room toward me.

"I don't need poisonous plants to get you to kiss me." And he proves his point, sweeping me up in an embrace as his mouth comes crashing down on mine. "Merry Christmas, Harper."

I push him toward the bed and jump into his arms. "Merry Christmas, West."

ACKNOWLEDGMENTS

I don't think I really knew what the "book of my heart" meant until I wrote this book. *Lease on Love* sort of felt like a fever dream of everything I ever wished for coming true. *Just My Type* pushed me and challenged me, and most of the time, frustrated me. But this book, this is one I kept coming back to when I needed little moments of joy. I'm so happy Emmy and Grayson found their way into the world and I hope everyone loves them as much as I do.

Many thanks, as always, to my incredible agent, Kimberly Whalen. You fought for this book to find its place, and I'm so grateful for all of your encouragement and support.

My unbelievably talented editor, Gaby Mongelli. Literally would not be here without you. Thank you for seeing the heart of this story, for helping me de-holiday it in a way that made sense, and for helping me take it to the next level.

Everyone at Putnam, you all are a dream. Samantha Bryant, Brennin Cummings, Kristen Bianco, Sanny Chiu, Shannon Plunkett, Hannah Dragone, Maija Baldauf, Leah Marsh.

Christy Wagner, Danielle Barthel, and Brittany Bergman, thank you for fixing all of my mistakes. I'm sorry I don't know the difference between "because" and "since."

Corey Planer, you loved Grayson and Emmy before anyone else. Thank you for your endless support, encouragement, and friendship.

Haley Kral, thank you for sliding into my DMs and texts right when I seem to need it most. Also, thank you for letting me steal your title.

Courtney Kae. Begging you to start *Happy to Meet Cute* with me was one of the best decisions of my life. I'm so grateful for the brilliant light you shine on the romance community. Basically the best partner I ever could have asked for.

Getting to chat weekly with other romance authors has been one of the biggest blessings of the past year. Thank you to all of the *HTMC* guests who have shared their stories with us. You have all made me a better writer, and I'm so thankful for the wisdom you've so freely shared.

I've also been able to meet more readers in person this past year and y'all continue to blow me away. Flying to San Diego from Brooklyn for my book launch?!?!? Showing UP for Summer Book Fest?!?!?! Sharing your reviews and your photos and your lovely, amazing, beyond kind, incredible words?!?!?! You are superstars and I love each and every one of you.

Booksellers and librarians, there are no authors without you. Thank you for all you do.

Bookstagram, you have continuously shown up for me and I don't know that you will ever know how much I appreciate you.

All of my friends, IRL and online, thank you for being there for me even when I don't deserve it.

My family. Thanks for continuing to support me; I'm so blessed to have you all in my corner.

Canon, I love you. Definitely don't read this book.

Matt, I have no love stories without you. Thank you. Love you the most.

DISCUSSION GUIDE

1. *Right on Cue* takes a look behind the scenes at how a movie is made. Were there any elements of the filmmaking storyline you were surprised by?

2. While Emmy built a successful career as a screenwriter, she's always had a passion for acting. Is there anything you've been passionate for a long time and wanted to pursue? What would encourage you to go for it?

3. Grayson is worried that he will get stuck being typecast into certain sorts of roles. Why does he feel this way? Talk about how his perspective on this shifts, and if you agree or disagree with his concerns.

4. In the novel, Liz is both Emmy's coworker and her best friend. Have you ever had to collaborate with a friend on a creative project before? How did it go?

5. Talk about Emmy and Grayson's first interaction when they were teenagers. Do you think Emmy was right to react the way she did to Grayson's behavior? How would you have responded?

6. If you could star in your own romantic comedy, who would your dream costar be?

7. Emmy is the daughter of Hollywood royalty. How does her family background play into her insecurities in the novel? How does it provide a source of strength?

8. Did your opinion of Grayson change over the course of the novel? How so?

9. Name some of your favorite romantic comedy films. What is it you like about them? Do they have anything in particular in common?

10. What do you think is next for Emmy and Grayson?

ABOUT THE AUTHOR

Photograph of the author © Brianna Mowry

FALON BALLARD is the author of *Lease on Love* and *Just My Type* and cohost of the podcast *Happy to Meet Cute*. When she's not writing fictional love stories, she's helping real-life couples celebrate, working as a wedding planner in Southern California.

VISIT FALON BALLARD ONLINE

falonballard.com
 FalonBallard
 FalonBallard